Journey By Fire

Bruce W. Perry

More Fiction

Gone On Kauai
(The second book in the Karl Standt detective
thriller series)

Accidental Exiles
(A young Iraq veteran is torn between escapism and
self sacrifice when he flees the Middle Eastern wars
to Europe–available in paperback and ebook)

Devastated Lands
(A dystopian thriller about young people who fight
to survive an eruption of Mount Rainier, and the
resulting epic lahars and chaos.)

Table of Contents

PART I: THE ROAD

CHAPTER 1

He got off the last train at dusk. He was in Denver, pulling into the ruins of the old city. He could see the tall skyscrapers with their lights off. Black sentinels against a purple sky with a faint glow of fires pulsating behind the distant peaks. Then one light on in a tall building; some squatter who's climbed the long flights of stairs and lit a cooking fire, he thought. Thinks the height of the building in and of itself will protect him.

The station platform was all but empty; he saw a few people but nothing organized. One remaining lamp flickered a jaundiced light onto the littered asphalt. The sun hadn't quite gone down.

He stood up and hoisted the heavy backpack onto his shoulder. The train slowed, almost soundlessly, then ground to a halt, wheels screeching, pushing him against the empty seat in front. He paused, more out of habit, before he entered the aisle, like he used to when he'd traveled on airliners and let other people go ahead. Out of an old-fashioned courtliness. Probably got it from his father, a normally circumspect and cheerful man who seemed to have predicted all of this. *We're falling into another Great Depression*, he'd said before he died. *That president, he's opening up the gates of hell.* Even though he obviously didn't want all of this to happen, he was proud of his late father's prescience and wisdom.

Now, it was just him and the old man sitting on the other end of the train.

He'd had the window down on the trip across the territories of Kansas and Nebraska (he refused to call them by the new names). He'd watched the countryside go by; he enjoyed the moist evening smells of long wet grass and tilled soil and the general wind and emptiness. It gave him pause. He was wistful, almost relaxed. Limitless fields with islands of woods dominated the few ratty remains, falling down billboards and abandoned malls and decrepit townships and torched filling stations. Here was a semblance of Nature reborn, growing back over the crumbling, graceless sprawl. The train knocked along as if on automatic pilot, except for the ludicrously cheerful voice that kept announcing the stops over a speaker wired to the train car.

He didn't know whether that was recorded or not; it had to be. No one could really be like that.

He'd passed some work details in the flat fields, hundreds of young men and women baking in the harsh sunlight. They were up to middle-aged and some teenagers, herded along by gruff overseers who gave off the vibe, even as Wade trundled along quickly by in the train, as being loutish and utterly stupid. They took revenge for something, for being born. So they sided with the lunatics when everything went to pot.

The train slowed into the siding and he stuck his head out the window, for one last look. The fetid smell that met his nose was of rotten food no one would scavenge, and worse things. He scoured the platform for people, still deserted. He found that reassuring. No one, these days, was always a better bet than a crowd.

He felt a stab of insecurity and patted around for his weapons and things. From now on it was going to be mostly walking.

# # #

The old man didn't move from his seat, which folded down near the exit from the car. He sat still as a statue. He had thick, white eyebrows and a white beard down to his coat lapels, which were part of a dark and dusty old worsted suit. Another previous generation, making sure they're dressed civilized no matter what has gone down, Wade thought.

The man held a black book in his lap, *The Holy Bible*, King James version. Finally he nodded in greeting.

"Aren't you getting off?" Wade asked.

"Where're you headed?" the man said after a pause.

"South…southwest of here."

"I suggest you turn around, young man. There's nothing that way for you. Only heat and wreckage, the worst of it is down there. What's your reasoning?"

"I'm looking for my daughter."

"Oh."

"This here's the last stop so…"

"I know that. What's your daughter's name?"

"Kara. Kara Wade. I have a picture of her." He fished into a side pocket of his pants and removed a zip-locked bag, from which he carefully took out one photo among a stack. He handed the photo to the man, who leaned forward and grasped it gently with his boney, blue-veined hand. The white

4

laundered shirtsleeve slipped forward from the suit coat when he reached with his arm. He took the photo and fiddled with his glasses as he stared at it. "Tch-tch," he said, disapprovingly, that the world could lose such a girl.

"A delightful looking girl. Radiant. I won't forget the face, even at my age." He handed the photo back. "May God's good fortune be with you. I have a good feeling about this one–the reuniting of your kin. But one can't do it alone." He wagged a liver-spotted, gnarled finger at Wade. "It's too much out there for one man only," he said in a gravelly voice. "The wickedness under the sun; the chaos, a world come apart at the seams...the darkness and fires," he intoned, as if giving a grave reading of Edgar Allen Poe.

Wade placed the photo bag back in his backpack and carried his belongings towards the door. "You should..." he fumbled, trying the give the old man some advice, knowing that in Denver began an "uncontrolled territory" of mostly free-ranging human predators.

"Mr. Wade," the man called him back, using both hands to hold up the black book. "I want you to take this book. I've no need for it anymore. It will offer you solace, nourishment, and maybe some protection."

"No, I don't have any room for extras," Wade said. He picked his backpack up again and strapped it on. It was heavy but well-organized, including a crossbow and quiver bound to the outside of it with cords and carabiners. He had only a dozen arrows and a small bag of replacement arrowheads; his methods involved recovering the arrows.

A rapid hiss of compressed air escaped down by the train's wheels. Steam rose to the window; he thought of the hot smell of an iron left too long on the cloth. He was impatient to get going.

He turned toward the exit then looked back. "Aren't you

coming?" he said. "Where are *you* going from here? There's no place to go. Maybe another train is going east. You should wait for that one and get on it…this is no place…"

"No need," the man said, shifting in his seat. "I was born here. 1940. This is where I'll finish my days."

Wade did the math; it was 2025, hardly worth remembering since a grotesque timelessness had descended upon the world. That made the man 85.

"I have this notion I can find my childhood home, and curl up beneath the apple tree in the sun…" He shook his head bemused. "I *never* thought I'd make it this far."

He put the thick book into a leather satchel. Then he reached his boney hand across the aisle and Wade took it and shook it. It felt brittle, light as a feather. "Don't trust anyone along the way, unless you're sure of it," the man said with a sudden, fatherly, grim change of tone.

"And you're going to need help. You shouldn't go down there on your lonesome. *Two is better than one*," he quoted. "*For if they fall, the one will lift up his fellow, but woe to him that is alone.*" He removed his hand, set it in his lap, and resumed the statuesque pose. "There is great wickedness in this land. Be careful." His chin and long beard trembled slightly. "God bless your daughter. For it's the innocent that must be spared. The innocent, the humble, the righteous…will inherit this near Godforsaken world. I say *near* because God still exists out there, despite our sorrows…"

Wade nodded. "If you see her, my daughter, Kara Wade, tell I'll be back through these parts." A pneumatic door opened and the train idled. "Last stop…" the loudspeaker croaked again. "Have a nice evening."

Wade walked down the metal steps into a strong gust of arid wind that almost blew the boony hat off of his head. The platform had fallen into shadows. A lone lamp fizzled and blinked, giving off a pallid, faltering light. He'd been staring at his map a lot of the time he was on the train. So he knew the direction he would take from the train station, but not his mode of transportation. He could steal a car, which would be a rare stroke of luck, or he could catch a ride with someone, which would be even less likely. Little fuel was to be had anywhere.

He kept walking along the platform to its exit, and when he looked back, he saw the old man in his black coat standing next to the train with his arm upraised. He waved back. He had to walk south to the outskirts of the city. Absent a car or pickup truck, maybe he could find a bike or a cart.

# # #

When he reached the end of the platform he heard voices from inside the neglected terminal. A low laugh, brisk cocky comments, then a door burst open and three young men came onto the platform. Wade ducked into an alcove, looking for an escape.

The old man sat down on a wooden bench down near the end where the train idled. The men wore t-shirts and bandannas; one of them was bald, the other two had long greasy hair and patchy beards. They were heavily tattooed. They laughed vapidly, looked around the platform, sizing it up and aching for trouble. Wade figured they were on something strong; a lot was available and around. It seemed more so than food. When they spotted the old man, they walked quickly toward him. He turned his head from the bench and Wade saw him cross himself.

"What do we have here?" the balder of the men said. He flicked a cigarette he'd been smoking into the greasy train-track bed.

"It's Grandpa Jed."

"Jed Clampett!" said a shorter hanger-on with a high

voice.

"Or Moses," the cueball said. He stopped near the bench and stood over the man. He reached out and ruffled the white hair. "Is that real? I'll be darned. When'd you get your hair done?"

"Sump time back around 1919 I figure," the other hairy one said.

"It's a wig!" the third one said in his high-pitched tone, pathetically trying to keep up with the juvenile commentary.

The bald one gave off a "leader" and instigator vibe. Then the man who had just spoke kicked out at the old man's legs, and the force of the kick uncrossed them so that he slumped down on the bench. The priest put up his hand. Wade heard him say something, faint and even. Wade looked around the platform, forming a plan, then laid the backpack gently against the wall of the alcove where he hid.

The third one reached for the leather satchel, and the elderly gentleman put his hand on it, saying all the time, loud enough for Wade to hear, "You're barking up the wrong tree lads. I don't have any food. No water. I'm looking for them, just like you. I'm just an old man at the end of his journey."

"I'll say," the stout head of the gang quipped.

Then the medium-height one who'd tucked his pants into a pair of black Army-issue boots unbuckled his trousers and began to urinate on the old man's pant leg. The shorter one, who was insanely scratching himself, burst into his high, idiotic laugh. The bald one gave the back of his hand to the scroungy kid with the unbuckled trousers, so that he fell to his knees, and he shoved the other one, whose laughter shrank to a whimper.

"We're wasting our time! Listen *Methuselah*, cough up whatever you have, food, cash, pills…I know you're on something. Show me the meds. Let's see them!"

"I have nothing but my faith," the old man said quietly. Then the burly bald one grasped the old man by a thick lock of his hair. Wade saw the elderly man wince. He pulled the bowed head closer and removed what looked like a truncheon from his bulky trouser, which he brought down abruptly on the side of the man's head.

He raised his club again. "You've got about three more seconds Methuselah! Show me the goods! One, two…" But the "two" came out all choked and gargled just as the sharp end of an arrow, now painted crimson, jutted out just beneath his chin. The arrow had rent the air with a whir that lasted only a second. He stood frozen with a look of blatant shock in his flat red-rimmed eyes, as his companions went dead silent. Then both of his hands flew to his neck and he fell to his knees, making the gargling noises and the hands fluttering around the foreign object coming out of his throat, as if out of curiosity. He fell over on to his side and Wade could see the feathered end of the arrow coming out the back of his neck, and he'd rearmed his bow. The old man lay on the bench bleeding from his head and pressing a kerchief to it.

Wade didn't want to waste his arrows. Neither did he want to use the handgun, as he was almost out of ammo. Precisely two .38 Special bullets left, hidden in his backpack.

Wade stepped out of the alcove and the other two men, standing with mouths agape, turned and ran in the opposite direction. Wade lowered the bow, looked quickly behind him for any more city denizens he had to deal with, then walked toward the bench and the old man.

He sat up, and he didn't seem too badly hurt. He was now tying the kerchief around his head to tend to the wound near the ear.

CHAPTER 2

When Wade got to the old man his breathing was raspy. He held up the hand not holding the kerchief to his head, as if to signal, "Don't bother. I'm alright."

"You should come with me," Wade said.

"Nonsense. I'm too old. I'd be a burden to you on the open road." He caught his breath again. His tone was stoic and weary. "You have to find your daughter. I'll go to the Church of the Ascension. It's only a few blocks away. They'll leave me alone in the church. They usually do. Remember that. God maintains his influence, even with what the world has become."

"Okay," Wade said, then he moved to the big body sprawled on the asphalt in a spreading pool of blood. He wanted his arrow back. First, he checked for a pulse on the carotid artery, then determining the man was dead, he put one of his knees on the body's back and gripped the feathered end of the arrow and summarily drew it out. It felt like pulling a stiff plant up by the frozen roots. Then he wiped the blood off the steel arrow and carefully placed it back in its quiver, with the bow. He made sure everything was tight again on the backpack. He'd become fastidious and organized in a way he'd never been before.

Then they began walking slowly together through Union Station. Night had fallen. Things were consequently more treacherous. The terminal was empty and echoing, save for a few sleeping and destitute residents who weren't targets because they'd lost everything already. They were wrapped up in old sleeping bags and shipping boxes and had slunk to the shadowy corners of the terminal. They didn't even bother to raise their heads.

The interior was fetid and humid and it was a relief to push through the shattered front door to old Wynkoop Street.

The regime had failed to reclaim Denver and probably wouldn't, due to the fires, Wade thought. Everything had been left to burn out because the resources didn't exist anymore to fight an inferno nearly one-third the size of the North American continent. Even if they did exist, the rising temperatures would simply relight the smoldering landscape, and all its ashen homes, businesses, and cities. It was a vast complex of interconnected fires and no one could tell you when it would end, not even Wade, who knew forests and maps.

Denver was no doubt hopelessly looted, when it came to food and necessities.

They stood beneath the Union Station sign on Wynkoop Street; the sign had been drilled with rocks and bottles and the "Union" part of it drooped precariously. All Wade thought about was getting outside the city and heading south, by any means. Find Kara.

"Where's the church?"

"That way," the priest pointed.

There used to be bars and restaurants here, lively neighborhoods in the cool, dry, glamorous Rocky Mountain evenings. Wade mused that a cold glass of beer would taste great right now. All the big American cities were like that. Cold drinks and cafes were vestigial luxuries of a lost time. Best not to think about those things.

The street was wide and unlit and littered with trash and unfueled cars, rusting and missing their tires. Wade looked up into the sky and saw the glow and pools of burning slopes along the Front Range. It was beautiful, like a Northern Lights, save for what he knew it represented which was profligate destruction.

It didn't matter that they walked down the sidewalk because everywhere was dark; there were no streetlights. He saw lights far down the boulevard which he figured were cooking fires and the meandering headlights of the few operable vehicles, much coveted targets for the crazies.

He really should have his handgun out but he reminded himself that ammo was precious; he'd get the priest to the church, then he'd go all night to get out of the city.

# # #

"What's you're name?" the old man said.

"Michael Wade."

"Saint Michael, the archangel. The protector. I can think of two fine shrines, in Italy and in Russia. I truly hope they still stand."

"What's your name?"

"Jedidiah Rutledge. So my young man, the southwest. It's a vast territory. How do you know which direction to go in? Where exactly are you going?" The priest shuffled along with one arm on Wade's shoulder. He talked steadily, like he'd recovered his energy.

Wade was silent for a moment. The whole trip from Vermont had blown his mind so far.

"A place called Sierra Vista. That's where I'm going. Because I have Kara's last location, the border of Mexico and Arizona. We talked. Her cell phone ran out. I told her to stay put if she could, or..." He didn't want to think or talk about the needle-in-a-haystack, quasi desperate quest he was on with the priest, who couldn't help him anyway.

"The church is there," the priest pointed with his gnarled hand. It looked gloomy and hulking, unlit as it was, but in surprisingly good shape, a square brick structure with unbroken, stained-glass windows that reflected back the shimmer of the distant inferno. They couldn't tell if anyone was about but a tiny pale light glared from the interior.

"This is fine," the priest said. He leaned on Wade's shoulder. They stood on a walkway overgrown with grass and just inside a wrought-iron gate. "I can make it from here. They know me. It's shelter, at least. I know you need to go. I'll be praying for you, and Kara."

"Thank you."

The man bent over tentatively and took the bible out of his satchel. "Take the book...please...the least I can do, along with prayer and hope. It contains the essentials."

Wade accepted the gift, just to get things moving.

"You sure you're okay?"

"Yes, I'll be fine. Because of you, and your actions. I'm home now." Then he half-turned and he said "God speed, I hope we'll meet again," and he shuffled over to the stairs that led to the church's shadowy alcove.

Wade watched him go, then assured that the old man had made it through the front door, he shoved the book, which seemed light for its thickness, into the top of his backpack, then turned left in a direction he'd already worked out. It led past the ballpark, the old Coors Field, toward Interstate 25.

# # #

He had to regroup, in a place that had some light. He had to take stock of things. He heard dogs barking in the distance. There were stories of roving packs of feral dogs preying on people in the uncontrolled territories, especially in the cities. You couldn't sleep out in the open.

Oh, for a train that went south into the old New Mexico…

He walked in the darkest part of the street, where the trees hung over the sidewalk. Pools of light moved about in the darkened urban landscape like oversized fireflies. He was so hot he pushed his hat off his head and let it flop around on the strap behind him.

After about 20 minutes of leaving the priest, he came upon an apple tree's branches that had left piles of mushy and rotten fruit on the street. He ducked beneath the branches and gorged himself with mostly small, tart, green apples for what seemed like an hour. He stuffed some of them in his pockets.

No one was about, but he kept moving toward the interstate and as he got closer to the stadium, he saw small groups huddled by the exits. Maybe a tenth of the lights were on inside the stadium; generators powered by natural gas, he guessed. People had to be living there. He heard someone talking on a loudspeaker; it was too gruff and authoritarian in tone to be trusted, so he made his way past the stadium as quickly as possible and soon he was on an entrance ramp to Interstate 25.

I-25 was deserted. The only thing that came by was an open-topped Jeep over-loaded with riffraff of the type he'd just dispatched back at the train station. He walked fast but stealthily down the emergency lane, which was covered in fine dust, ash, tumbleweeds, and broken glass. He'd never been a killer before in his life, nothing close to that.

CHAPTER 3

When he'd left Vermont going after Kara, he'd packed a loaded handgun with a box of ammo, the crossbow, and a quiver full of arrows. He'd never owned a gun before, and he was a sport shooter exclusively with the bow. As in, go into the 17-acre block of woods behind his little home, on a hill above a village, and shoot at trees. He got pretty good, hitting any tree and any spot he'd wanted from 100 or 200 meters away. In Vermont, you were either a hunter or "not a hunter"; there wasn't a mediocre middle. He didn't shoot at an animal once, not even at the copious deer, but he did keep it in the back of his mind that if his family needed protein in an emergency he'd take down some deer.

He was good enough to do that, but then he was almost nauseated with anticipated sadness to imagine how the poor animal, just trying to get through its day like him, would jerk, flail around, and probably squeal after being impaled with one of these steel arrows. He was sensitive, not squeamish; it just wasn't in his nature.

# # #

He was actually a fairly dull, keep-to-himself guy, until all this chaos and mayhem transpired.

The state of Vermont had a forestry/map app that academics and wildlife regulators and citizens could use, and it was his job putting the maps online and making sure the app worked. He got up early in the morning, drove 20 miles to an office outside of Burlington with a to-go cup of coffee, and sat in a cubicle pouring over maps and code most of the day. He took walks at breaks; he lifted weights some nights. His wife Lee was younger than him and was a teacher. He had one kid in college (Kara) and one in middle school (Shane). He was a burly former lacrosse and football player; Shane played hockey and lacrosse and shot a bow with him. Wade was forever looking at the handful of fat on his gut and thinking, "Nah, I'll deal with that tomorrow."

He mostly drank with his wife. He was, as he thought then, calm and unremarkable, and Vermont had a tranquility and predictability and sameness to it that fit him.

# # #

He certainly had no trouble seeing global warming coming. The forests told him that, acres of toppled over, diseased trees that conveyed an over-the-top climactic stress; something profound was happening. He liked the term "drunken forest" and he used it a lot when describing this problem to whomever would listen.

But nobody saw coming what came. Not in its timing, the ferocity of its speed. Even the preppers were overrun. The California governor said in a paternal tone to his constituents "the state of California will burn" if they took no action on their emissions, and darned if it didn't.

The heat trend moved down from the Arctic (which was

already 13 Fahrenheit above average), the Golden State continued its epochal drought, then the entire state burned down, everything that wasn't desert. Cash-starved during a terminal recession, the depleted fire crews didn't stand a chance, then chaos and mayhem was unleashed as the fires "complexed" in a nightmarish cascade and began to take out the Pacific Northwest, Nevada, Arizona, Utah, Idaho, Montana, Wyoming, and Colorado. Feeding on itself, the atmosphere just got hotter and the society that vitally depended on it more fragmented and destabilized, and politics followed suit. As millions migrated east and thousands died along the way (most of the troops were deployed, fatefully, fighting the fires in vain), people wanted someone and groups to blame and scapegoat, and they found someone blunt and charismatic to do the blaming and the scapegoating.

Even the headstrong president with the velvety voice and his bellicose handlers could only go with the frightful flow, however, and martial law became the norm. The internet went down, except for regionally, and there were news blackouts. Back in Vermont they heard terrible stories about mass crowds of starving people being herded into vast, sprawling open-air camps, the likes of which had not been seen since the Nazi POW camps on the Eastern Front during WWII, and certainly had never been seen before on the North American continent.

This was the inferno that some foresaw but nobody had predicted for this century, in the year 2025. In Vermont, it still rained. Once in a while. Everything was relatively okay for the Wades with the exception of one terrible problem. Kara had wintered in Baja, Mexico for a semester abroad in marine biology and when she'd needed an airliner home there was none to be had.

Wade had considered himself pretty well prepared for anything, but it was more like a hobby. He kept a first-aid kit that contained wraps, bandages, gauzes, ibuprofen, aspirin, two rounds of antibiotics; scissors, tweezers, iodine pills, and a tiny bottle of propylene glycol. He had a Swiss Army knife with a five inch blade and features that could open cans and act as screwdrivers. Their land included a pond with about 80,000 gallons of water that could be boiled if the well ran out. The woods behind his house were stocked with unlimited supplies of wood for heating and game animals; they had an orchard full of apples and blackberries and a 20-by-20 vegetable garden in season; he bought raw milk from a farm four miles away. Lee would poke fun of him with quips that he was "prepared for the end of the world."

Now his backpack contained the Swiss Army knife and the first-aid kit, but he'd left the antibiotics with Lee.

CHAPTER 4

His eyes drooped, begging for sleep. He trudged along the side of the highway. The smoke from the fires had risen like a blanket over the mountains and it blocked the stars. He could smell it in the air; the charred effect lingered in his sinuses. The flames poured like water through the ravines and along the creeks and were on their way to Denver and Boulder.

Not a single car had passed him. He mused how nice it would be to have a motorcycle and some gasoline. The orange glow was still pretty and it looked like the sun was coming up, permanently. Somewhere down the end of the road was Colorado Springs and Pueblo. He felt helpless and inadequate; he was still light years away from Kara. He didn't know where the hell she really was. What time was it; maybe 1 a.m.?

He saw the flickering of a small light up ahead on the highway. Then a second one. He thought they might be flashlights so he decided to duck down a culvert. But the lights didn't move; they stayed in one place and whipped around in the night winds. He didn't hear any voices. He cautiously approached. The culvert was dark and dropped down to dried up berms and rocky drainages and clusters of woods before the broken and abandoned highway sprawl started to flood the darkness again.

He crept closer and saw that they were two torches aflame. The road was full of debris. Rusted pieces of other cars and small junky appliances and boulders and piles of wood and tires obstructed the breadth of the highway, with a lit torch on either side of it. Whoever made this pile wanted to block the highway and was taking a break now, he thought, probably to sleep. When he got closer, he saw a sign leaning against the junk pile and crudely spray-painted: "STOP!! LYV ALL YOUR VALUBULLS! SCRAM!!"

So they, whoever *they* were, had erected a kind of ad hoc toll plaza and the price was probably your life. But none of them were around; they were most likely collapsed off in the culverts somewhere. Zonked out on that nasty weed…

He looked down the highway north in the other direction and he saw two headlights, approaching in the distance. Going highway speed. They were higher off the ground, like those in a sizable truck. He leaned his backpack against a rock and took one of the torches and walked twenty meters north towards the on-coming headlights. He waved the torch back and forth, and as the truck cab approached it slowed, but he was just going to think Wade was one of the crazies, he thought.

Rather than stand in the middle of the highway in a pugnacious way, he crept to the side and began making the international distress signal, waving his arms back and forth. He'll just have to trust that the driver will notice him; view him as a friendly.

The sixteen-wheeler flicked on its high beams, slowed

down with a burst of released air from down around the axles, and threw the disordered obstacles in its path into stark relief. Wade made a sign with his hands to cut the high beams (he didn't want this new band of highway robbers to come down on them, but surely he thought that they were already discovered).

The driver, bearded and wearing a bandanna, reached over and rolled down the passenger window, showing a sawed-off shotgun. Wade looked up at him and said, "If we move some of it, I think the truck can do the rest."

The big truck's engine idled and rattled beneath its metal hood. The driver thought for a moment, then leaned back toward the driver's door and opened it, dropping down onto the pavement. He still held the shotgun, but less in a threatening manner. They stood in the pool of his headlights with the fire's reflection quavering above the mountains.

"Wiley," the man said, and stuck out his hand, which looked big with long fingers.

"Mike." They shook and headed wordlessly over to the pile of wreckage. Together, they lifted and moved some of the more pliable things: a small fridge, a jumble of wood, and car tires, which Wade rolled into the dark culvert.

"Where're you from?" Wiley said.

"Vermont."

"You've come far."

"I've got a ways still."

They needed to move two more small cement blocks, then it looked like the truck could plow through the rest.

"Where're *you* from?"

"'riginally, Buffalo, Wyoming."

"What do you have in the truck?"

"Idaho potatoes." Then Wiley looked off into the darkness suspiciously. "I'll betcha they'd love to get 'em. It would keep these gangs eating for a year."

Wade picked up the crude sign and using both hands winged it to the side of the road like it was a giant Frisbee. The both of them rolled a junked motorcycle out of the way. A tipped-over VW Bus covered the other half of the highway, and it looked like they could maneuver around it. Wade looked back at the other man.

"I can ride with you, can't I?"

Wiley sized him up for a moment, partly in jest. "Well I guess you can, if you aren't some kinda serial-killer hitchhiker, like they show in the movies."

"Nothing of the sort…" Then Wade saw Wiley nodding in the direction of the mountains. He saw a line of torches coming quickly across a distant field toward them.

"Let's go!" he shouted, but Wiley was already climbing up the steps into his cab. Wade ran over to where he had left his backpack, hauled it onto his shoulder, then made it over to the truck and climbed up into the passenger seat. He slammed the door behind him.

He heard a shot ring out, then another. The second bullet clanged into the metal of the cab. "I guess they think we're unfriendly," Wiley said. The engine growled and shuddered into gear as Wiley hauled on the gear shift. With a kick the truck moved forward slowly, through the area they'd cleared then through another small pyramid of tires and wood and metal debris. They heard two more clangs of bullets hitting the cab and the side of the truck. Wade swallowed hard. He looked and saw that the row of torches was within about 200 meters of them. As they painstakingly pushed through the debris, the headlights illuminated a pile of adult bodies slumped in the breakdown lane, all necklaced with car tires and badly burned.

"Good God," Wiley muttered. "It's a fuckin' death

factory." Then he stopped the truck again.

"What are you doin'?"

"The Goddamned cable there! And we've got to get our asses out of here!" He looked behind him quickly, and his eyes were bugging out. "I knew this wouldn't be as easy!" He thumped the steering wheel with both hands and picked up his shotgun. "We're in a mess of trouble, we are!"

In the headlights, they could see that a metal cable had been strung across the highway, only about a foot high, but a formidable and inconvenient impasse. Wiley took the truck out of gear. Wade dug out the handgun with the two shots left, the .38 Specials in his backpack, opened his door, and stepped down to the black tar in the grim shimmering light of the smoke and stars.

He smelled burned, rotting flesh.

"How many shots do you have in that shotgun?"

"Two," Wiley said. "A few more in back."

Wade looked quickly behind him and saw one torch running ahead. They might have a minute. They reached the cable and Wade bent down and lifted it up. It had a tightly strung weight. "Take it out." Wiley put both barrels of the shotgun against it and shot once, twice, two loud hot cracks, and Wade let go of the wire on the second one just before it tore out of his hands and clanged across the tar. Then they both ran.

A head grinned in the red rear lights and yelled "Hey fucker!" and raised the barrel of a rifle. A guy running along behind him held a torch. But Wade raised his Beretta first and shot him twice in the chest and he fell dead in front of his partner, then Wade scrambled up into the cab and he hadn't closed his door yet as the engine roared into gear. Wiley was laughing and cackling with crazed relief as he moved the big diesel engine from low to higher gear. The driver put his head down and laughed uncontrollably and Wade, exhausted, just looked at him with his mouth agape.

"What's eatin' you?" Wiley yelled over the energized motor as they watched just trees and barren highway go by. "They didn't even shoot our tires out!"

The view exuded a relief-filled emptiness as the toll station from hell receded in the rearview mirror.

"We just escaped death, by the narrow margins, by God!" When his own mirth began to run out of gas, Wiley just shook his head and sighed.

"I think I just killed another person," Wade said. "I killed two people tonight."

Wiley looked at him, then back to the highway, newly somber. "Ever been in the military?"

"No. You?"

"No. But I have plenty of friends who have. The feelin' must be the same. You come to terms with it. Wouldn't feel bad. I wouldn't. You killed outa self-defense. You seem the good sort. There isn't a fine line these days, it seems. Just bad. And good. We wouldn't be alive...you seem to really think quick. It's the ones who are quick on their feet that stay alive. Damn if it isn't the damnedest time we're livin' in."

Wade rubbed his face with his palms as if he was washing it. His vision was blurry. He figured it was the trauma. And fatigue. He decided he should be grateful, although all he felt was numbness.

"How much gas do you have?" he mumbled.

"Three quarters tank. I filled up at one of our stations in Laramie."

"No fires there?"

"'Aint nothin' to burn."

"I guess that's good."

"I guess so."

"I have some water," Wade said. "What did you say your name was again? I'm just terrible with…"

"…Names. I know. I know, everyone says that. Ever noticed? Wiley James is my name. I'm the product of Wiley Coyote and Jesse James. Heh heh."

Wade handed him a blue Nalgene bottle of water, and they shared it. "Well, that's all I have. We'll get some more."

Wiley took a deep breath and watched the highway hurtling by. Then he began to hum a tune, more to himself. He nodded his head affirmative when Wade said, "Mind if I sleep?"

CHAPTER 5

He went out as soon as he shut his eyes, a heavy sitting-up sleep. When he opened them again, the real sun, not just the glow from the fires, crested the high ridges.

"How far's Colorado Springs?"

"We passed it. I have to pull over in a sec."

"Thanks for taking me in."

"No worries. Well, I guess you saved my life. Alone, I think I would have tried to blast through that mess. Might a' worked; might not 'ave."

"Where're you taking these potatoes?"

"Supposed to be taking them to Mexico, where I fill up with TVs, microwaves, some such things, then make the return trip. But the way things are, well, you tell me. It's too dangerous, and outright foolish. I might just end up driving east. I'll have to get some fuel though. Don't you think there might be some workable diner around here? My eyes are about to slam shut. I have to pull over."

Not far outside of Pueblo they pulled over in the emergency lane. Their windows were open. It was eerily quiet.

"Maybe you should hide the truck better," Wade said.

Wiley nodded, put the truck into gear again, then pulled off the roadside and onto the dried-up dusty gravel and grass. He nestled the cab and its bulky trailer beneath a dark copse of trees. Without any streetlights they might be hidden well enough, Wade thought, or be mistaken for an old, wrecked truck body with nothing to loot.

Wiley shut down the engines and the lights and crawled into a sleeping space behind the front seats of the cab. He seemed beyond exhaustion. "I'll take watch," Wade said. He was hungry and tired himself. Wiley handed him the shotgun with fresh shells loaded into it, then he fell asleep and started snoring loudly. Wade opened his door and stepped down onto the road.

The sky, as the sun came up, flickered behind the mountains and the blossoming light, like someone turning lights off and on. He could smell the fire still, but it mingled with a piney, pleasant tree smell. They'd seen no one coming north on I-25; it wasn't a good sign for gasoline in Pueblo. He stretched his arms in the cool air; all he heard were crickets and flies. It was a little warmer but not that much different than a common summer dawn. Nothing much thrived in the land of the fires. You hardly saw flocks of birds anymore; scores of animals had fled to the plains, or been killed in the inferno. The birds had gone north or east, and if it wasn't for Kara, he'd be headed in the same direction.

He heard a guttural engine roar coming from up the highway towards Denver. The road was still largely cast in the mountain's shadow. He walked to the back of the cab and saw lights in the distance, getting closer. He thought he better wake Wiley.

He went back to the cab and shook Wiley's boot, which stuck up over the seat. Wiley rose up with an embittered, bearded grimace, and Wade said, "We got company."

"Stay hidden and don't turn on any lights." Wade handed the shotgun back to Wiley who gathered himself and ducked down low in the cab as the sound of the engines got louder. It sounded like a motorcycle club used to. They didn't have "clubs" anymore, Wade thought. They had marauding bands of savages.

"We'll have to take to the woods if they see us," he told Wiley. He pulled his backpack down from the truck, but leaned it up against one of the huge tires and hid it behind the cab. He couldn't lose his gear if he had to take off into the roadside forest. He readied his bow and crept behind the trailer to around its stern. He watched as the first of at least two dozen Harleys roared past, headlights and chrome and oversized twisted exhaust pipes blazing in the dawn light, the men and the women in studded black leather and without helmets. *They're going too fast. It's still too dark to see us.* Not 40 meters away, the bikes had red and black flags attached to the seats, with leering renditions of skulls and bones and Swastikas. The bikers seemed to be going somewhere in a hurry. They raised the dust and ash off the road. He felt a slight breeze tainted by exhaust. It only took half a minute. He breathed easier and thought that it was a shame that they were all going in the same direction; toward the southwest and looking for gas and nothing else really, because nothing but emptiness and desolation awaited them.

He waited until the lights disappeared down the road south.

# # #

"Even our little pond is getting dried up and parched."

Standing on the roadside, he recalled that conversation he'd had with his wife Lee. It was even dry in Vermont, but they weren't having wildfires because global warming had rather increased their precipitation during the winter. He remembered Lee's warm, accepting eyes, a look that could bear any burden. Her long auburn hair and country stylish, fairly antiquated habit of wearing dresses over cowboy boots. He'd dropped her and his son Shane off in Ottawa, Canada, and she'd given him a hug, both arms thrown around his shoulders, that he didn't want to let go.

"Get ahold of us whenever you can," she'd said. She smiled but looked at him wearily. And warily. It was nuts, really, what he was doing, but they had to get Kara back. It was a last-resort kind of effort. He kept texting them until the cell phone ran out; he used his charger and found some electricity before they got into Chicago on the train and ran into all that business, but there wasn't any cell-phone service anyways. Even the regime lost that in many of its territories and was too dumb and religiously orthodox and authoritarian in its methods to employ technical people within its ranks to keep the technology going.

He took one of a half dozen flashlights out of his backpack and sat in the passenger seat and poured over a folded out map of the southwest. They had a decision to make in Pueblo; they could go east on 50 toward Grand Junction as an alternative. The route they were on continued to the deserts of New Mexico. He had to go east and south anyways to get closer to Sierra Vista in Arizona.

Wiley started up the engine, and they backed slowly out of their hiding place. Then rode over the dirt and back onto the highway. It wasn't far to Pueblo.

CHAPTER 6

They didn't see anymore of the bikers that day, and Wade figured that to be very lucky. His stomach was growling and he needed water, by at least the end of the day. He figured they should probably pull over and cook up a big batch of potatoes, maybe find a stream and use the matches in his first-aid kit. Maybe Wiley had a pan among his gear. One thing there was plenty of was dry wood around. He figured Wiley was hungry too, because he hadn't said anything for a while.

Wiley had to be worried as the gas gauge was going down and there were few opportunities to refuel. There *was* an advantage to being able to haul all that food around.

Once they pulled into the Pueblo, Colorado city limits they saw a person standing on the one of the highway entrance ramps. It was as though she was waiting for a ride. When she saw the truck coming down I-25 she waved and stuck out her thumb. She had long, light-colored hair and carried a small backpack, and she looked young, to be out on the road alone. Wiley put the truck into a lower gear and slowed down. So far, they weren't leaving the highway at Pueblo, so Wiley aimed to pull the truck over near where the entrance ramp connected with the highway.

Wade could see that she was smiling and had bent down and lifted up a pant leg to show them a little calf, and he smiled in spite of himself, because not much up till then had been amusing. He found a young woman hitchhiking here incredulous and outrageous.

Pueblo was the beginning of a ghost town and there weren't any other vehicles or people around. They stopped the truck, and she trotted up the entrance ramp to where Wade had opened the passenger door. She was pretty and had long hair and freckles on her face and bell-bottomed pants. Her clothes were a bit heavy for the heat, he thought, and made of a funky patchwork of other garments. She smiled and stopped short of the truck.

"Fee fie foe fum…friend or foe?" she said.

"Friend."

"Thought so. Thanks for stopping…I mean, you mighta' been the only car or truck for days. My name's Phoebe Tate." She stuck out her hand. He took it gently.

"Mike Wade. The driver's Wiley. Come on, get in."

"Oh, many thanks." She took his boost up the steps and climbed into the back of the cab.

"What are you doin' out there in Crazy Land girl?" Wiley exclaimed.

"Trying to get from Point A to Point B."

"I guess we all are. Did you see some bikers come through here? Glad they didn't see you…"

"Yeah, I saw 'em." She settled down on a cushion that Wiley slept on behind the front seats. Wiley restarted the truck and angled it onto the highway again. It coughed and a loud spurt of black diesel exhaust came out of the oil-stained pipe that stuck out of the back of the cab.

"I was camping under those trees over there. Then they came in like a flock 'a vultures and parked in a field and had some kind of weird funeral...they were burning a cross."

"Figures," Wiley said.

"Did they leave?"

"Early this morning."

"Good."

Wiley looked over at her; she had energy and a pretty sparkle in her young, green eyes. "Seen any working fuel stations around here?"

"I know where we can get gas...and food."

"Where?" Wiley said.

"Over west past Pueblo, if you take the exit for 50 coming up."

"What is it?"

"The old Southwest Grill. It's half burned down, it doesn't look like anyone would be there, which is good obviously...but I know the family that runs it. The Santiagos. Real nice folks. Kindly and caring. They still live over by there and they can keep the grill going and they have all this used grill oil that a truck can use for fuel. They have fuel."

"You don't say..."

"Yeah."

"You can find it from here?" Wade asked, looking back at her as she leaned eagerly between the two seats.

"Yeah...take the upcoming exit there."

"I'm starving," Wiley said.

"Me too."

They got on 50 and headed west towards Grand Junction. Wade got out his map again. He felt uplifted by simply going in another direction.

"Gee, I really could use a Starbucks about now," Phoebe said, bouncing along on her perch in the back. "Or a Seattle's Best."

"What about Green Mountain?" Wade said, thinking of his home state.

"That too…"

"As long as it's dark and strong," Wade said.

"You drink it black, too?" Phoebe said, hopeful of a another connection between them.

"You bet, dark roast, black…"

"Will you guys quit talking about Starbucks and such?" Wiley said, staring straight ahead through the windshield. "It all kind of rubs it in…reminds me of a diner they had in Buffalo that had better coffee than anyone in the morning…wash down a plate of eggs and hash browns with it."

Then he looked back at Phoebe half serious, and smiled. "Yeah, one of them coffee-house lattes would go over good about now."

"What did I used to get…" Wade said. "A chocolate machiatto on ice."

"Chai latte," Phoebe said.

"I figured you for chai," Wiley said. "That's a complement." They'd seen a half-burned green sign for Starbucks, out in front of a crumbling mall in Denver. It'd be worth it to stop and harvest the stainless steel, Wade thought, with a practicality he couldn't resist. Thinking of favorite franchises and restaurants and the habits of eating out of malls and parking lots seemed like a very recent past that wasn't coming back. Who knew what would arise from the ashes.

"Did you see the bikers go this way?" Wiley asked.

"Don't think so," Phoebe said. "Think they kept going

south." They were getting close to the block containing the Southwest Grille and Phoebe told him to slow down. She pointed to a building that was one-third blackened with its roof partially collapsed. The neighborhood, a failed chunk of suburbia, looked like a riot had taken place, then it was picked over for weeks afterward.

Wiley slowed the big truck then turned into its parking lot, which had a few junked car bodies lying about.

"This is it, huh?" Wiley said.

"Yeah." He turned off the engine and they sat quietly for a minute.

"Where are they?"

"We'll see them soon," Phoebe said.

"How do you know 'em?"

"I was a waitress here once."

Wade opened his door, stepped down from the cab, and shouldered his backpack. He got his bow out. He already thought of the truck as his sanctuary; he was wary moving too far away from it.

He looked around the emptied blocks and saw nothing moving. The sun blazed above the floppy rim of his boony hat, and the air was tangy with hot ash. He figured the fires would flow down here eventually and feed on this long dry grass and the clusters of trees and the wooden homes.

Phoebe put thumb and forefinger into her mouth and whistled loudly toward a spot of woods behind the old grill. Wiley virtually jumped out of his shoes. "Sh-sh girl, you'll wake the dead!"

"They'll know it's me."

Then three people emerged from the trees and walked tentatively around the side of the building. It was two adults and a child behind them. When they recognized Phoebe, they smiled with a tired relief, and the little boy began to run.

"Hey little guy!" He ran right into her arms. She hugged him then let him down and then hugged the man and the woman, who were short and had friendly, proud, put-upon faces, probably given what they'd seen so far, Wade thought.

"This is Carmen Santiago, Javi Santiago, and the kooky Pepe," she said, ruffling the little kid's black, bowl-cut hair.

"Mike Wade." It felt good to smile and shake this kind-looking couple's hands. He was beginning to think people like this, and Phoebe, had ceased to exist.

"These guys picked me up right off the highway!" Phoebe said. "I got nicknames for 'em. This ones Latte and this here's Machiatto. It's too hard to remember the real ones anyways." Wiley chuckled and smiled bashfully.

Carmen wiped her hands on her dress and shook Wade's and Wiley's hands and Wade thought she looked brave and pretty.

"I'll bet you you're hungry," Carmen said. "We can go over there and cook something up." She pointed to the part of the building that still had its intact roof. It was a one-story, fairly long restaurant in the typical, memorable roadside style.

"I'm *famished*," Phoebe said. "Man oh man, remember the all-day breakfasts, and those truckers would come in and order the same thing but three-plates worth every time?"

"We might be able to cook up something like that," Javi said.

"Wow," Wade said. "Do you need some potatoes?"

"Yes."

"You need potatoes, we got potatoes," Wiley said. "I just need a couple of boxes."

"Inside."

It felt weird and nice to be doing *anything* casual, like stand in a parking lot and chat. But Wade was glad they were going inside.

"Anybody been by lately?" Wiley said. He regretted the remark later; he hadn't wanted to destroy the rare goodwill that permeated the gathering.

Partly grimacing, Javi looked at him and said, "We had'a group come through two weeks ago, then nothing."

"Good."

They had gone farther into the foothills to reach this place off 50 and Wade looked up into those hills and saw bits of whitish gray ash floating in the breeze, like snow.

He hadn't seen snow in a while, not even in Vermont, where they had rare winter storms in the small mountains that topped out at 4,000 feet. Where he was from, it used to be Snow Land.

CHAPTER 7

The last thing he'd gotten from Kara was a postcard before the mail services collapsed and stopped delivering. She wrote "Daddy I'm okay..." She'd never used to call him Daddy since she became college-aged and had matured quickly as young girls do. Then she probably thought that it wasn't too cool. She wrote that she was with a small group of other students and that they'd paid some guys to truck them over the Mexican border to Arizona. That part scared the shit out of him, amongst all the other scary details of their predicament. It was then that it became an easy decision to go and he vowed to not come back without Kara. He felt bad about leaving the rest of his family, but Lee understood.

Kara said they were going to Sierra Vista. He thought of snows years ago in their backyard and pushing Kara down a hill on a sled they called the Swiss Bob, and of Kara laughing her sweet giggle as she tipped over in the powder. How distant the memory seemed in this charred, broken-down restaurant and parking lot. They hadn't heard anything else after the postcard.

# # #

They walked around into the back of the good part of the Southwest Grille. Javi pulled back a screen door that hung loosely on its hinges, then he took out a key, unlocked an inner door, and they came through a back way into a kitchen. The stainless steel gleamed, Wade noticed, as he thought Carmen had tidied up the damaged kitchen, aiming for a sense of normalcy. Javi took some eggs out of a fridge and removed two frying pans from a shelf and they had some butter and they began to cook the eggs on the top of an old wood stove. Wiley and Wade went back to the truck with two wooden crates, and they opened the truck rear door and filled the crates with potatoes that still had crumbly flakes of soil on them, and Wade liked the loamy smell the piles of potatoes had. It made him think of sticking his head out of the train window when they crossed Kansas and Nebraska. Some of the potatoes on the very bottom of the piles had gone bad, but they filled the crates with good ones and carried them back to the kitchen.

Carmen was already making a second batch of eggs, and they cut up the potatoes with two kitchen knives and threw them in with the eggs and butter, then she began to scoop the piles of eggs and potatoes, nicely fired in the butter, onto plates.

Wade was beyond starved and it seemed so delicious.

"Wait," Carmen said, as he picked up his plate and fork. "Don't you want some sauce?"

"Yes."

She squirted some Mexican hot sauce from a plastic container onto his eggs and potato pile. "That's fine."

They were all standing in a circle eating, as if they'd never eaten before.

"Just like home!" Phoebe chirped out.

With his mouth full, Wade asked, "Where'd you get the eggs?"

Javi put a skillet down. "Farm down on 50."

"They still have a farm? A working farm here?"

"It's off the road," Javi said. "You'd have to know where to find it. They have chickens, and dairy. They milk the cows by hand now. They've had to butcher some of the cows for meat, but the last time we were there we came back with some milk."

"Amazing."

Javi went back over to the fridge, which had no electricity but provided some insulation. He opened the door and pulled out a clear two-liter jar of milk.

"We have to finish it in a few days or it goes bad."

"We will make yogurt from it," Carmen said.

"We will."

Wade looked over at Phoebe and Wiley, as if seeking their approval. "Can I have some?"

Carmen pulled a small glass off a shelf and poured the creamy milk into it and handed it to Wade. He put his plate down and accepted the glass, then brought it up to his mouth and drank; it tasted thick and sweet and like a milk shake. It was warm but still delicious. He put the glass down on a stainless steel shelf and watched as the creamy residue clung to and slowly drooped down the side of the glass.

"Can we go back to this farm?"

"Yes, I think so," Javi said. Wade thought they could load up on eggs, some milk, at least temporarily, and maybe meat, in return for potatoes and whatever else the farmers would take. Maybe they could work for it; the vision of a farm in a field back in the woods, and working on the farm, had made

Wade think that there could be texture in a day again, not only thinking one hour ahead. To spend a day beyond survival mode.

Pepe sat cross-legged on the cement floor spooning eggs into his mouth. When he was finished he put the plate on the floor, and said "We chased the chickens. The barn was full of yellow hay and baby chicks, and we jumped in the hay. Then they cut the chicken's head off..."

"Okay Pepe, help your father collect the plates, if the people are finished," Carmen said.

"If you don't mind..." Wiley brought his plate over to the skillet, which still had leftover, hash-browned potatoes in it; with black-crusted sides where it had griddled in the melted butter.

"Please," Javi said. Wiley shoveled the rest of it on to his plate with a spatula.

Then Javi said, "Can we go with you on the truck?"

"Where?"

"To the west. Grand Junction."

"Why sure you can. Do you have any leftover oven grease?" There was a bit of it in the iron skillet from the butter, eggs, and potatoes.

"We have a lot of leftover grease," Javi said matter-of-factly. He walked into a side room of the kitchen, and came out with a gallon-sized or so bucket that had a brown, rheumy grease floating in it with small pieces of debris.

"That's the ticket," Wiley said, giving the bucket a studious but sluggish inspection. "I'm down to a quarter tank. It's worth a try, isn't it? Never tried it before with the truck." He scratched the whiskers on his chin. "How much more of it do you have?"

"Twenty gallons, thereabouts."

"Do you have tops for the containers, so we can transport

them?"

"Yes."

"We'll load them into the back of the truck."

"Good."

Then everyone was quiet, sated and fatigued by the food.

"Let's move the truck to behind the building," Wade said. "It's too visible, and we can load it up from here."

Wiley nodded, distracted. He turned to Javi. "Why do you want to move from here?"

"We want to go home. There's no future here."

"Guess not. Where's home?"

"Nicaragua, near Managua, on the coast."

"No kidding?" Wiley's eyes lit up. "I drove down there about thirty years ago with some pals and ended up on the beach, camping out and surfing. Best weed I've ever had…"

"You can go back sometime." Javi smiled.

"I just might, I just might. That's a long way from here."

"Everywhere is a long way."

"True."

Phoebe yawned strenuously and tossed her hair behind her shoulders. "Many many thanks for the food, and I have to grab some zees."

"*De nada,*" Carmen said.

"Do you still have the booths out in the restaurant?"

"It's wet and moldy and exposed to the elements," Carmen said. "But you can try. Do you want to lie down?"

"*Si,*" Phoebe said, and stood up. She stretched and ground both her eyes with her fists, in a way that made Wade tired too. They couldn't get too complacent and comfortable at the Southwest Grill, he thought, or they'll be snuck up upon.

Wiley went to move the truck and Phoebe left for the evacuated part of the restaurant.

"When you get the truck back here, we'll load up the

grease," Wade said.

"When do you want to leave?" Javi asked. Carmen wiped the dishes with a towel, and Wade wandered over to help her.

"Don't go far!" she yelled out to Pepe, who followed Phoebe out of the kitchen. "He's usually not allowed to be alone."

"Pepe's my pal, right compadre?" She put her arm around him. "I'll keep a close eye on him. We're just going to have a nap…"

"If you hear me yell in there that we have to go, you two are going to have to move fast," Wade said. "Do you hear me, Pepe?"

"Yeah." Then Wade turned to Carmen. "We might as well stay the night…load up the truck with food, grease, and what you want to bring."

"I think that will be okay."

They could hear the guttural cough of the truck starting up and the loud engine and springy suspension as the truck angled over the dirt and gravel behind the restaurant.

CHAPTER 8

They lit a small fire behind the restaurant at night and Javi came out with a jug of Chianti. Carmen brought glasses and gave each of them one. They were cooking the last of some slices of beef and bacon that the Santiagos kept in the old fridge, and they ate them with potatoes and cheddar cheese. Javi walked behind each person and filled their glass. They planned to leave first thing in the morning. The truck was already packed. The night was silent and comforting by the fire, with an evening breeze that blew through the leaves of the trees they huddled beneath, and the sound of crickets. They could see anyone who was coming close, due to the lights of the vehicles from far away.

Wade watched the distant flickering in the sky over the ridges, like a faraway fireworks display.

The food was delicious, freshly grilled in butter and olive oil, and the wine was better. It loosened their tongues;

everyone began telling stories. The Santiagos talked about how they rode on the roof of a train from Nicaragua and entered the U.S. by crossing a desert at night in Baja. Then they ended up in Colorado working long hours at the Southwest Grill, and had the baby Pepe and the original owner died and left the restaurant to them, as they had full citizenship. They wanted to go back home and the fabric of society fell apart before they had a chance to sell. They wanted to get to the southwest and the border almost as bad as Wade did.

Phoebe worked as a waitress in the Grill and she also sold desert jewels with "special powers." She scoured the desert outside of Santa Fe, New Mexico and in Utah for special rocks and made artwork out of them and sold them to tourists off the road and at a Taos gallery. She became adept at journeying through the desert. She read the poetry of Pablo Neruda from Chile and she tried peyote in the arid parts of the Sangre de Cristo. She's been going through boyfriends; she finds them easily and tires of them quickly, about one every six months.

She had no particular destination when Wade and Wiley met her, but now she was seriously considering going to Nicaragua with the Santiagos. Wade just wanted to get to Grand Junction in one piece, then head south after his daughter.

Wiley told the story, as if it was his favorite one, about the surf-bum trip to Latin America, where the food was mostly fruit and marijuana. Then everyone got their wine glasses filled again and the Chianti was gone and Wiley talked about how he went to North Dakota about ten years ago as a roughneck in the oil fields for the good money they paid.

Phoebe quoted from Neruda:

Now they have the ocean

The cold and burning emptiness
The solitude full of flames.

Wade liked the sound of it and he asked her what the name of the poem was and she said it was *The Old Women Of The Ocean.* She said both of her parents were dead and used to live on the coast in Northern California. She asked Wade for a picture of Kara and he got up and found one inside his backpack. He handed it to her. Pepe was asleep in his mother's lap.

"What a gorgeous chick," Phoebe said, and she passed the picture around. "I want to meet this soul sister."

"Maybe you'll get a chance to."

"Where did you come from again?"

"Vermont." Wade took a small stick and began poking around in the fire absentmindedly. He thought it was just a little weird that they'd lit one on purpose, given that vast territories were already aflame. The little campfire still imparted warmth and helped bring them together. Somehow it eased his mind. They'd put it out soon.

"Then you took a train?"

"Yeah, I made it to Denver, where I met a priest." He hadn't even looked at the Bible, so he reached into the backpack and removed it. "He left me with this Bible."

He handed it to Javi, who had sat down next to him on a log.

"Did he try to convert you?"

"No, we had a little dust-up in Denver, with some men, and he thought he should give me something."

Javi began leafing through the pages until he came to a part of the book that had been hollowed out into a compartment. Things were firmly packed into it.

"I'll be darned," Wade said. "I hadn't noticed. The priest

acted like he really wanted to give it to me. What's in there?" Javi removed the objects delicately, like an archeologist.

"Medicine," he said. He took out a plastic bottle and shook it lightly; some pills knocked around inside. He handed it to Wade, who got out his glasses and read the tiny print on the label.

"Doxycycline, two rounds. That will come in handy. So he gives me a Bible, and it contains antibiotics..."

"A bottle of virtue," Phoebe said. "What else?"

Javi next took out a zip-locked bag that had a white powder inside; it was labeled "For Pain" in black ink.

"Enough said, I guess," Wade said. "Keep it with the pills." He'd put them both in his first-aid kit.

Then Javi brought out a gold-colored medallion. The compartment only contained one more thing after that. He held the medallion out and it dangled at the end of a red cloth band. The medallion glinted in the firelight.

"Let me see," Phoebe said, excited. She reached across the fire and he handed it to her. She examined it closely, then she said, "That's a Saint Michael medal, and an old one, too. It will protect the wearer from evil. It's powerful magic, that one."

"Put it on, let's see how it looks on you," Wiley said. She put it over her head and the medal slipped into the space left by an unbuttoned denim shirt. She rearranged the cloth so that the medal lay near her clavicle, then looked around and smiled. The fire crackled and the breeze lifted some embers up, which swirled into the dark trees.

"It becomes you," Wade said.

Finally, Javi removed a small cloth bag from the Bible, and it too contained something of value. A string of pearls. A tiny crinkled line of paper, like you'd find in a fortune cookie, came out of the bag with the pearls. Javi gave the paper to

Wade, who handed the pearls to Carmen.

"They're so beautiful," she purred. She ran them through her fingers; she put them on.

Wade read from the paper, "Genuine pearl jewelry made by the Maori in New Zealand...Okay..."

"They are priceless," Carmen said.

"You can keep them."

"Oh no."

"Yes."

"Muy bonito."

Wade felt the darkness closing in around them and their fire, a homy yet fearful impulse. He got up because he wanted to look at the road again out in front of the restaurant. Once he left the sanctuary of the fire it was incredibly dark; he thought he might walk straight into a tree. He couldn't see the road itself, yet its evident emptiness and inactivity was reassuring. He listened to his boots crunch on the gravel of the parking lot and sensed the unlit restaurant as a barely discernible, crumbled hulk beside the road. Clouds covered the stars and the distant fire flickered lightly over the ridges. He felt they were well-enough hidden for now, yet someone high up could still notice the campfire inside the black night.

He was ready to leave the next day, and he thought he would sleep outside on a pad he would unroll beneath a tree and a cotton blanket.

He walked back to the fire and all the wine-glasses were empty and everyone seemed to lean into the weak flame and embers. He could only see their faces well. Javi was translating Spanish phrases and Wiley asked him what *A mal tiempo, buena cara* meant, and Javi said, "To have courage, and hold your head and chest high, when times are bad."

Wiley just nodded, then he looked at Wade, who took the seat on the log where he had eaten and drank.

"Will you come back here again with Kara?"

"No, I haven't figured out the return route yet."

"I figured you two could get on that Denver train and head east, back to Chicago." It was nice of him to discuss that scenario; him and Kara coming home. As if assured that it would definitely take place.

"Best not go to Chicago."

"It was that bad, huh?"

"Yeah."

"What happened? I thought the regime owned that city, not the crazies?"

Wade picked up the same charred stick and dug it into the fire and stirred it around, not taking his eye off the glowing embers. "I don't need to go into that here."

He was a different man before Chicago; not a killer.

After a while, Wiley got up and went back to the truck and returned with an old folk guitar. He tuned the guitar and strummed it for a moment as they all stared into the fire and listened. It was sleepy and calm. "You know Harvest Moon? Neil Young?" he said.

"Yeah, I do," Phoebe said. "That song is like a great kiss." They sang it together, a delightful duet. Phoebe had a pretty, high voice. Carmen rocked Pepe to the rhythm. They all just wanted to continue doing that, and not have the sun come up the next morning on the world they now lived in.

CHAPTER 9

Wade woke up with the first light. He pulled the blanket off and refolded it and put it back into the backpack with the bedroll, then he found the tin pot of coffee they'd made the night before still sitting by the fire. He used some warm coals to heat it up so that it was at least lukewarm, then he sat on the stoop of the restaurant and drank it and watched the sun come up. None of the fires were flaming in that direction and had effected the sunrise's color.

The others began to stir. Then he heard Pepe's plaintive voice from inside the restaurant where the Santiagos slept. They'd all decided to go to the farm on their way west. They needed to pack away more food. Javi would show them where it was. Wiley wandered out in a few minutes from where he'd slept in the truck, looking disheveled.

"Did you sleep?" he called out, when he saw Wade.

"I did. I got some unbroken hours. You?"

"Yeah. That wine, it had more kick than you'd think. It made me forget. That and the music."

"Forget what?"

"Darn near everything."

"Do you want to put more fuel in the truck?" They had plastic buckets of the unrefined grease packed away in the back of the vehicle.

"Let's start it up first."

The truck had started up fine when they'd poured the first gallon in the night before. They'd be walking if the truck doesn't start, he thought, but the engine turned over with a familiar and reassuring metallic shudder. The elongated pipe spit out a clod of black exhaust, then the engine settled into a steady noise. The air smelled of strong sulfur. The Santiagos came out of the shell of a restaurant with a duffel bag and Carmen carried a small suitcase. The Santiagos would all have to cram into Wiley's sleeping space behind the cab's front seats with Phoebe.

She'd slept on her booth in the falling-down restaurant. She came out with her hair tied back with a yellow bandanna and the same denim shirt, which she'd just pulled over her head, and the Saint Michael medal dangling between the open shirt buttons. "Bless your heart," she said, when Wade handed her a mug of still warm coffee. Then she climbed up into the cab.

The farm was located at the end of a long dirt road. They spent about fifteen minutes on Route 50 until the turn-off. The two-lane highway was cracked with weeds growing through the fissures and covered with dislodged lumps of tar. Scorched subdivisions wound through the parched yellow foothills above; it was as if the homes, some large, had been dropped from the sky. Many of the hillsides had swaths of black ash.

They passed one empty and windblown Shell station. Its

windows were smashed and the walls burned and it had a black scar on the concrete where fire had spread from the gasoline tanks to the building. It didn't seem worth stopping; it was apparent that scavengers had stripped away anything usable.

They turned off on the dirt road, which was dry and dusty, and after about a half-mile they saw the horses. They stood in a field feeding on grasses that were still long and green. Some grass actually grew better in the deposited ash, due to the nutrients, Wade thought, and if it rained, which it did once in a while, the grass grew well.

The three horses had white or brown coats and grazed against the horizon. Like the campfire the night before, the scene was like things used to be.

Wiley slowed down the truck; the horses raised their heads nonchalantly to watch them pass. Then they went back to nibbling the grasses in the breeze over the fields.

"They're wild horses now," Javi said.

"They're beautiful," Phoebe said. "Oh, can we take them with us, if we find some saddles?"

Wade shook his head, and Wiley said, "If the truck broke down or stopped running on garbage, we'd have to. Yeah, a horse is really worth something again."

They drove past the horses and they could see the farm buildings in a distance; a large house, a paddock, a barn.

"Where are the folks I wonder?" Carmen said.

"They must be lying low," Wade said. "What's their names?"

"Corsair," Javi said. "This is the Corsair Farm."

A wooden gate was open. A bicycle and an upturned kid's wagon lay beside the road. "Do they have kids?" Wade asked.

"Yes."

"How many?"

"Two," Carmen said. "Like the age of Pepe."

The truck didn't fit through the gate so Wade jumped down from the cab onto the road and opened the slatted gate all the way. It creaked and swung to the side. He looked around the grounds. He listened. Nothing, just the hot wind across the baked ground. No other vehicles were around, save for a tractor parked in a field. He waved the truck in past the gate.

It parked in a cleared-out area, then everyone got out of the cab and began walking toward the house.

"No one's here," Wade said. "They would have heard the truck."

"We'll knock on the door—you see, they weren't expecting us," Carmen said. She had Pepe by the hand and he was looking very alertly all around him. It was weirdly quiet, Wade thought. Wiley shrugged his shoulders.

"Maybe they're out in the fields, cuttin' wood or herding the cows."

"I don't know...I don't know. I'll check the barn," Wade said, and walked over toward the paddock. "Maybe you should stay with the truck."

Wiley seemed disappointed. "If we find some eggs in the kitchen, and milk, maybe we can take some and leave some crates of potatoes and a note—promise to come back and do some work."

Wade walked over to the paddock. The wind was on his back. It was hot; he took off his hat and rubbed the sweat from his forehead. He headed for a screen door that opened onto a middle section between a barn and the paddock. When he got close, he smelled manure, and something else, rotten and fetid. He stuck his head through the screen door and yelled, "Anyone? Hello!"

The room contained a large, stainless steel tank and had a

cement floor with a drain. A fridge stood in the room with a sign that read "Eggs," but he opened it and found it empty. The steel tank had a nozzle at the floor level; a white trickle of liquid led from below the nozzle to the drain. A plastic cup sat on top of the tank, like a cup from a thermos, and he held the cup beneath the nozzle and used a lever to open the valve on the tank. The metal screw-cap for the nozzle lay discarded next to the tank. A trickle of milk went into the cup but stopped when it was filled halfway. Empty.

He drained the cup of the delicious milk, including a blob of cream at the end. Then he heard a cow's bellow from the paddock, and the clubbing of its hooves on a wooden floor. He wanted to look at the barn first, so he opened that door and found an empty office. "Mr. Corsair!" he yelled. "Mrs. Corsair!" Still nothing.

He crossed the office to another door and opened it upon a small barn or stable, where he figured the horses lived, because he found two saddles hanging from hooks, and it smelled of hay and manure and the stalls contained the kind of wool blankets you might use with a horse. He walked across the stable's wood floor to another sliding door that was partly open and saw no sign of the Corsairs, but he saw the others walking toward him from the house.

"Where's Pepe?" Carmen cried out. She approached at a half run and Javi and Wiley were on either side of her.

"He got away from us, temporarily, curious little bugger," Wiley said.

Wade walked back through the stable and the tank room and he noticed the door to the paddock ajar. A foul odor met him when he went through the door and off to the side of the large open space lay a slaughtered cow. It lay in a huge pool of blood and a blizzard of flies, with its eyes open and big tongue lolling out on to the floor. Gouges of flesh had been cut away from its haunches, shoulder, and thighs. Another cow stood over the carcass dumbly, and when it saw Wade it vigorously wagged and nodded its big head.

The stinking paddock was dim, dusty, and airless, and when he looked up he saw Pepe standing at the very end of it. "Pepe!" he yelled, and ran down past the empty stalls to where Pepe stood shivering on the wooden floor and staring into the last stall.

"God almighty," Wade muttered. He picked Pepe up into his arms, kicked open the last door to the paddock, and stepped out into the sunshine. Pepe's little jaw trembled and he was silent.

"They were just sleeping, Pepe, you understand me? Only sleeping." He put the child down and leaned down to his level and said, "Don't ever run away like that, okay? Don't do that again. Stay with us."

Finally Pepe nodded. Carmen ran around the paddock and grabbed him; she hugged him and ran her hands through his black hair, but Wade thought Pepe had a thousand-yard stare. "You didn't see that," he said, more to himself.

Wiley and Javi came through the paddock door; Javi looked stricken.

"We gotta scavenge whatever we can and get the fuck outta here," Wiley said, then he spat on the hard ground.

"Is that the Corsairs?"

"Even the children," Javi said, with a bitter Spanish accent. "Even the children..." Flies buzzed furiously by the open door.

"You didn't see, dear boy," Carmen said, gently rocking him. Wade saw Phoebe carrying a stack of two boxes and she put them down and came running across the yard.

"Just sleeping..." Pepe muttered, catatonically.

"Yes."

Wade walked quickly through the paddock past the stalls and the cow carcass and the tank room to the barn, where he took one of the saddles down off the wall and brought it to the truck.

"Best to get anything we want that's left in the house," he said to Javi. "I saw a water pump back there."

"It's dry; I tried it."

"What were the Corsairs using?"

"The horses and cows are drinking something. Maybe there's a little pond or stream back there."

"We don't have time."

Carmen stayed with Pepe. Wiley gathered some tools he found in the paddock: a scythe, a pitchfork, and two axes. They'd opened the trailer door and he put them back there where Wade had heaved the saddle. Wade also took the blankets from the stalls, folded them, and piled them in the truck cab. The whole time he kept his eye on the road.

"Fuckin' savages," Wiley said, then he slammed the trailer door shut. He looked at Wade forthright. "This is a damned fucked up world we're in."

"That's why it's better to keep moving."

He wanted to look in the office one more time. He walked there quickly as the others made their way back to the truck. Phoebe had found a stuffed horse in one of the rooms in the house, and she'd given it to Pepe, who clutched it to his chest. She knelt beside the boy and used her fingers to comb the hair out of his eyes, which still mirrored an awful aftermath.

She took the Saint Michael medal and draped it around Pepe's neck.

Phoebe had found a cardboard box and loaded it up with some old unopened cans of kidney beans, two bags of brown rice, and some cups and dishes.

She looked up at Wiley. "I feel bad taking this."

"Don't."

Wade went through the shelves and drawers of the office as quickly as he could. Lo and behold, tucked into the back of a shelf, he found a small box of bullets he could load into his pistol. He strode back to the truck and stepped up into the cab. Then he removed the pistol from the pocket of his backpack, opened the bullet box, and one-by-one slipped a new bullet into the empty chambers. He knew he needed a loaded gun for the days ahead.

Wiley got back into the driver's seat.

"Don't you think we should bury the dead?" Wade said. "Give them a decent burial."

Wiley thought for a moment, then looked down regretfully, as if addressing his knees. "Yeah, I do." He looked at Wade and his face was sweating around the scraggly beard, his eyes bloodshot. "That would be the decent thing. But we don't have shovels, and whoever did that is probably nearby, and we have to think about Pepe and the Santiagos and just get the hell out of here." Then he looked away and started up the truck.

They drove back through the gate and out onto the dirt road. Wade could see the farm buildings recede in the sideview mirror, through a cloud of yellow dust. When they drove past the fields where the horses had grazed the animals were gone.

CHAPTER 10

They got back out on the two-lane Route 50 and headed west, towards Salida. They passed through the outskirts of Canon City, Colorado pretty quickly, and it was empty and abandoned, the old town in shambles. Wiley floored the gas pedal and never took his eyes off the highway, as though he was afraid the engine would fail if he did. Wade, who sat in the passenger seat, got out his maps and studied their route.

The sun baked him through the window, so he pulled the boony hat down over his forehead. Once semi-arid range land and developed suburbia, the landscape outside had rapidly given over to a rocky desert, littered with shells of buildings, vehicles, and falling-down signs. He unfolded and draped the plastic map on his lap.

In the old days, he was wedded to maps and it was his career, but he never had to plot his survival using one. He used to consult the U.S. Drought Monitor map every week on

Thursdays, when the government renewed it. Orange regions meant severe drought, red was "extreme," and very dark red signaled "exceptional," rather, apocalyptic. California, week by week, was covered in dark red, and the seeming contagion spread like a blood stain across Oregon, Washington, Nevada, Utah, Arizona, and the rest of the west. It was obvious that the data indicated a longterm, implacable trend. There was nothing to be done; it was like geology and history playing itself out. The drought then the fires resisted human engineering, and when the wildfires exploded this had been predicted but only on a scale measured in centuries, not a few years.

Wade traced his finger from Salida on Route 50 into the mountains–over the continental divide and then on to Montrose and Grand Junction. Beyond that was only unknowns–he would still lay hundreds of miles from Kara and Sierra Vista, Arizona. Was she even still there?

He looked back and Phoebe had opened one of the side windows and she sat looking thoughtfully out at the rocky flatlands that filled the valley, the wind blowing through her reddish blond hair. He found her presence comforting, for more than one reason.

"It's about 180 miles from here to Grand Junction," Wade said, talking over the engine. "Think we have enough fuel?" It was only waste grease, but "fuel" sounded at least like they had a chance.

Wiley took his hand off the wheel and scratched his head. "Maybe. We could head south at Poncha Springs, instead. Avoid the continental divide. That would save on mileage, and get us south."

"But there's nothing down there but desert." *And roving bands of hungry crazies,* Wade thought.

"Probably."

"What kind of mileage do you think we're getting?"

"I'm lucky to be getting five m.p.g. with this garbage."

"So we need at least thirty gallons to get to Grand Junction."

"Yeah, and what's there when we *get* to Grand Junction? A pile of rubble, with desperadoes making some home out of it. And we're a truck full of food and provisions. By the way, keep your weapon handy. Don't forget..."

"The *Colorado River* is in Grand Junction." Phoebe had been listening in.

"Fine," Wiley said. "Why don't we put on our best duds and buy six tickets for a trip on the River Queen. Dammit, all I want to do is do my job. Get this truck and my load down to Arizona." It was weird that he was talking about *his job*, under these circumstances, Wade thought. Wiley just wanted normal back.

The truck entered a canyon on Route 50; it had crumbly, beige rock walls rising on either side of the highway. Flinty rockfalls littered the roadway, and the large river ran below it, not deep but rapid and boiling over rocks in the sunshine.

"We need more water," Javi said, watching the river from the backseat, like they all were. "We should stop here. We're all out of water."

"Yeah," Wiley said, looking from side to side. He slowed the truck down to about twenty; the engine coughed and sputtered and the pipe pumped black smoke into the arid, shimmering air.

"That's the Arkansas," Wade said, looking off to the side, away from his map, and the sight of water, not only the ruins of scorched towns and hillsides, gave him cause for hope.

They approached a dirt turn-off on the left above the river, and Wiley geared down and steered the truck into it. They just fit, then he shut the engine off. All they could hear was the white noise of the river below.

"Let's pour the rest of that grease into the tank," Wade said. "And we'll get some water."

The road had been completely empty, not a soul came by in either direction. The people might be on I-70, Wade thought, which intersected with Grand Junction north of there, but that area, including Vail and Aspen, had been engulfed in flames.

They all got out onto the roadside, including the Santiagos. Wiley walked to the back of the truck and unlatched the door and started taking down the plastic buckets of grease. Wade helped him. Javi, Phoebe, and Carmen took all the plastic bottles and canteens they'd brought with them and climbed carefully over the embankment down to the river.

"I need a bath," Phoebe said.

"A wash will be nice," Carmen said. "The water looks good. Pepe needs one." Wade held the bucket steady and Wiley poured the grease into a filter they'd stuck into the truck's fuel tank.

"How big's the tank?"

"Hundred-fifty gallons," Wiley said. "Plenty of room for as much garbage as we can find." Wade thought that they were lucky to find Phoebe and the calm, generous family, and that he and Wiley alone would have probably run out of gas somewhere on Route 25 near the New Mexican border. The old priest was right, about people depending on each other. About not going it alone.

The grease had an almost savory aroma; it left solids in the filter that they flung onto the roadside. Then they put the empty, dirty plastic buckets back into the truck and latched the door.

Wade looked up and saw a hawk or an eagle hovering in the sky above the cliffs of the canyon.

"Think someone should stay with the truck?"

"No," Wiley said. "But bring your pistol."

They both climbed sideways through steep, loose dirt down to the riverbank. Wade took his hat, shirt, shoes, and pistol and left them in the weeds by the river. He stepped into the water, and it was cold and refreshing. It ran quickly over his ankles and numbed them. He used to swim in cold rivers in Vermont with Kara; he thought of the chilly river and of Kara dog paddling and smiling through a calm shallow current, as just a tiny girl.

The Arkansas River bed was mostly flat rocks smoothed over by decades of water flows, and it had sections of sandy bottoms he stepped through amongst the stones. He rolled up his pants and waded in and cupped his hand and started drinking. Carmen filled a bottle by dipping it in the river, and Pepe made a little pile of rocks by the riverside, lost in play. That made Wade smile. He realized he hadn't been smiling much.

He was so hot he just went all the way in, soaking his pants, and let the cold current take him down river. It wasn't fast or deep because of the epic drought or lack of snowmelt, but it still moved. The water lapped around his neck and numbed his body. He submerged his head and opened his eyes and it was miraculously clear. Nature had a way of renewing itself, he thought, amidst the inferno it had become.

He came to the surface and steadied his bare feet and legs on the rocks, and he could see Phoebe bathing. She was back to him and her back was smooth, brown, and freckled. He long hair was wet and plastered on her back. She gathered the hair behind her head and smiled in the sunshine. The sun shone brightly on the flawless, moving water.

He submerged himself and drank some more and returned to the embankment.

#

All the bottles were filled and lined up by some rocks. Wiley had a floppy hat on and was standing knee-deep in the river and staring off into the distance. Javi lay back and slept by the river. Wade wanted to make sure they weren't vulnerable, getting complacent, but he still understood what everyone was doing. He went over and fetched his pistol and sat on a rock in the shade.

The sun was burning and stifling outside of the river. He felt that they had cooled off and had gathered enough water for several days, but that they were driving into the unknowns and closer to the core of the fires.

CHAPTER 11

They'd decided to spend the night by the Arkansas River. They made a small fire out of an old crate from the truck, and some scrappy desert growth. They boiled potatoes and mixed it with the kidney beans and the rice.

The sun went down behind the cliffs; it was abrupt, shifting from bright sunshine to a sudden mauve dusk. It cooled off. The stars came out while they ate and sat by the fire beneath the truck. The vehicle was a dumb and metallic object sitting silently above the river, and it was almost easy to forget about it. The stars were incredibly bright in a velvety black sky. The winds must have blown the ash clouds in another direction, he thought.

Wade sat with the pistol in his lap and he put his metal plate and fork onto the ground beside him. Wiley had left to fuss with the truck and keep watch. He might sleep in the truck, Wade figured. The Santiagos were getting their campsite put together and were using the horse blankets they'd found. Everyone transitioned to sleep as the sun went down; it was as if they lived in an earlier era, when people didn't stay up to all hours watching cable TV and staring at computers.

Phoebe was sitting across from him. She had combed her hair, and let the yellow head-band fall to around her neck like a scarf.

"What happened to your parents?"

"We lived in Shasta, California. We lived off the grid when I was a kid. My dad hunted and planted and did odd jobs and sold skins, and I learned the magic-rock jewelry trade from my mom. But we couldn't exactly make ends meet so..." She brushed the hair out of her eyes and Wade could see the sadness in her eyes, glinting in the firelight.

"...My daddy had to go work the tar sands in Canada, and he got something in his lungs and died pretty young, and my mom died I think of grief."

The fire crackled and the starlit darkness settled around the desert. She uncrossed her legs.

"That must have been hard."

"Goodness," she sighed. "I don't think about it much anymore. I went out into the desert and spent some time chillin' and searched for my precious rocks and my mom would have liked that. She would have done it, too."

"Got any siblings?"

"An older brother but he went bumming and surfing in Bali and Thailand and I haven't heard from him since. I think we have the wandering gene in our blood. What's your wife like?"

"Beautiful, maybe like your mom was because you got it from somewhere. She's loyal, and *sane*. It takes rock hard patience to live with me, and she's got it."

"You're not so bad."

"Think so?"

"I feel safe with you. You guys are my saviors. Latte and Machiatto."

"Hey, I'm so glad we ran into you."

"I hope you find your daughter soon. I want to meet her. Somehow I think we should be best friends."

"I hope you get the chance." The fire they'd built collapsed onto a brittle structure of ashen sticks and a whippet of embers blew off toward the river.

"Why do you carry that pistol all the time? I mean, I *know*, but everywhere?"

"You never know who's going to show up."

"You weren't always like this, were you."

"No."

"What happened in Chicago?"

He put the gun next to his plate on the ground and picked up a stick and began fidgeting with the embers again.

"I brought the handgun as an absolute, you know, last resort. Never had been a gun guy; I'd shot it on two occasions in the woods to see how it worked."

"Chicago was just supposed to be a connection; stop, pick up some people, go on with the train to Denver. I was asleep when we pulled in. I'd left my hand on my gun; I was nervous. It was lying beneath my coat next to me. We'd passed a lot of burnt-out towns in Pennsylvania and Ohio and some of the gangs were waiting in the stations to see if the train would stop, and they looked very bad, but the train never did, and one time the train blasted through some old railroad ties that someone had piled up to derail us, and anyways the whole trip to Chicago was very dicey. I didn't want to stop there long.

"Then I heard a woman crying, hysterically. I woke up. The train was pulling into the Chicago station. A woman outside the window was standing on the platform with a baby in her arms. A toddler was holding her hand." He cleared his throat and he looked up and he saw Phoebe looking at him raptly in the shadows.

"She was saying, what was it?...*I won't give them up. I won't give them up.* One of the regime's uniformed guards had a gun to her head. She was standing there on the platform, with the little boy looking up at her and she clutching the baby to her chest. Then the guard took the gun away from her head and I couldn't quite see them completely through my window, so I got up in the aisle and walked down to the exit door and stood on the top steps to see what was going on. And the lady screamed *No!* And just as the train starts moving forward...he grabs the baby with both hands and she's fighting for her child and he rips the baby out of her arms and turns...and in this one casual motion, heaves it like you would a shovel-full of sand under the train, and the lady collapsed on the concrete and I shot him...I don't remember thinking...I shot him from the steps, two, three times...might have missed once...then he's lying there crawling and the train gets going and I shot him a couple more times as we pull away..."

"My word," Phoebe said, but in a murmur that expressed sympathy for him.

"The lady got to her feet, still hysterical, understandably, and ran away with the boy. I used up most of my ammo then. That's why it was good that I found that box back at the farm."

CHAPTER 12

The next day they climbed to the continental divide. The truck could only muster about ten m.p.h., but they made it. It snowed at first, cold wet snowflakes spitting onto the concrete road and frozen ground, then the clouds opened up, proffering a view.

Wiley was so relieved they made it that he stopped the truck at the old tourist turn-off. They were at eleven thousand feet. Phoebe got out and, using a spray can she'd scavenged from the Corsair farm, she wrote "Nicaragua or Bust" on the side of the truck. Everyone hugged themselves in the sudden cold, but it felt good to get out of the truck, breath the chilly but clear air, and let Phoebe's high spirits enliven them.

Cirrus clouds composed of smoke from the burning forests trailed off most of the mountainsides. The San Juans, he thought. Some of them had snow on the peaks but there was remarkably little snow at the high elevations. The warming had given the Rockies a minimal, almost nonexistent snowpack.

He didn't like not knowing what they were going to do after Grand Junction; it felt like they were being pursued, rather than actively seeking out a destination. They were making things up will-nilly. He still had about 700 miles to Sierra Vista. Then came the fire.

Just outside of Montrose the forest erupted on both sides of them. At first they drove through drifting smoke and the woody smell in the truck cab almost clogged their nostrils. Wiley, who'd been flooring it once they'd seen fire evidence ahead, had to slow down. They couldn't see. The headlights stabbed into the fog of wood smoke.

"Jesus," Wade said, looking out the window. "Speed up. Speed up if you can, *now*." Beyond a small meadow and a band of trees, on the righthand side, an ominous wall of black, billowing smoke, sitting on top of a whorl of vicious yellow flame, rose up. It hung above the trees like a towering wave. A hellacious red glow pulsated in the forest. Just ahead of the truck, they could see flames leap the road and light up the other side of the highway.

The sun went down at the same time and everything went black. Wiley turned on the headlights, and the glowing cinders stretched to the tops of the trees.

Carmen whispered her prayers in the backseat. Wade could feel the heat on the window; he feared that the truck's gas tanks could explode or its tires melt. They would surely be dead then. The fire seemed to suck the oxygen from the air. "All we can do is outrun it," Wiley mumbled grimly, steering the wheel with both arms like a besieged ship captain. The trees sparkled all around, as though the branches were encased in yellow ice.

Blazing homes and buildings reared up in the darkness, and the power lines lay limply about the road like dead, melted snakes.

Now to the left the monstrous flames were traveling and scouring the land. Then they were out of it, as one could drive out of the periphery of a tornado's swirling winds. The flames died down as suddenly as they appeared, even as the conflagration flared in Wade's sideview mirror. He saw Carmen cross herself. They drove through the blackened landscape with wisps of gray smoke trailing off the embers.

They crested a hill and began to descend the road to a valley. Behind him, Carmen smiled, calm and beatific. The valley brimmed with a lake of clouds.

#

They saw a man standing on the side of the road. He had a big dark blanket over his head, then the blanket came down and he waved his arms at the truck. Wiley looked at Wade, who nodded. "We could get some information off of him."

They slowed down and Wade cranked down his window.

The man's face was bearded and covered with black ash. He had dirty jeans and work boots and the kind of t-shirt that Wade recognized worn by the work crews he'd seen from the train.

"Howdy folks!" he called up to Wade's open window. "Thank God you stopped! I almost didn't make it back there, when the fires came. I lay in a brook and soaked the blanket and pulled it over my head. Presto! It worked! The flames go by, I feel my arms, my legs, I'm alive. I got a buddy down the road and he's injured. Can you help us? What do ya got in that truck there? Can you pull down the road a piece and pick up my buddy?"

Wade looked at Wiley and shook his head. Then he opened the door and hopped down. He looked all around the truck and didn't see any signs of anyone else; or an ambush. He noticed the outside of the truck was covered in white and black ash.

"Where'd you come from?" he asked, looking over the t-shirt again.

"I ain't gonna lie. We escaped the regime crew and stole a motorcycle. Been driving non-stop. Ran out 'a gas. We came from out in eastern Colorado. Once you get away, they forget about ya, at least it seems so. Can we get a ride, to Grand Junction at least?"

The man unfolded the blanket, letting it dry in the arid air, and Wade noticed a big "C" logo sewn into it.

"Where'd you get that blanket?"

"Oh, down the road, back before the continental divide."

"Was it a farm? Did you get it at a farm?"

"Yeah, that was it. It was a small farm, real nice people, and they let us borr'a some food and this here blanket. Then we moved on."

"Was it the Corsair farm?"

"Yeah. Think so."

"Did they have any kids?"

"No didn't see any kids." Wade looked at him for a moment silently.

"Maybe we should be gettin' off to Gee-Jay, 'fore it gets too dark and the fires get over here."

"What do you know about Grand Junction?"

"They say somethin's happening there. A small society; a community. They have food, beds, work, maybe fuel for that truck. No regime groups there. Sounds promising. Can we get a ride?"

"You can get a ride. But you'll have to ride in the trailer. We're not picking anyone else up."

"You gonna leave 'im?"

Wade glanced up at the cab; Wiley had an impatient expression.

"Yes. Now turn around."

"Turn around…okay. No problem." Wade patted him down, top to bottom. No weapons. The other guy, in waiting, must have those, he thought.

Then Wade walked over and unhitched the trailer door, and held it open. The man had a mopey look. "Alright, if that's all you got," he said. He jumped up into the back of the trailer and dragged the blanket after him.

"This place have air in it?"

"There's plenty of ventilation. It might get a little hot. But we're stopping soon." Then Wade shut the trailer door and hitched it.

CHAPTER 13

"You put him in the back of the truck?" Phoebe asked.

"Yeah."

"He seemed like he was in trouble." Now they were about five miles out of Grand Junction. It was the river Wade was looking forward to; the Arkansas had seemed like a lifeline. The Colorado River.

"He had one of the Corsair's blankets."

"No kidding?" Wiley scratched his beard and kept driving.

"What did he say?" Phoebe said, leaning her head forward into the front seat.

"He said they gave him the blanket. He admitted it came from the Corsair's farm. It's awful fishy. He said they didn't have any kids. I think his friend was going to ambush us."

"So what are we going to do with him?" Phoebe said. She seemed to partly, but only partially, concur with Wade. "We're going to let him off at G.J., and be done with him.

Probably…" Wade was truly undecided on that matter.

They could see the semblance of a town ahead. Route 50 ended abruptly at a makeshift wooden gate, and two men stood on either side of it.

Rather than being ruinous, Grand Junction had sprouted a busy, if rickety, shanty town. The heat shimmered throughout a broad plateau where the town, once burned down and raked for its valuables, had been partly rebuilt. Horses and carts and bicycles plied the flat streets, a scene from a bygone era. Wade saw lots of people milling around and huddling in tents and under canopies, a rare sight. It's the Colorado River, he thought. You can rebuild life around it.

The truck rolled slowly up to the gate. A pot-bellied man with a beard and a boony hat like Wade's wandered up to Wiley's window. His bulbous cheek betrayed a chaw of tobacco.

"Got any gas here?" Wiley asked. That was wishful, Wade thought, as if they could "fill up" and head on down to Arizona.

The man sized up the truck with a proprietary once-over. "That's quite a rig. Where're you coming from?"

"Wyoming and the Front Range."

"Got any propane back in the trailer? We could really use some gas here. We're down to mostly wood, and a little hydropower."

"No, only potatoes."

"I was hoping you'd trucked in some natural gas, coming from Wyoming." He spat some tobacco juice onto the dry ground. "You won't find any diesel here, or anywhere else for that matter. How many people you got? We're welcome, but food here isn't infinite, you know."

"Counting a guy we just picked up, seven. But we can haul our own weight. We've got the potatoes (*what's left of them, he thought),* and other food and water."

"Well, come on in then. Welcome to River City. It's the same town, believe it or not, without the gas and sundry amenities. So you drove through those fires?"

"We did."

"Well you dodged a bullet. We always have our eyes on the horizon. We're lucky in that this is a plateau and not a woodsy town. Otherwise, we'd be done for. Come on in. If you have cash, silver, or some other kind of barter, we have a couple of stores, a boarding house, and a saloon."

He spat some more of the tobacco juice and stuck his thumb up in the air, and the gate rose up. Wiley jerked the truck into a low gear, and he maneuvered it past the gate and into a vacant lot on the edge of town. Wade could see the Colorado, a deep blue ribbon winding through the sparse aridity, in the near distance. There were piers built along the sides, which indicated some river activity, at least.

Wiley shut down the engine and stepped down from the truck on to the hard-packed earth. "What do we do now? The tank's almost dry." He looked at the truck sadly, as if it had already been abandoned.

Wade could see the Mesa and the the ornate tracery of woodsmoke clouds threaded amongst the blackened hillsides. Their own prospects didn't stretch much beyond the ramshackle settlement and the river. He wondered if they'd all split up here. He'd gotten out his backpack; it was time to head south with the river, get closer to Kara.

"Why don't we pack some things together. Have a look around. Maybe that fella back there is wrong about the fuel outlook."

Wiley had unlatched the trailer door, and the man inside dropped down to the ground sheepishly, displaying an almost demented grin through his beard. "Obliged," he said, and took the blanket with the "C" on it and wandered off towards the town.

Wiley set some of the tools and potato crates on the ground.

"Do you want to come with me?" Wade said.

"Yes." Phoebe followed him down a hill, toward the river.

"I'll come back with some food," Wade said over his shoulder to the Santiagos, who had sat down wearily beside the truck on a pile of their luggage.

The closest spot to the highway on the river already supported a thriving flotation trade. Both Wade and Phoebe had the same idea simultaneously.

"We'll head south, on the river," she said excitedly, brushing the hair out of her eyes as a breeze came off the baked plains. "Yes siree. We'll catch one of those wooden boats and take it as far as the Colorado goes. Heck, maybe all the way to Mexico...I like Mexico. I *love* Mexico! Oh I can't wait–I love boats." Wade found her girlish glee infectious, a kind of pioneering happiness amid the stricken landscape.

They sat down on a piece of grass on the riverbank.

"There can't be much left of the Colorado in Mexico."

"But you're going to Arizona."

"I am."

"The river will take you into the desert."

"It flows south into Utah, and it ends up at Lake Powell and Lake Mead, or what's left of those places." Both once giant reservoirs were in an accelerated process of drying up, the last he read. He unfolded the map on the grass. Then a creeping fatigue came over him, and he put the map down and lay back in the grass and put his hat over his head and shut his eyes. Jagged pentagons of red regions sailed across the blackness behind his eyes.

"You really going all the way to Mexico?"

Phoebe paused. "Don't know for sure. I'll see what's down there first. Might stop in Arizona. If there's a community there, you know. It's divine, the desert."

"You're welcome to join me, all the way to Sierra Vista, to find my daughter. I like your company."

"I like yours' too Wade."

"You're a resilient whipper snapper, I mean, amidst all of this."

"How kind of you."

"I guess we should look for some food."

"It's okay to look at the river a while."

He opened his eyes and lifted his hat. She'd crossed her legs in the grass and offered her face up to the sun, which baked and reflected off the dark blue river. She had her eyes closed, a sleepy smile. The water flowed calmly past the embankment. You'd hear only an occasional trickle. It soothed him, the river, in that it was all its own and paid no heed to whatever business the humans left on its shoreline.

Then he closed his eyes again and moved his leg over the map so it wouldn't blow away, and he fell off into a black sleep. He dreamt that he was with Lee in Ottawa, Canada, and it was hot and sultry, and they walked through strange streets at night trying to find the train station where Kara was to arrive but only getting more lost, and when he opened his eyes again it seemed only minutes had passed but he felt refreshed.

He sat up. Phoebe was down on the grassy riverbank, talking with a man. He wore a cowboy hat and boots, and smoked a cigarette. It seemed to be a friendly conversation; he smiled and flicked the cigarette away into the reeds. *How can you do that? Wade thought, while living in the age of fires?*

Phoebe asked him questions, then she smiled and dug her hands into her pants pockets and walked back up the embankment. Across the river, near the far bank, he watched a wooden raft float by, carrying a few seated people and a guy in the stern steering it with a long tiller. It looked like the raft used 55-gallon drums for flotation. The river depth, at least at this point, couldn't support much bigger boats, he thought. They'd have to travel leanly, as the rafts won't leave room for many provisions–it wasn't like having a tractor trailer at their disposal.

He hadn't given up on the truck 100 percent, not yet.

He got up and took one more look at his map, following the course of the river southwest past Moab and into the Utah desert. It will be quick, unless the river runs dry, he thought, and it could potentially be nice traveling on the river. *Divine*, as Phoebe put it. And maybe safer. He folded up his map again, and put it away in the backpack. Then Phoebe and he walked over to a plain wooden building that the gatekeeper had said was working as a kind of general store. Wade still had the gold coins he'd packed in a small cloth bag that tied at the end.

They all could get started again, after they'd reached a kind of end of the line in the truck.

"You can buy tickets for one of those rafts," Phoebe said. "They leave once a week, I think he said."

"That all? Where do they sell the tickets?"

"At the store." Wade wanted to leave right away. He saw an old beaten and dusty Harley parked outside. On the back of the seat was strapped a small rucksack and the folded-up Corsair blanket he'd seen the man with.

Wade hadn't put the Corsairs behind him at all, it was just that the others had decided to stop talking about it. They walked up from the grassy riverbank and he stepped up onto a wooden platform out in front of the building and Wade pushed a door aside and they both walked inside the store.

It was humid inside and moats of dust floated through a

square of sunshine. The wooden floor was sawdusted. Sitting off to the side at a round table was the man they'd given a ride to, next to another man who wore a black scarf around his long, graying greasy hair. They were hunched over whisky glasses and drinking from a dark bottle of Bacardi rum. Wade shot a glance their way, then headed for the counter.

"We're here about the raft tickets. We need at least two on the next one."

"We're sold out," the woman behind the counter said, perfunctorily. She was short and squat and wore an apron. She had a blunt, dismissive air. "Nothing till next week. Need anything else?"

"No." Wade heard a chair scrape across the floor as one of the men got up. People came through the door behind him.

"When's the boat leaving next week?"

"Thursday."

"What's today?"

"Wednesday."

"So one's leaving tomorrow?"

"As I said, fella, that one's sold out. Those two men bought the last two tickets."

"Where do the rafts go?"

"Lake Powell."

"What about beyond that, like to Lake Mead?"

"What do you think we are, Greyhound? That's a kind of no man's land out there. Maybe another outfit's gotten started. Don't know; it's none of my business anyhow."

"What about Vegas? It's close to Lake Mead."

"What about it? There *is* no more Las Vegas. It's gone, I heard, back to the desert. The Mexicalis and gangs have taken over, and the coyotes, and the Indians…" Then when he didn't reply right way she said facetiously, "Oh sorry, the Native Americans."

He looked over his shoulder and the two men were leaving. The one he didn't know had a bandage on the back of his neck caked with dried blood, and he laughed and nodded toward Wade and shoved a cigarette into his mouth as they swung through the door into the scorching afternoon.

CHAPTER 14

Phoebe wandered to the other end of the counter and she gazed at the motley collection of goods arranged on the shelves above it. Nestle's Quick, Gold Medal Flour, Saltines, Campbell's Soup, Kellogg's Corn Flakes, dusty bottles of rotgut bourbon and rum, cans of peas and carrots, powdered milk, a small pile of Mars and Snickers bars; a few iron skillets and tea pots, and a battery-powered alarm clock (Wade had to laugh at that one–there was no "time" anymore). They even had an aluminum can of extra-virgin olive oil.

"I want that biscuit mix," she looked at Wade hopefully. "…And the olive oil."

"How much?" he said. "And six tickets on the raft for next week."

"What do you have?"

"What do you take?"

"Cash and valuables–no junk. This isn't a pawn shop."

He pulled out a piece of gold bullion–a Canadian Maple Leaf–from a pocket in his backpack and placed it on the counter in front of the woman.

"Think that's enough?" she said.

"That's more than enough–how much cash you looking for?"

"Hundred each for the raft tickets and forty for the oil and flour."

"What you got right there is worth about a thousand or more–in fact, you owe me some change."

"We don't give change here."

Wade looked up at the shelves. "How 'bout that box of Saltines and the bag of coffee too. And some peas and carrots…" He placed his hand over the gold coin.

"Let me see that," she said. He moved his hand away and she picked up the coin and stared at it in the light. "Heavy enough," she huffed, then glanced back skeptically at her shelf of goods. Phoebe put her open backpack on the counter.

"C'mon Martha," she said. "You're not gonna get a better deal than that. That coins' worth a lot in the world, unless you're planning on spending the rest of your life in River City."

"How did you know my name was Martha?"

Phoebe reached out and ran her index finger along the woman's left forearm, which carried a tiny tattoo. Martha looked at Phoebe for a moment, and Wade noticed a measure of gruffness and hostility flake away from her.

"Okay," she said, and she went to the shelf and pulled down the flour, coffee, and canned goods and silently placed them on the counter near Phoebe's bag. Phoebe didn't have room for the olive oil, so Wade put it in his backpack, then the lady handed them six tickets of the kind you used to get at the county fair, the red ones with the little border decoration inside. "Don't lose those," the lady said. "We don't reissue tickets on the Colorado."

Phoebe and Wade walked outside. The guy in the black head scarf and tight greasy bluejeans leaned back against the motorcycle in the sun. He didn't say anything until they'd walked past, but Wade knew he would.

"My, my," he said. His voice was whispered and impudent. "One fine chikita." He stubbed his butt out on the motorcycle seat, then crossed his arms.

"Where did you come from?" Wade said.

"Leavenworth, Kansas. Ran outta gas. But I wouldn't a' bought those tickets if I knew things were lookin' up in River City, right sweetheart?" He smiled at Phoebe, his eyes avoiding Wade's on purpose. He had a hungry, filthy smile. "Name's Gillis. What's yours'?"

"Fuck off," Phoebe said.

"Let me handle it," Wade said, under his breath. "You got that blanket from a farmer, your friend said. He said you were hurt, back on the road. He was lying through his teeth. Where is your friend, by the way?"

"I dunno." The man seemed suddenly sullen.

"He told me all about your visit to the Corsair's."

"Yeah? He did?" Wade glanced around that baking patch of land and things had emptied out somewhat. The woodsmoke had meandered away from the white sun, which beat down onto the ground mercilessly.

"What'd you give in return for that blanket?"

"Nothin'."

"That all, huh?"

"We didn't bother."

Wade put down the backpack and fingered around the pocket where he kept his pistol.

"Wade…" Phoebe said steadily.

"…We gave nothin' back but the kindness of strangers." The man was trying to feign boredom, and he took a toothpick out of his breast pocket and went at his front teeth. "You see, as I said we come from Kansas all the way, we was a little threadbare. Toasted. Traveled out. We get there…nice people. Nice family. The Corsair's, you say? These must be generous parts, here in River City. That makes us lucky, doesn't it partner?"

"You said 'nice family.' But your friend said they didn't have any kids. Did you see any kids?"

The smirk vanished from the man's face. "Oh, they had kids."

They looked at each other for about thirty seconds without saying anything or blinking.

"By the way, I gotta go. It's been nice chattin' wit ya," he said, flippantly.

The man dropped his toothpick and leaned forward, and in a loud motion that startled Phoebe, pulled a steel sword from a leather sheath attached to side of the motorcycle. "I really need to get this sharpened, and I heard they truly had a real smithy around here. It's been a long time since they had smithies, 'aint it? Real ones, know what they doin'? So I'm goin' to pay him a visit. I really hope I see you all later…especially you miss." Then he nodded at Phoebe and using the sword like a walking stick, half-limped his away across the dirt past the general store, and into a vacant area between it and another building.

"You watch my backpack," Wade said.

# # #

No one was around outside by the river or the store building, and it was like some kind of siesta had taken place, he figured. They were down by the riverbank. He had the pistol to the head of Gillis, up against the black scarf. He had his foot firmly on the small of the man's back. Gillis was pleading with him. He made sure he had the steel right up against the man's skull.

"I'm going to show you as much mercy as you showed the Corsair family."

"Get off! You're making a mistake." Wade dug heavier into the man's back until he shut up.

"I know you did it. You used that sword on them. You're an animal. It's your kind that's ruined the world." The sword lay discarded nearby in the dust and the grass where Wade threw it after he caught up with Gillis. "You're *lower* than an animal. You used that sword on children."

The man strained to turn his head to Wade; he had slobber on his beard, and his greasy hair plastered with sweat to his face. He grimaced and spat in the dirt, like an angry mongrel. Wade noticed a raft of timber floating past on the river. Someone must be using those logs, he thought, pressing the barrel of the gun into Gillis' head; yet the timber is on its own way to Moab.

"Wade!" he heard behind him, and he looked over his left shoulder and through the tall wavy grass saw Phoebe watching at the top of the hill. The timber knocked together with loud raps and cracks and he swore it made the wind come up off the river, and he smelled the woody scent and the man squirmed under the gun and he pulled the trigger once.

He was still conserving ammo. The wind blew hard through the grass but the riverbank was silent. The man's head had jumped when he pulled the trigger, then the body sagged. He didn't want to put Gillis in the river, so he dragged him into what was probably a flood wash and covered the body with rocks. Phoebe had turned and walked away. He went through the pockets first and found the two red tickets for tomorrow. The coyotes would take care of the rest, he thought.

PART II: THE RIVER

CHAPTER 15

They waited six days before leaving. He'd given the two tickets to the first Mom and group of kids he saw. They could use them, or sell them; he just didn't want them wasted.

They lit a campfire by the river, and it was a clear night. They were all going, including Wiley, the next morning. They were antsy; he mostly spent the week gathering food and other essentials such as plastic water containers and matches for the trip, packing and repacking and gazing at his map and trying to predict the movements of his daughter, somewhere in the desert.

He'd asked around a bit on the street and in the general store. He had Kara's picture with him, but everyone was either staying put or going south. No one had come up from Arizona or Mexico.

It had taken a couple of days for Phoebe to speak to him. She'd had enough of killing; he already knew that. So had he, for that matter. Somehow, she'd had the idea that she could handle Gillis herself, and on that matter he was in deep disagreement.

He sat by the crackling fire eating a can of peas. He ate straight out of the can with a spoon; they were small and sweet. Some butter would have been perfect, he thought. They all ate them with cuts from a ham that Carmen had found and for which they traded all but a few batches of their potatoes. The ham was salty and contained veins of delicious fat. They couldn't have carried the spuds on the raft anyways.

He stared at Phoebe across the fire; he didn't want her silence to last. He couldn't take that. He ate his peas and looked up at her thoughtfully. Carmen had handed her a piece of crusty bread they'd bought "in town." They were dipping it into the olive oil. The wavy flame lit up facets of her face.

"Do you believe in God?" he said.

"I've always believed in God," she said, quietly holding her bread. "My parents didn't. I loved them dearly. They were eco-heathens, [she said that facetiously] but I needed to know somebody was looking after me, somebody else, somebody holy. I still do, especially now."

"I know you don't think I'm God-fearing," he said. "But we all need to know that there's something else other than *this*, that *this* isn't all it is. I think that's where I am now. I've been reading in that Bible." He reached behind his backpack where it lay next to where he sat in the dirt. He pulled the Bible out from behind it. He wasn't a believer, in the strict sense, just because he read random Bible passages, he thought.

They never went to church at home in Vermont; it was the farthest thing from their minds. There weren't too many other books to read here, frankly. But the fear had grown in him, and he needed at least to be distracted from it, the *this:* the soulless marauders roaming the scorched land, the insipid, empty regime, and the plight of children, and the fact that he of all people had to kill. They all needed to be saved and redeemed.

He put on his glasses and read a passage out loud. "This part here, *the race is not to the swift, nor the battle to the strong, neither yet bread to the wise, nor yet riches to men of understanding, nor yet favour to men of skill; but time and chance happeneth to them all...* It's about what happens to all people being an accident. They can't take credit for it, or be blamed. It's in Ecclesiastes. That's how I see it, anyhow."

"It's not your fault," Phoebe said. "At any rate, let's put it behind us." The river moved past them below in the night. You knew it was there in the dark, purple and alive and solemn. And that you'd be on it tomorrow.

#

The wooden raft was about 350 square feet, Wade figured, sizable for the depth of the river. The water had gone down in the drought and moved slowly south among riffles and small rapids. The floor of the raft was made of plywood. For flotation, it had a combination of logs and 55-gallon drums, and even some Styrofoam glued to around its edges. It seemed sturdy enough, to him. It had a little compartment with a mast and canvas top that looked a bit like a sail, even though it only acted like one when the wind was right. They already had the current to move them downstream, even though Wade had heard it was only a few miles per hour.

Right next to the mast was a large green plastic drum full of potable water, and a jug to use for ladling hung from a chain attached to the container.

All of them were on the raft with one man on the tiller; his name was Winston Jones. "Everyone calls me Jonesy," he said when they first met. He had short cropped white hair; strong forearms, wrinkles at the corners of his eyes, and he seemed dependable. He wore a floppy hat and talked a lot when they first met him; he seemed happy to have a group of *nice* people this time to take down the river. He had big hands and he was strong. Jonesy said Wade could probably take the tiller some, plus others.

Jonesy didn't even look at their tickets. He said they actually had one other stop before they got to Lake Powell, and that was just past Moab at the intersection of the Green River.

Wade didn't think there was room for anymore, but Jonesy thought he had a chance to pick up more ticket fare. Pepe was curious about the tiller and sat cross-legged beside it. Jonesy called him "captain." He let Pepe hold the tiller. It felt good to be floating away from Colorado, even though Wade didn't know what they were going into.

It was a one-way trip as far as Jonesy was concerned. He was just going to sell the raft or live off it when he got to Lake Powell.

It was desert country that they were heading into, and only becoming more so. Wade didn't know what they and people like Jonesy were going to live on once they got there. It was next to impossible to grow anything in that terrain, and the only water resources for hundreds of miles around were in the river or the lake.

The cleanliness of the river water was suspect, and that's why they had to carry their own. The river had a reddish tint with all the sandstone that had washed into it, and it was silted with ash and charcoal from the adjoining forest fires. The river used to be fed by snowmelt from the Rockies, but that hardly ever happened anymore, so now it often received an ashen sludge in the run-off from infrequent rains.

Lake Powell and Lake Mead were rapidly evaporating, Wade knew from his research. They said you could stand next to the lakes and literally watch the water go down. The cliffs on the shore of each lake had giant white bathtub rings hundreds of feet high along their sides, showing where the depth of the water bodies used to be 25 years ago.

#

The first day passed quickly and was calm and the river contained no dangerous stretches. In the old days, the river might have upended even a raft of this size, depending on the season. But now just getting it through the shallower stretches was a challenge. Jonesy had two gaffs for helping nudge the raft through shallower sections. Yet the raft moved steadily along the river that curved through red cliffs and hillsides covered with thin dry grass and brambles.

Its movement made a slight breeze under the sun. There was a thin cloud cover, and it was pleasant just watching the cliffs go by. The passengers seemed safe, for now. Wade sat cross-legged under his hat and silently watched the shore and listened to the river's calm burble. The water was copper brown and didn't look drinkable, but he let his hand dangle in it and it was a good if cool temperature for swimming. He was already barefoot, so he took his hat and white t-shirt off, emptied his pockets on to the plywood, and lowered himself over the side into the water. The cold was a shock then felt like immense relief. He'd only bathed in the Arkansas since he arrived that day on the train in Denver.

"Don't go floating away because I don't have time to catch ya," Jonesy called out, looking like a ship captain as he steadfastly eyed his tiller. Wade hung on to the side of the raft where it was wood and Styrofoam and let his feet dangle in the current. He felt the cold water all around his legs and the bottoms of his feet. Then he dunked his head but kept his grip around the edge of the raft. He opened his eyes briefly but the water was dull and murky below the surface. When he raised his head out of the water the cool immersion had washed away some of his bad feelings, and he saw Pepe and Phoebe leaning over the edge and smiling at him.

He was tempted to let go, so he did.

CHAPTER 16

He pushed away from the heavy raft and swam along with the current. It was easy and there weren't any rocks and he kept the raft to his righthand side. "Don't stray!" Jonesy yelled out. Wade knew why he was nervous. If they lost touch with Wade, Jonesy wouldn't want to pull to the side to get him, and if Wade lost the raft, he would have to survive in the desert alone.

He swam hard to the raft and grabbed the side again, and he noticed that Phoebe had stripped down to shorts and a bra. She had an ornate tattoo on her belly, in the shape of a dark green embroidery, that he hadn't noticed before.

"Can you swim?" he called out.

"Yes!"

"Well?"

"Of course!"

"Just asking." Then he let go again and let the current take him. He looked up and saw a hawk or an eagle floating above the canyon. He watched it until the bird disappeared behind the high ledges, with the sky dark blue and empty. You never saw aircraft anymore, he thought. The cliffs were steep and fragile looking, and they had small washed out beaches beneath them. He wondered when they were going to stop the raft for the night.

Leaves floated in the water, which sparkled and riffled in the sunlight. As he swam, he could see just over the water surface and he thought of swimming with Kara when she was small, dog paddling bravely in the current of a Vermont river, her chin set and out of the water but her eyes merry, and he thought of his daughter and his heart sank some, and he stopped making himself forget everything by immersing his head in the cold river.

He heard a splash and Phoebe came up out of the open water laughing and he heard Jonesy say "Dammit, this isn't a holiday. I need you to stay close to the raft!" He had a rope coiled close to his feet and Jonesy tossed the rope close to the edge of the raft, but Phoebe had one hand on the edge and seemed to be in control.

Wade could see Wiley sitting off the side sulking, beside the mast. He missed his truck, and Wade figured that he liked being in control. He'd locked the vehicle and hoped to return to it sometime; he was going to make his way into Arizona and see if the outfit he worked for still had any operable vehicles left. Unlike Wade, he'd had no one at home he'd abandoned.

#

Phoebe let go and floated with the current, her head above the surface. She shook the water free of her eyes, smiled, and kicked to the middle of the river. Wade looked downstream and he could see a bend in the river and it was still calm. He moved over closer to the side of the boat and hung on to the side. The sun was bright on the water and when he squinted against it in Phoebe's direction she just seemed like a chunk of formless floating debris. The shoreline still looked rocky and empty; not too many places to pull over.

"Where are you going to moor the boat?" he yelled over to Jonesie.

"I'm keeping an eye out for the spot now."

Javi Santiago stood up by the mast and was looking downstream. "It's getting a little rough ahead," he said to Wade. "Phoebe should come in."

"Come on in," Wade yelled across the water to the swimming woman. It seemed like the raft had picked up speed. He looked ahead about 200 meters and saw some white water torquing above the surface.

"Now!" he said. She began a crawl toward the raft but it turned partly sideways and floated out ahead of her. Jonesie frantically waved her on. Wade boosted himself up onto the raft and picked up the rope and threw it out toward where Phoebe was now actively swimming. "Grab the end!" he screamed over the flat moving water. "Hold on!"

The rope landed limply and slowly sunk into the water. Wade jumped in feet first holding on to the other end; the rope was strung through an iron loop that was screwed into the raft's plywood floor. He sunk into the muddy, coppery water and saw nothing but murk then came up and could first see Phoebe's arm coming up out of the water. He could hear the rapids in the background and feel the pull of the raft on the other end of the rope.

"Keep swimming!" he yelled, then he thrashed against the slow current with the rope in one hand. She floated off to the side then made her way to the middle of the river, with the surface of the water roiling with the beginning of the rapids.

He reached out for her and he could feel his feet strike the muddy bottom now of the river and he was shocked it was so shallow, and afraid of breaking bones on some rocks, then he had her by a chunk of her shirt, hair, and right arm and he made the rope around both of them.

He could see Jonesie at the tiller madly gesticulating at Javi and Wiley as they pulled on the rope. Wade kicked in the river water hard toward the raft then he had one arm up on the wood and the water was turbulent and getting in his mouth and they were pulling Phoebe up on to the raft. He boosted himself up and rolled over onto the raft; he could feel the floor of the craft bounce in the turbulence. It was going through strong but not steep or violent rapids, perhaps Class II or Class III, he thought.

The shoreline went by quickly, then the cliffs gave way to an open green grassy section, and he started laughing. It just came out, lying there on his back. The faster motion of the boat made a breeze that was refreshing. Phoebe sat on the floor of the raft with her hands around her knees, dripping, quietly smiling.

"You dopes," Jonesie said, almost parentally. "I told you not to go too far." He seemed tired, simmering.

"Do you want me to take the tiller?" Wade said. Jonesie had been at it all day.

"I will," Wiley said. Jonesie handed it over without a protest. The raft had sidled through the narrower passage, around a bend, and now sailed through a wider, flatter section of water.

"We'll pull over and camp for the night soon," Jonesie said, and he stretched out on a mat on the wooden floor. "Just stay away from the rocks if you see any…and if you can't avoid 'em, hit 'em with the side rather than the front of the raft. That's one of the reasons the Styrofoam is there." Then he pulled the hat over his face and fell asleep.

CHAPTER 17

They pulled over as the sun was setting. It seemed as if they'd entered the barrenest of lands. He'd seen no animals along the river, not even a bird or a red squirrel, beyond the eagle that time. Outside and beyond the cliffs was Utah, a burnt and burning cauldron. The sun dipped toward the cliffs and Jonesy aimed the raft for a muddy bank, and they grounded her.

Wade jumped into the shallow water with the raft's line in his hand, then he fixed it to the narrow trunk of a stunted tree that grew out of a waterside rock fissure. It seemed secure enough. The cliffs around them were steep and shaded the color of ochre. He'd had a desire to climb them, to see what was going on above them and this river, but he thought better of it. He considered the flaky nature of the rock and the gathering darkness.

Everyone disembarked from the raft onto the riverbank.

Javi Santiago tossed the backpacks and duffels that contained his family's possessions onto the narrow shoreline. There wasn't much room on the riverside, just a slim embankment until the cliff and rocks began. He lay down a small tarp, fastidiously in silence, and began to make camp.

"Maybe we ought to sleep on the raft," Wade said. He knew he would; he didn't trust the cliff or rockfalls or the small beach's air of vulnerability. Something about the river made him feel safer, but he wasn't going to force Javi to do it Wade's way. The sun dipped behind the cliff, throwing their landing site in cool shadow.

Javi gave his bags a look, as if having second thoughts, then he said, "I think it will be more comfortable on the ground, beside the fire."

"I'm staying in the captain's quarters," Jonesy said. "But first I'm going to eat. And drink. I'm hungry enough to eat a dead horse and thirsty enough for many a flagon of cold brew."

"I could probably find you a dead horse up there," Wiley said, nodding upwards. "But I can't make any promises about the flagons of frosty lager."

The top of the cliff was beautiful against the purple sky, Wade thought. Beauty hadn't been at the front of his mind much lately, despite the scenic and austere landscape of wind- and fire-scarred mountains and river valleys, which still had a life to them. He'd lived at merely a meagre level of survival, minute by minute, no room for reflection; punctuated by a few vengeful killings. It didn't make him feel at all like himself; he was doing it for his daughter, ultimately. He then felt a wave of longing for his wife Lee, for the true beauty of times they'd spent together.

Wiley already had a small fire going on top of a circle of stones Javi and his wife had meticulously arranged. Wade could hear the crackle of small sticks and dry grass; sparks flew up into the air, to which the fire had given a slight scent of cedar.

He thought of the time he and Lee had gone to the Alps together for their honeymoon. Flew Air Canada to Zurich, back when the world was somewhat normal. No kids yet. They lived in a tiny spotless hotel and sat in a cafe by a large lake. They stared at the mountains with the sun reflecting on the water. Some of the mountains still had snow on them, and wore wispy clouds that looked like hats. The lake was clean and clear. They were quiet part of the time, just holding hands, or laughing about stories from college or their silly childhoods. The alpine sun was hot but nurturing; they wore sunglasses and sipped ice-cold Fechy wine and swam in the cold lake afterward. They dived in from warm rocks, and Lee came up out of the cool water shaking her head and laughing. She had a big smile; lively eyes.

Wiley threw bigger chunks of wood onto the fire, and this cast more sparks into the sky. It was very dark by the river. Wade's eyes had misted up, and he stood up and walked over the to the cliff-side and put his hand on the rock. It was warm too, which he found oddly, universally reassuring. All he wanted to do was bring his family together again. But the world had gone mad.

# # #

"Yeah," Wiley said, coming back to his thought flow. "I could find horse and cattle, up there in that desert. Picked clean by the buzzards."

"What are *we* eating?" Jonesy asked.

Carmen looked up, having quietly accepted the lead-food-provision role from the days before.

"Kidney beans and rice, and some onions all cooked together…"

"We don't have any chicken, any meat?"

"Just in cans. Chicken soup," Carmen said, looking down into the fire.

"Let's open them."

They really had to do some hunting and fishing, Wade thought. They all needed more meat to keep their strength up. He wondered whether there were any fish left in the Colorado; probably not. But maybe...

"What about coffee?"

"We have some coffee left," Javi said. "We save the grounds in cans."

"Good."

That reminded Wade of the morning, and he promised himself that he would climb the cliff. Maybe there were left-over settlements or vehicles; something more to scavenge. The canyons made him claustrophobic; the climb might provide relief. But he knew there was nothing up there but desert sand and scrub and an old, desolate highway that was more dangerous than the river.

Moab was close, then it was 200 miles or more to Lake Powell and Page, in the former Arizona. He thought he'd probably get that far on the river, before he had to track south to Sierra Vista.

Phoebe stood on the bank with a blanket over her shoulders. She had a faraway look, the expression of a girl who had just woken up.

"How far's Moab?"

"Not three mile from here," Jonesy said, looping the raft's line into a tidier bunch in his hands. The raft tugged gently against the line in the current. Night fell abruptly; you couldn't hear anything but the trickle of the river. Wind soughing through the cracks in the cliff wall.

"Given the quiet..." Wade said. "There must not be much

going on in Moab."

"Not exactly jumpin' these days."

Jonesy shrugged. "It ain't what it used to be."

"I loved Moab years ago," Phoebe said. "The golden desert. It was so spiritual–I found some of my best rocks and jewels there. So much to do, so enlightened. The restaurants, the music, art, the desert walks. An oasis..." The flames from the fire leapt; you could see the shadows on the cliff wall. They seemed engulfed in desert solitude.

"We stopping there?" Phoebe asked, looking around as if having emerged from her reverie.

"No," Jonesie said, sitting down on a blanket he'd laid by the fire. "Back at G.J., they said 'don't moor at Moab. Too risky.'"

"In what way?" Wade said.

"Used to be okay, a trading post. Then it got robbed, least the story goes, and the bad types took over. They take a cut of everything that passes between people. It's not a trading post anymore, it's a robbing and graft post, or worse. The lowlifes came on from the city...Tucson or Vegas...or Phoenix..." He looked over at Pepe; he didn't want to scare him. But Pepe was playing a game with a couple of stuffed animals over by a bush. "They wear red bandannas, and no ones been able to dislodge 'em. Too bad; Moab, it was turning into a nice stopover."

"Maybe the good folks up in Grand Junction could do something about it," Phoebe said.

"Maybe...doubt it somehow..."

"I'm going to cook something," she added, with a burst of good cheer. "What'd ya say, señorita? What else do you wanna whip up?" A couple of pans filled with bean-and-rice mixtures leaned against the rocks by the fire and simmered.

"What else..." Carmen repeated, sifting through a bag at

her feet. "We have a few potatoes left, and parmesan…"

"Yeah!" Phoebe said. "Let's do it!"

Wade went up on the raft to fetch his bow and watch the river and the cliff as the ladies cooked. When he stood on the raft, it seemed unsteady, like an old pier. The river lapped against its sides. At least there would be no fierce storms that night, he thought as he looked at the stars.

He unfurled his bedroll and lay down on it, using his backpack as a pillow. He could smell the food, and his stomach growled. He'd eat and try to get some sleep, then push for them to leave at first light.

After he ate he slept on his back and in the middle of the night he heard more thunder in the distance. He figured it was a passing storm in the desert. He sat up and looked toward the riverbank, where the sleeping people lay quietly by the dying embers. When he looked over the top edge of the cliff, the sky was still purple with bright webs of stars. The stars seem to envelope you in the desert, he thought.

Flashes and flickers of light accompanied the thunder. He figured it was lightening, but the thud of the thunder had a different nature, like something being dropped from the sky. He listened for a few minutes then pulled a blanket back over his head. The horizon was always alight, commonly from massive fires, and this phenomena appeared as nothing new.

CHAPTER 18

In the morning, he pealed back the blanket and sat on the edge of the raft and watched the river. It was dark-blue and cool; it seemed to change color, lighten, as the sun came up. He reached down and splashed some of it on his face.

He always woke up in the minutes just before sun-up, which is about the only thing the present had in common with the past. He stepped off the raft onto the wet riverbank, where the others slept in silent lumps under their blankets and tarps. A pot sat on the campfire rocks with leftover grounds and coffee from the night before, and Wade went about re-starting the fire.

Pepe exclaimed from beneath his blankets a few feet away, thrashed around, then seemed to go back to sleep. Wade dipped a pot into the river to make some weak coffee from the grounds; he figured the water was okay boiled. He otherwise distrusted it and wouldn't drink it; he feared it was contaminated by deposited ash and the bodies of animals and people, among other things.

The raft tugged lightly against the line, the river flowing past in the shadows thrown by the cliff. He got a small fire going and put the pot directly in it, and when the water reached a spattering boil in the pan, he poured it over the grounds using a filter he carried with him. Then he sat on a log and sipped the coffee looking up at the cliff.

He thought about the thunder and flashes from the night before. As the light bloomed on the river and the rock, he was momentarily taken by its preternatural beauty.

When he was finished with the coffee, he put the cup down on the ground and stepped over to the cliffside. He looked straight up the cliff and plotted a number of hand- and footholds. Partly motivated by the caffeine and his own curiosity, he started climbing.

The red rock felt cool and flaky. A muddy moss and a wet kind of lichen filled its cracks.

As long as he didn't fall, he thought, listening to his own breathing, he would make the top in minutes. And he shouldn't climb a pitch he didn't think he could safely descend, he thought, from all the times he'd scrambled over stony climbs, often with his son by his side, in Vermont.

He crested the top of the cliff and as the sun rose over the mountains in the distance, he had some kind of a revelation, as if he was still asleep. He thought he saw Kara walking across the desert in sandals and a wide-brimmed hat. Her image shimmered in the heat and the indistinct light. He got to his feet and stood up in a warm wind that smelled like burning pine.

He had a good view of the river below, snaking through the narrow canyon, shallow and blue with small rapids breaking out on its surface. Smoke rose in the distance towards Moab.

The red hills rose out of the yellowish brown sand and had sculpted and contorted shapes. When he looked longer, the image that he took as Kara was actually a cactus, a common kind that dotted the flat, windswept landscape.

Then he heard the helicopter, tearing through the sky from Moab's direction. It pierced the dead silence with its rotating blades, and flew a path between the river and the highway. Its course took it east towards Grand Junction. It had a black body and a red tail, like a bird. It was headed right towards him, and he ducked behind a rock.

Gun turrets and missile launchers hung from its belly. It was the regime's, he thought, crouching down. The sound was deafening when it flew overhead and churned up the sand and pine needles and mesquite into a dust devil. Then it was gone as quickly as it appeared, going at a speed of at least 180 m.p.h.

Whoever it was, he hadn't wanted to be seen or to betray the location of the raft. It couldn't possibly be friendly or neutral; it was on a kill mission, and everyone was trigger happy those days.

The regime had a minimalist way of killing to a make a point, he thought, but neither the will nor the resources to fully eradicate the human pestilence that had infected the scorched southwest.

The chopper was only a tiny dot along the old empty highway. Wade stood up and brushed himself off. He pulled his buff down from his face. The smoke was oily black coming from Moab, and he thought he could see the familiar reddish yellow flickering of burning buildings.

There seemed nothing of value above the cliff, only rock, sand, cactus, and weeds. The horizon warbled with a heat shimmer that reflected off the sand. He fingered his bow; if he saw a rabbit or prairie dog…then he heard Phoebe call out his name.

"I'm up here! Moab's on fire…"

"What are you doing? Trying to run away from us?"

She was at the bottom of the cliff, and when he peered over, she grasped the nearest projecting rock and started climbing toward him.

"Don't do that!" he said, pointlessly. She was stubborn and driven in her own way. She deftly covered the rock, dressed only in sneakers, a t-shirt, shorts, and a scarf holding back her hair. She was at least as good a scrambler as himself.

Then she threw herself into his arms with an outpouring that startled him.

"I woke up and you weren't there!"

"Calm down."

"I thought, where's Machiatto?" she said breathlessly. "You weren't going to leave me, were you, with cranky old Latte and Jonesie?"

"Of course not." Chances are, we're going to have to separate at some point of this desolate road we're taking, he thought to himself. She's acting like my daughter. That made him think of his mirage.

"I thought I saw Kara."

"Where?"

"Out on the desert. I think I was hallucinating."

"It's been known to happen among desert dwellers," she said, with a half smile. "You miss her, don't you?"

"Sure yeah." He picked his head off her shoulder, where it was beginning to feel mighty good; a feeling of warmth he missed, in this new cold world.

"By the way, how do you keep your hair smelling so good?"

"I crush flower petals and keep 'em in a glass bottle. Sometimes I bathe with them."

"I need a bath in the river," he thought out loud, wondering how gamey he smelled.

Phoebe shielded her eyes and looked across the expanse at the black, growing cloud, which besmirched the dark blue Western sky.

"Something happened in Moab..."

"Yup. Best we better get past Moab on the river. Only one direction to take."

"What's that, dogs? No, coyotes!" Phoebe said, dropping her arm to point. Three of the mangy gray animals stood over a prostrate form in the sand about three quarters of a mile or so away.

"You're right, coyotes. They've got something, too. A carcass." Two of the mutts nosed around whatever body they had, while the third stood stock still and stared at Wade and Phoebe.

"I'm going to see what it is," Wade said, picking his bow and quiver off the ground. "If it's an antelope or some such, I could take back a couple of the legs and we could eat some meat, if it hasn't gone bad."

"How savage of you."

He shrugged. "If you want to survive..."

"Hey you two nature explorers, we're leaving soon!" It was Jonesie from below. "What do you think this is, river-raft adventure travel?"

"Give me twenty minutes," Wade yelled back. "We might have found food." It was a stretch, but something compelled him to reconnoiter the coyotes' spoils. It wasn't far. Maybe he'd even pot a coyote with his bow.

"Can I come?" Phoebe said.

"Yeah, but watch out for snakes, okay?"

"I know the desert," Phoebe snapped proudly. "Maybe better than you do."

They began walking, he in well-worn boots, Phoebe in sneakers. He was glad it was nearby, because otherwise they'd need water, Moab seeming to be not the oasis it once was. The carcass also gave him a purpose for climbing the cliff, which seemed to him the manifestation of rash and anxious restlessness.

"Do you miss your old life?" Phoebe asked, as though they were taking a calm stroll in a national park.

"Sure I do. I miss my family..."

"That goes without saying."

"What about you?"

"I was a nomad to begin with. This feels like an extension of what I was doing."

"Really?" That surprised him, seemed almost phony or dishonest. Everyone else he encountered appeared numb, paralyzed, terrified, or all three. But it made him think about what he didn't like about the past, the delusions and complacency.

"The old life, you say," he said, keeping an eye on the coyotes, silhouettes on the burning horizon. "What I saw that was happening to the climate, in the hands of humans. And some of the companies and agencies I observed, they were run by speculators and kleptos. You got the sixth sense that it had to end some day, and something not so great was coming up behind it."

The coyotes watched the two of them raptly. When they got within about forty yards the animals yipped and tossed their heads and trotted away across the desert.

Wade got to the corpse first. He put up his hand.

"You can stop right there."

"Oh my god the smell."

"The heat will do that."

He was a gray-bearded and white-haired man, eyes closed and collapsed on his side. His jeans and a funky t-shirt were caked red with dried blood and ripped and chewed up. He had a backpack hanging off his shoulder.

"He died before this happened to him," Wade said as much to himself as Phoebe. The coyotes had definitely gotten to him, below the rib-cage, and Wade knelt down and gingerly maneuvered the backpack away from the shoulder.

"He was trying to get away from Moab, I figure. Jesus, it's so hot out here...he just collapsed. Those animals, they're scavengers. They don't prey on wandering people. Usually..."

"Scavengers...like us?" Phoebe stood off to the side; she'd put on sunglasses and a visor. She was watching the horizon, which was dark purple and vermillion above the desert floor. Actually beautiful.

Wade crouched on his haunches and removed a bag of snacks from the backpack; Saltines, processed cheese, and raisins. "We can use this..."

"You're picking him over, just like the coyotes."

"What do you want me to do, give 'im a twenty-one gun salute? We have to do what we can, where we are, with what we find."

The coyotes watched them afar, waiting for them to leave. They are opportunistic, Wade thought, just like me.

"Shoo!" Phoebe yelled at them and clapped her hands together. They turned and ran but only for a moment. Then they stopped and continued monitoring. They were gaunt and their sides were ribbed.

"I wouldn't want to be stuck out here at night," she said. "Let's go back to my friend, the river. Old Man River."

"Okay. It's a stove-top on high out here." He rummaged around in the pack once more, and came up with a document, laminated in plastic. It was a poster, professionally designed. It pictured the leader, who he thought of as El Commandante, of the regime. Wade wondered if they were dropped from the helicopter. He stood up and looked it over.

"What is that?"

"More bullshit." He handed it to Phoebe, after looking at it for a minute. The lantern-jawed Strongman of the former USA had heavy eyebrows, unusually close-set eyes, and a disingenuous smile. Far from reassuring. Wade remembered his appearances on cable TV, before he shut them off forever; his clever gift for voluble speeches that appeared off-the-cuff and unscripted. He appeared oddly good-humored and soothing as the West began to burn down, and the Arctic boiled over (thirty degrees Fahrenheit above average, which melted all sea ice and made North America even warmer).

El Commandante (Wade refused to use his real name) had an uncanny way of hitting every hot button held dear by the anxious Everyman; and before you knew it, he had control of the military and had assumed an authoritarian rule, "to protect our beloved land and our Democracy."

He sowed fear...of everything, particularly foreigners and immigrants, who were blamed for everything that had happened. The old world was gone with a nightmarish speed, and was replaced by martial law, black helmeted and armored storm troopers, and helicopters of the ilk that had just raced over the desert floor. He created a dread of free speech and an obsession with control; "shoot first and ask later" for any form of legal trespass; and an embrace of the "bad old ways" of doing everything.

Of course, anyone who had crazy or psychotic tendencies, the "crazies," embraced this atmosphere of dictatorial anarchy. They were already armed to the teeth but...all that was water under the bridge. Now everything, to him, revolved around finding Kara.

Phoebe read the document out loud, in a spoofing tone. "Calling on all the good people of Moab to vacate the town while we cleanse it of the miscreants, robbers, and rapists…"

"That's putting it mildly," Wade said. Those bad guys in Moab must of robbed the wrong guys, to bring the regime down on them way out here.

He ran his tongue over his lips and they were cracked and salty. They walked, but the super-heated air wouldn't move. "The world burns up and we have this…" he nodded toward the oily smoke rising from Moab. "…To make it worse."

CHAPTER 19

They clamored down the side of the cliff to the embankment, where the others were already moving the stuff back on the raft.

"What did you find up there? Spiritual enlightenment?" Jonesie asked, flip and gruff.

"Almost," Wade said. "We found a dead man…"

"Poor soul," Phoebe said, slinging a bag of food onto the raft. When she stepped aboard, her weight pulled the raft away from shore, and it tugged on its line.

"The coyotes were getting at him. But he was already gone," Wade said. "I found a flyer on his body. It seemed the regime shot missiles into Moab."

"You don't say," Wiley said, looking up from what he was doing with an astonished expression. "So *that* was what the helicopter was all about."

"You saw it, yeah I thought you did. They burned out the

town and no doubt killed a bunch of people, to root out the gangs, the flyer said…"

"Destroy the town to save it," Wiley grunted.

"I figured that chopper was up to no good. Here, grab the rest of the stuff."

He and Javi passed the rolled-up tarp and sacks of goods to Wade, who stood balanced on the raft.

"The people there…how horrible…what if we see someone suffering or hurt on the shore?" Phoebe said. "Can we give them a lift?"

"We can't take anyone else on," Jonesie said, trying to put the subject to rest.

"What if they're in need? What if they're kids who've lost their parents?"

This was a problem, Wade thought to himself. They had a crowded raft already; they were scraping around to survive. But if they saw some kids on the shore…it was a deviation from his goal, but he couldn't stomach just leaving them there.

"We don't have the room, the provisions," Jonesie said, without taking his eyes off the river.

Phoebe took her shoes off, sat on the edge of the raft, and pouted.

Shoving off involved only re-entering the current. The water was flat and slow, the current indicated only by fan-shaped ripples. They'd pass Moab within the hour.

Wade put on his boony hat and kept his bow and handgun handy. He didn't know what they'd encounter drifting past those blasted moorings.

# # #

The river was barely thirty meters across at its widest; sticks and logs floated into it from the various flash floods off the desert. Sparse shrubs clung to the shore, which led up to the red rocks and the wind-scoured sands. It would be hardcore desert from now on in.

CHAPTER 20

Wade knew from his map that several tributaries entered the Colorado River along their route. The next big one was the junction of the Green River and the Colorado. That was about twenty miles downstream from Moab. Then there was the Dirty Devil River at around Hite, Utah, a small town further south that used to be on the shores of Lake Powell, before the drought took most of the water. Wade didn't expect all that much to be left of the giant lake in the desert, or the tributaries, which had probably been reduced to mud flats.

He was just hoping that the Colorado had retained enough flow to stay navigable. He trusted Jonesy's knowledge of the river, that they wouldn't all just be forced to walk the desert, because the current and the depth run out.

"Stick to the left bank," Wade yelled out to Jonesy, who was at the tiller. He didn't want any desperadoes leaping onboard from the shoreline near the torched Moab remains, or attacking them. They rounded a bend in the river and saw nothing but an untouched wooden pier. A flag with the old state of Utah insignia hung by a pole inserted into the end of the dock. He guessed the pier and its moorings hadn't been targeted, but it was surprisingly empty, save for a dog.

A small gray, mangy mutt stood on the muddy shore and stared at them as they drifted past. Any boats that were moored were gone, they couldn't see any people, and lightish gray smoke rose above the rim of the small canyon above the river.

"Here boy! Here!" Phoebe yelled out, her eyes lighting up. "Oh poor thing! C'mon!"

"Don't call the scrawny cur over!" Jonesy cried out, hands still on the tiller. "God dammit, I told you we can't take on anymore passengers!"

"I know but…" The little dog stared at them rigid as a statue, then he barked twice, and as they passed he began to run along the shoreline.

"Oh can't we take him on?" Phoebe said, now pleading.

"Mommy look!" Pepe said, pointing to the dog.

Carmen sat cross-legged in the sun, under a broad straw hat. "It looks like it hasn't eaten in days!"

"And we don't have the food for it!" Jonesy answered her.

"Might be good for the boy," Wiley said, weighing in. "Keep his mind off everything that's been happening, that a child shouldn't see…"

"Aw shut-up Wiley…" Jonesy shot back, as if he felt too alone in his opinion.

"I call him Latte, by the way…" Phoebe felt the need to referee.

"I'm just sayin', a dog like that could almost take care of hisself," Wiley shrugged. "Might even nose around these parts and find us some more food."

They rounded another corner in the slow current, and the dog leapt into the water and paddled along desperately in their wake.

"I'm going in after 'im," Phoebe announced, leaping onto her feet and taking her sandals off. "Poor thing!"

"Oh no you're not!" Jonesy said, and Wade thought he sounded like a crotchety dad who knew he was losing another family battle.

Javi had moved to the back of the raft, removed his hat, and now he was holding out his hand for the dog. He looked back at Jonesy.

"Let's just slow down a bit, let him catch up," he said diplomatically. "We can't disappoint Pepe...now that he's seen the dog and everyone yells for him..."

"Christ," Jonesy barked, then he leaned on the tiller and forced the starboard side of the raft to turn and face the current, which slowed the boat down. "You guys want to get to where you're going, right?"

Wherever that is, Wade thought to himself, staring at the steel blue, cloudless horizon. It'd be stellar under different, less desperate circumstances. There'll be nothing useful in Hite, Utah, he guessed, except for more carcasses of cars and falling down structures.

Who knows what Vegas has become? It's a hellhole now, collapsed ruins in the desert...

When the dog reached close to the raft, still frantically paddling with its head pushed above the lapping water, Javi grabbed him by the scruff of his neck. Phoebe rushed over and helped pull him aboard. The dog landed on the deck boards on all fours, shook himself, then looked up and twitched long whiskers and wagged his tail.

"Perro pequeño," Pepe squealed, delighted. "Perro pequeño!"

"What does that mean?" Wiley asked.

"Scruffy little dog."

"Peh-kaynyo, then that will be its name…it's as good as any other, right Pepe?"

Si, the boy said smiling.

Pequeño had already laid down on the deck in the sun. He peered up at the people gratefully, as the raft slipped right-side into the current.

They had entered a land of beautiful bone-dry ochre-colored buttes that rose from the desiccated ground beside the river. Wade could see the layers of geological time in the walls, like tree rings. Few plants grew on the riverbanks; everything was red sandstone and desert, like photos of Mars. The sun burned relentlessly onto their heads and their backs during the day, when they sought shelter under hats and umbrellas.

The water supply was low, and Wade began to worry about firewood. They would need a fire to boil the water in the river, once they ran out of drinking water.

"So you're telling me there's no resupply depot on the river anymore?"

Jonesy lay on the deck with a hat over his face. Wiley steered now.

"No. Not with Moab out of action. Hite's a ghost town, I'd bet."

Hite…Wade referred again to his map, unfolding it on the deck. It was roughly halfway between Moab and Lake Powell, right near the Dirty Devil. He couldn't lose this map, he reminded himself, because it was just about all he had to lead him along the southwest and to his daughter.

Wade let the fishing line dangle in the water; as a lure and bait, he'd tied a yellow tassel Carmen had given him along with a tiny cheese chunk onto the hook. Now he watched the hook break the greenish water in the current. A somnolence had settled over the raft. Everyone slept, and all he heard was the wind and an occasional strum from Javi's small guitar. Javi came over and sat down beside him. He wore a wide-brimmed hat, too, and he was shirtless and barefoot.

"Did you change your mind about where you're going?"

"No. We will still return to Nicaragua. But not by the desert. No, I don't want to make this trip again, through Mexico. I want to go by boat, in the ocean, follow the Colorado all the way to the sea."

"Didn't like Mexico, huh?"

"Mexico was fine; it's what the world has become with the migrations of desperate and dangerous people. It's too bad for a family to cross there."

"I hear you."

Wade bobbed his line up and down in the water, hoping to feel a tug from the other end. They sailed along steadily past the high red buttes, which he couldn't see over except for the flawless sky, marked only by the occasional stray, wispy cloud.

"I'd have liked to be on this river thirty, forty years ago. Can you imagine the flow then?" he said to Javi. "Cool clean snowmelt water–probably deep enough to come halfway up that canyon wall. They had true run-off streams flowing into it, not these parched mudflats…the river's just drying up."

He could still see the evidence on the surfaces of the canyons of flash floods off the desert floors, but now the desert could go years without the rain, and all the arroyos were perpetually dried up.

"The damn at Lake Powell, up ahead…" Javi said. "That changed everything though."

"The Glen Canyon Dam. Correct." He was talking about

what had happened about sixty years before, when the federal government built the dam and flooded the canyons. "Those sublime canyons were full of ancient artifacts…they're being exposed again though…" Wade gazed out to the water aimlessly, then he had a tug on his line.

He stood up on the deck and pulled back on his flexible pole, and then he let some of the fishing line out. He was careful not to fight the fish too hard, because this line was all they had. A sizable river trout broke the surface and flopped on the water and exposed its shiny belly to the sun. Then it dived down. Wade reached out and guided the line to the side with his free hand; by this time the fish fought and splashed and its tail hit the side of the raft.

"Help!" Wade said, laughing. Javi put the guitar and his hat aside and went on his belly, where the line went into the water. Wade pulled back a bit and Javi pulled the fish out of the water with both hands and tossed it flopping onto the deck. Wade gave it a blow on the head with the back of a small axe, then he removed the hook embedded in its mouth. They wrapped it up in an old newspaper wrap that Carmen had kept, and prepared to cook it for that evening's meal.

CHAPTER 21

By late afternoon the horizon had filled with burgeoning, fiery orange clouds. They appeared to have nothing to do with wildfires this time. It was just an ordinary, stunning sunset. He sat on the front of the raft, as composed as he would be on a stonewall in his Vermont backyard, as the craft meandered down the river toward Lake Powell.

They'd probably get there by the evening of the following day. Maybe there was electricity power still being generated at the lake's station. Then he could charge up his cell phone and check for messages…maybe…he ruminated on a lot of things.

It was a lovely evening. They'd just finished a nice meal, considering, of the fish, rice, potatoes, and cheese. He'd caught three fish total. Then he'd gutted them with the Swiss Army knife, cooked the whole thing over a fire, then tossed the brittle bones with the oily skin and shreds of clinging, cooked flesh to the hungry dog.

He was sated and sleepy, but he didn't think he really had the right to relax.

The sky was angry, roiled, and inspiring; it cast splashes of fading sunshine on to the rugged canyon walls. The raft flowed towards nothing but the unknown, Wade thought, glancing over at the others, who seemed equally struck by the sunset.

The breeze over the river had a coolness now in the early evening, with a scent of mesquite.

They reached the junction with the Dirty Devil River, but there was nothing left of it but a space in the canyon walls where it used to flow. There was no sign of Hite, Utah, and its meagre inhabitants, nor did they see any other boats. This continued to surprise Wade; he'd thought the river would be busy. It only traveled in one direction; south. Trying to walk the desert was a death sentence, more or less.

It left a bad taste in his mouth, the sense that no one wanted to head south on account of what they'd find there. As if everyone knew something he didn't.

Then just as he was thinking this, and as the light had sunk to dusk, they spotted a submerged boat ahead. The prow stuck out of the water near the right side of the river. Wiley was at the tiller, preparing to hand it over to Wade.

He'd volunteered to take the tiller for most of the evening as they slept. He thought steering the boat would help assuage a restless energy.

Wiley looked back at him. "Should we check it out?"

"Yeah, just get close."

They floated past the wooden boat slowly, but no one seemed to be around, or on it. The shoreline was empty, just rocks, riverbank, and the silent canyon walls.

"It's a battered boat–I wonder how that happened?" Wiley

said. "'Ain't no storms or flash floods of late."

"Maybe it's an old wreck," Wade said.

"This isn't a rough river on these stretches," Wiley said, reaching over and grabbing part of the hull. The raft gently nudged against the side of the sunken boat. "Seems stove-in on purpose. Why don't we scavenge some of that wood...give me a hand..."

Wade, Wiley, and Jonesy were able to tear off a few planks of wood for campfires later. They piled it on the deck of the raft, then they untied the line Jonesy had temporarily secured to the wreck, and they floated off again.

The river wound like a snake through the narrow canyon. "Do you think maybe someone sunk it from above?" Wade asked. "By starting a rockfall?"

"Yeah, could of," Jonesy said.

"Ain't that a fetching development," Wiley said, gazing over the rim of the canyon, which hovered precariously above them. He was really missing his truck, Wade thought; he was still second-guessing its abandonment back at Grand Junction.

"It's best that we keep going at night...cut the lights...I can steer by the stars," Wade said. He had already shifted the tiller to move the raft into the current, into the middle of the river.

Then abruptly the sun dropped behind the tall cliffs and mountains and everything was enveloped in a calm darkness. The cliffs were black, but he could see the water's rippling reflections and it reminded him of watching the sea at night. The sky was dark purple with congealed webs of stars. When he looked off to the side, he could see two forms on the deck and the light from a candle; the eyes shined. It was Phoebe, who pet Pequeño who sat by her side.

"Can you put that candle out?"

"Do I have to?"

"It's probably best…" He scanned the empty rims of the canyon. At his feet was a canister of lukewarm coffee to help keep him awake. He reached down, picked it up, and took a sip. The black canyon walls drifted past on both sides. Wiley had sulked back to his bedroll, and Wade could hear a murmuring from Carmen and Javi Santiago over on a part of the raft where they'd laid out their sleeping things.

"Careful," he heard Carmen say. Pepe wandered over a part of the deck to pet Pequeño. "He's okay…" Phoebe said, then she lay down on her back and looked at the stars. Wade kept his eyes on the river.

CHAPTER 22

He heard the splash in the dark, then Carmen screaming "Pepe! Where's Pepe! Pepe!"

Wade had no idea what time it was–somewhere in the depths of the evening. The tiller had needed no more finessing than a steady grip. The stars glistened and the tall black cliffs drifted by. He let go of his grip and ran to the back of the raft and jumped in.

The water was cold but not icy. He faintly felt his feet touch the river bottom before he bobbed to the surface again, treading water in the dark current. He heard Carmen splash into the water and Phoebe screaming at her to get back on the raft. Their voices echoed stridently in the canyon silence.

Then he thought Phoebe went in too…but by then he was swimming upstream looking for Pepe.

He looked one way then the other, sputtering and feeling the cold blue blackness all around him. He noticed the mass of the raft drifting into the night. He figured Pepe would be splashing and panicking and moving with the current, but much slower than the heavy raft with its gear and seven human passengers.

He swam upstream for about 10 meters, stopping every few seconds to look around. He kept seeing black, blobby shapes of what he thought was Pepe. He felt winded and like an idiot trying to sprint upstream. He stopped and treaded water, carried up by the current again; he saw a tiny light on the raft and heard voices fading over the water. He recalled that Jonesy had no heavy metal anchors on the boat, because he didn't want to carry the extra weight, and he thought they wouldn't be needed.

As he drifted closer to the shore in the current, he heard a boy whimpering.

Pepe was visible about five meters away over the water; he cried out and struck the water with the palms of his hands, thrashing about. Swimming hard towards the boy, Wade thought, *Thank God he kept himself afloat. Thank God.*

Pepe was wet, shivering, and crying when Wade got to him. Side-stroking and clutching the boy, he took them both to a narrow, sandy shoreline, after feeling his way in the dark for several meters amongst some rocks. Wade got to his feet and the current swirled around his pant-legs. Pepe was water-logged, limp, and heavy as a sack of sand as Wade lugged him onto the muddy shore.

#

The raft had vanished and the moon had set into the desert. They sat at the bottom of the cliff and clung to each other until the sun rose. He caught only snatches of sleep as Pepe slept in his lap.

They were sheltered from the wind. He waited until morning when sunlight hit the canyon, then he spread their shoes and clothes across the few flat rocks on the slim shoreline. The dry red sandstone rose on all sides. They were trapped, hemmed in, except for the river that drifted past over the shallows they had just struggled through.

Wade wrung out his shirt and his pants and laid them next to Pepe's, which he'd gently stripped off as the boy stared vacantly at the river, and at the man standing in the sun in his underwear and untied shoes.

"Where the hell is the raft?" Wade said out loud. His voice seemed to violate the silent chamber of the canyon.

Pepe had wandered off the deck in the dark. *Why the hell wasn't Carmen watching him?* he thought. *What the fuck was going on?* He climbed up part of a taller rock to get a better view downstream, but saw no sign of the others. The flat river disappeared around another bend, entering the next canyon. He couldn't climb the cliff with Pepe, and getting up there probably wouldn't help them anyways. *God dammit to hell!* he thought, *what about all the gear I left behind? This rescue trip is shot to hell!* He vaguely kicked at some stones and sat down and put his head in his hands.

Everything was on the raft: his pack, pistol, bow, phone, maps, even the old Bible with its emergency meds, everything. Except for the knife, which had still been in his pocket when he'd dropped into the river. Well I still have that–that's something, he thought.

We'll find the others soon. He calmed down a bit. Or maybe another boat will pass that'll take us downriver.

He sat on the edge of a rock and watched a hawk circle the rim of the canyon, waiting for the clothes to dry and looking for he knew not what amongst the sterile rocks and cliffs.

#

There wasn't much they could do, in his mind, but cast themselves back into the stream. Desperate measures…this was the way to catch up with the raft, which couldn't go in reverse.

They were boxed in by the canyon; in fact, looking around, he considered themselves lucky at all to have found sanctuary in the dark on this paltry spit of riverbank. The sun spread like yellow liquid on the sandstone. The clothes were drying but would get wet again; maybe he'll make a ball of them and they'll go in half-naked. *No not that...the river's too cold.* Pepe sat on the rocks and stared at the greenish-blue water, and the current fanning across its surface. The kid must be exhausted and starving, Wade thought.

"What I'm going to do now, kid..." he said as much to himself, as Pepe seemed traumatized into silence, "is build a cheap raft so we can float on out of here." Keeping busy leaked away his anger and frustration; he'd never find Kara if he got marooned in this canyon with the Spanish kid.

"I'm going to call you *kid,* like Billy the Kid, okay?" In his soul, he regained a semblance of good humor. "You can help me build the raft, okay?"

"*Si...*" Pepe said.

"Alright!" Wade exclaimed, and even hearing words from the kid helped calm him. *But not even a thank you for fishing him out of the river...I guess I can't expect that as the kid wonders why we're on this awful voyage in the first place, including visiting the slaughter farm.*

Wade began to collect anything he could mass together into a crude flotation device; he found them on the shoreline or floating by–shrubs and branches that had been uprooted the few times the Colorado had breached its banks.

Clouds eventually moved in. They looked like giant bags of gray water. He knew they had to get moving fast.

He made a big pile of the debris on the riverbank.

"For a fire?" Pepe said.

"No kid…that's our new raft…"

"No raft!" the kid said, for the first time with something close to a smile.

"Yeah, it is…"

"*¡Mamá! ¿Dónde está mamá!*"

"Mama is where we're going, kid. You just have to be patient."

He had to have some way of binding the motley flotsam he'd gathered, so they could float at least their upper bodies on it. "You stay here…" he told the boy, then he began to scramble along the shoreline, looking for more debris for the raft, or if he got lucky, a discarded rope…

He waded barefoot, mostly in the river shallows. He found a can, which he kept, and then an empty plastic jug, which he thought he might be able to use. This was survival–scavenge and collect absolutely anything you can possibly use, even if it seems like garbage or dead weight.

He didn't find a rope, but he had the mass of a raft put together and yet little to tie it up with. Or to keep it floating with their combined weight, which would be at least 100 kilos or 220 pounds.

He took his pants off, again. He looked at Pepe and said, "Don't laugh…" Then he tied the pant-legs together. The pants tied this way offered some buoyancy. If he could combine that with the jug, and bind it all together with the mass of his raft debris…it was really more of a nest than a raft.

He wanted to leave the same day, but the gray and now black clouds appeared at the canyon rim at noon. They were a part of a monumental cumulus that rose from the desert, like a billowy mountain on the horizon. Wade thought the clouds were stained with wood smoke from the endless fires. When it started raining, the puddles turned black. He couldn't capture it for drinking.

It was like blood from the sky.

CHAPTER 23

They found refuge under a shelf of rocks, up against the cliff. Wade moved all their drying clothes into the refuge, along with the stuff he wanted to make a raft out of. The temperature might have dropped 20 degrees F., and the canyon went dark. Pepe started crying; Wade had to remind himself that not only were they marooned on the riverside, but the kid had lost his parents.

"That's alright," Wade said. "This one doesn't look like it will last long. We're safe..." *For the moment*, he thought. Their clothes were barely dry, and he pulled them on the shivering child. He thought again of the raft, now miles down the river unless they moored. The Santiago's must be suffering now over Pepe; the raft could even be tied up not far around a bend in the river.

He wondered what Phoebe was doing; he wondered if his friends were going to escape this desert tempest.

It began to hail. They were showered with what looked like black, ashen pebbles, buffeted by a cool wind. Thunder cracked. He held the whimpering Pepe, then fierce lightening bolts struck different parts of the canyon. Explosions reverberated off the canyon walls, and flashes lit up the swollen river, making it look greenish yellow in the intermittent light.

Then it was rain, coming down in sheets and pelting the rocks. Rivulets of water ran at their feet, this time, unlike the hail, not black. Spouts of flood water sprouted from the canyon rim like hoses. Wade jumped up with the jug and stuck it beneath one of the flows, capturing some drinking water. He got soaked doing it but it was worth it.

Pepe watched him intently. He thought of the potential for flash floods; it was still pouring a torrent. At any moment, a savage flood could sweep down the river, now fed by countless ad hoc streams from desert arroyos above.

He looked around; there was no escaping it, no place where he and Pepe could climb to safety. The river had already risen about half a foot. Then just as he was about to consign them to the vagaries of fate, the rain stopped. There was a clean, pristine moment as clouds shifted over the canyon and the breeze died down.

The sun came out, bringing silence, a calmness like the eye of a hurricane. The scrubbed, newly chilled air had a scorched scent. He immediately took Pepe and led him into the sunlight so that they could both stop shivering. The spouts and waterfalls still cascaded down, but with less volume.

It's all run-off, he thought. The desert, parched and rock hard, won't absorb the water, which almost all flows into the river. The river needs it, he mused, but not the blood-like, burnt wood particles that have blackened some of it.

They both sat and drank from the jug. It was cool and

delicious, with just a bit of grit. He felt them both coming back to life. But they were still starving. Clumps of sticks and logs floated past on the river; he knew they weren't out of flash-flood danger.

They sat by the riverside near Wade's makeshift "nest" and watched the green swollen river. With the sun back out, it was harsh; he needed his hat, which he pulled back onto his head. He moved them back into the shade. Maybe it was the slaking of his thirst, but for the moment he had time to think. *Where were they?*

Close to Lake Powell. The Glen Canyon Dam, or what was left of it, was going to block passage on the river...it would take a major portage to work around it and back down into the river heading south. But Jonesy had heard rumors that the dam had been breached, and that boats could get past the structure and into the Colorado going south. Wade wanted to go as far as Lake Mead, through the Grand Canyon, but somehow that wasn't looking very likely right now...the task at hand was getting them off this riverbank...

When he looked up, he saw a disturbance in the middle of the river. It was like a group of fish thrashing around near the surface. The frenzy of splashing moved towards them in the current, and he could see the heads of snakes and their slithering black bodies. Some of them struggled, their bodies making an "ess" motion, to reach the shore. But the flood-swollen river swept them downstream. Wade got his knife and a heavy stick handy. He felt himself filled with a predatory lust.

He went down to the river and got on top of a rock where the water swirled past and slapped up against its sides. The swarm drew closer and when it came alongside, he struck into the snakes with the stick, over and over again, aiming for the heads. He felt like he had stunned one or two of them; he gingerly pulled the slimy bodies out of the water by the tails. One was still alive and he swung it over his head and hurled back into the river.

He took two of the beaten snakes onto the flat rock where he struck them further on the head. Then he plunged the knife into the back of the skull of the first one, then the other. He turned the blade of the knife into the rock, and their heads rose with the mouths gaping open.

He had two snake bodies lying still on the rock next to him.

He looked at Pepe, who stood on the riverbank staring at him and aghast at the swarm of snakes that receded around a bend in the river. Then Wade burst out in impulsive, relieved laughter. "Well, this is breakfast boy!" *And more...he thought, we can possibly use the skins...*

He cut the heads off the snakes, and set the heads aside. Then he turned the bodies over on the flat rock, and slit each snake down the middle of the belly. Pepe came over and watched with intense curiosity.

"Don't go near those heads!" Wade called out. He'd bury them in the river mud later.

When he'd finished slitting the snakes down the middle, he carefully tore each skin off of the muscle, bones, and entrails. He made sure to do it slowly to get each skin off intact. It peeled back stiffly like duct tape off of a roll. He left the gooey muscle, spinal cords, and guts on the rock in the sun. He assured himself it was highly edible, even as he had no matches for a fire.

The skins he also left to dry on the rock. Then he stepped back off the rock to admire his bloody work. "I wish I got more than two," he said. "But I guess beggars can't be choosers." He bent over and washed his hands in the river. He went back to inspect the skins, which were taut, scaly, and slick on their undersides. He turned them over so the insides faced the sun. They began to smell odorous, but not as stinky as he'd smelt some dead animals before.

The battle with the snakes left him suddenly bone weary, so he took the opportunity to lay back against the warm rock. He closed his eyes. When he opened them again, he watched Pepe toss small rocks into the river, which meandered by with a mellow current. A dry wind blew through the canyon. It's getting time to leave, he thought; we can't linger here forever and live off of snakes...he stood up, fetched the knife, and spread his shirt over the dry rock. He placed the glistening snake bodies on the shirt and cut them up into small, bite-sized pieces, sawing with the knife. The two skulls lay with a reptilian, malignant stare off to the side.

Then he picked up one of the morsels and began to chew. It was tough and fibrous, but it felt great to have some nourishment in his mouth. "Delicious," he announced to Pepe, then smiled. "Here, you try one..." Pepe came over and he handed the kid a piece. The boy was so hungry he was willing to try it.

He looked at the snake meat skeptically in his hand, then he placed it in his mouth. It made a bulge in his cheek, and he slowly chewed around a scowl. Wade laughed, then uncontrollably, and the tension leached out of his body.

"Why that's a delicacy around these parts! We'll call it...a Utah taco! I'll have another one myself...hmm yum...one of the only good things I can get my son to eat is salmon," he said around his own vigorous chewing. "This tastes like salmon to me. Or chicken...Chew it up well kid, before you swallow..."

Pepe sat chewing in slow motion, unhappily, but at least he didn't spit it out. And they had a full bottle of water...then he looked at the river again, now moving swiftly toward Glen

Canyon, and the others in the raft somewhere downstream.

CHAPTER 24

He'd used the snake skins to tie together the collection of sticks and brush into a crude raft. It hardly had enough bulk to hold the two of them, even as its appearance didn't inspire confidence. As Wade placed it into the shallow water, Pepe stood on the riverbank, looking solemn and skeptical. They'd both eaten a handful of tough, squishy snake meats, and Wade had stored the rest of them in a fist-sized mass in his pocket. Then he stepped into the water, one hand steadying the raft.

A rock beside him slowed the current, then it picked up speed and swirled downstream about a meter beyond. "C'mon," he said. "We're going to see your family now." Pepe wandered tentatively into the water. When he got up to about his waist, Wade hooked him gently and they both settled down stomach first on what seemed more like a large shrub, about five by five feet, yanked out of the shore roots and all. Their feet dangled in the water, and it was with marginal relief that Wade pushed them into the current using his feet on the river bottom. He watched their riverbank sanctuary fade as they entered the stream.

They were going quite fast it seemed, but their weight pulled the raft down so that only the upper third of it showed above water. He told the boy to kick. He wanted them to continue facing forward, because he knew nothing about any rapids coming up ahead. For that reason, in part, Wade tried to steer them close to the shore. The water was not cold; it was lukewarm where the sun had been baking its surface.

Only occasionally would his feet touch the bottom, which he concluded was made up of rocks embedded in large stretches of sand and mud. He focused on keeping Pepe on top of the raft; he urged him to scurry farther on top of it, so that only his feet scraped the river's surface.

Wade tried to reason with himself so that he wouldn't revert to the prior angry panic; *we're moving in the right direction...we've had food and drink...the water is keeping us cool...there was nothing else I could do...* The sun was back out and beat relentlessly upon their heads and bodies. He also didn't want to torment himself with the ludicrousness of his plight, how a series of decisions had left him without his gear and with a failed ability to make any real progress towards his lost daughter Kara.

Pepe had a look of determination; his mouth was set and his brown eyes were open wide. The canyon had gotten deeper. The rock that rose on either side was yellowish beige, looking brittle and millennia old. Never touched by man.

The river had sweeping bends in it and Wade looked up at the vacant canyon rim. Occasionally a black bird flew overhead; he took it as a good sign that he saw no men looking down on them. The friends would be on the river, he concluded.

A crescent of sunlight breached the rim. He thought of the snakes; within minutes they entered a place where the water was more agitated, but on that spot the current only pulled them faster and farther downstream. The river flattened again. The snakes had to be far away now, he thought.

He really had no plan except to float throughout most of the day, until possibly they found someone.

At times he experimented with kicking and steering, and he reached the point where he could rotate the mass of sticks 90 degrees clockwise toward the shore. Then he tried it in the other direction; it worked. The raft seemed to be holding together, for now.

He took a deep breath; the river around them had no real scent, the air having been distilled by the recent rains. They'd traveled for a couple of hours at most, but that would be about eight miles. It was a pure desert river, he thought, an ancient passage that could have been known well by only hardy inhabitants from centuries ago. There weren't even any plants on the shoreline; it was water passing through stone. He and Pepe could only think about one hour ahead of them, and hope to survive.

Pepe was silent; he didn't cry or whimper. He did not quite understand how frail their mode of transportation was, Wade thought, but Pepe's spirits seemed to be lifted by the momentum itself, of their movement down the river. Wade was glad, because there was nothing much encouraging he could say anymore to Pepe. One time Pepe took his eyes off the river and he caught him looking his way, and Wade said, "We're in this together kid, just the two of us pal…"

The wind picked up. It offered some relief from the heat cooking their heads; he'd wetted and draped their shirts over their heads and necks. He realized that rough waters ahead had caused the breeze to pick up. The current quickened. "Hold on!" he said. The river seemed deeper and they bobbed up and down in a chop, which slapped against the sides of the canyon.

Then a kind of Vee appeared in the current, pointing downstream, and they were sucked down into its narrow chute. They were spat out into a stormy funnel, which rotated Wade's raft of enmeshed sticks out of control. He gripped Pepe with one arm and the fragile craft with the other. They were suddenly like two people who'd been ripped from the shoreline against their will. The canyon was thrown into shadow; they barreled around another bend.

Wade realized that the puny, fragile nest that they clung to would be smashed to smithereens against rocks that rose against the side of the canyon. He and poor Pepe would be flung into the current and separated in the maelstrom, which had taken him by surprise.

But it didn't...He kept one arm on Pepe and the other flung over the top of the raft, and for minutes it held together.

"Ahh!" Pepe screamed over the roar of the water, pointing with his skinny arm. "*Allí! Por ahí!* Look!" Wade looked up and around the bend ahead he could see Jonesy's raft moored against the rocks. It was near what looked like the mouth of a river. But the boat was empty.

CHAPTER 25

The river was fast and carried them past the raft. At the river mouth, the current slowed again. He couldn't see anyone on the raft's deck, but he did notice, from a short distance, piles of possessions and bedding.

"Hey! Anyone there!" he yelled out as they floated beyond the mooring. Then he frantically began paddling and rowing with his right arm, toward the riverbank. It seemed the river had become shallower where the nearly dried up, smaller tributary flowed into it. They still had to be miles from the Glen Canyon Dam, he thought, but finding Jonesy's boat was a major development. He sensed salvation; his previously low spirits soared over the empty canyon rim.

The landscape remained only sun-blasted rock with the river carving its lonely course. Nothing grew along the sides, and it would be featureless desert above. Still, he longed to be on solid ground again.

He continued to steer and row toward the shoreline as they drifted out of site of the raft, until he felt his feet touch the bottom. The current was gentle now. He was beyond exhaustion, but a raw gratitude flowed through him. He walked the "boat" to the riverbank, then he told Pepe to let go. Pepe waded safely ashore with the gentle water up to his thighs, and pulled himself onto a sunny, flat rock. He lay there motionless.

Wade stood with water calmly flowing around his knees. They would still need to make their way back to the raft along the shoreline, but it seemed not even 200 meters, and the river mouth they'd passed upstream offered dried mud flats for them to walk on.

He already thought of all the things he could do when they reached the raft, and they didn't all involve reuniting with his friends. That made him think of food; with one hand he felt around for the now water-logged snake meat.

He looked up into the sky, penetrating and blue. He'd grown what he figured was an uneven and matted beard; his longish brown hair was mingled with sweat and river water and plastered along the side of his cheek. The top of the canyon swooned and seemed to drift the more he stared at it, as if it too was connected to the Colorado's current. He had a wordless, nonspecific moment of prayer. He looked down, then he let go of his ad hoc raft, reluctantly. It was quickly caught up in the current, then made its way like flood debris to the middle of the river, rounding a bend and disappearing.

They ate the rest of the snake meat, chewing slowly until Pepe spit the last of his out. "I don't blame you..." Wade said, wondering what they'd find to eat on Jonesy's boat. Perhaps nothing...maybe that's why no one seemed to be there, yet maybe it was only a question of someone asleep under the canvas lodged like a sail in the middle of the raft. Maybe they hadn't heard Wade cry out.

They made their way barefoot along the side of the river. Wade had rescued the bloated pants that had barely helped keep his raft afloat; he untied the pant legs and put them on, then tied his shirt around his head to block the sun. They scrambled over a few rocks; each part of his body felt tender and strained, from his knees to his lower back to the neck. He was glad they didn't have far to go.

They walked across the hard-pan mudflats, which had dried into wafers of old river bottom. They still had to cross the other river to get to Jonesy's raft. It was shallow and he held onto Pepe's hand and they carefully made their way to the opposite shore. The water was warm and brackish; different than the river. They reached the other side and covered the rest of the distance to the raft; still no sign of the others.

Wade instantly felt utter exhaustion; the extent of effort required to scrape out survival with a child hit him like a ton of bricks. He muttered to Pepe to stay on the wooden deck of the raft, and when they'd climbed up onto it, he passed out completely. He lay on his stomach on one of the bedrolls that remained. He'd felt guilt that he didn't search for food or water for Pepe first, but sleep came to him violently, like someone pulling a dark cloth over his head and pushing him onto the floor.

He woke up to no noise or light, responding to what was like a natural signal that his body was somewhat restored. He propped himself up on one elbow. A bearded man stood over him, smiling maniacally.

CHAPTER 26

"You mangy old catfish—look what the cat dragged in! By God, I didn't recognize you. I thought you was long gone, done for, with the boy! Carmen and Javi are going to be just ecstatic. Jesus, I can hear her now!"

It was Wiley. Wade was bleary and didn't recognize him at first, then he was flooded with relief.

"The boy's around right?"

"Pepe? The little squirt. You bet he is. He's over there eating. I scraped him together some grub."

"You have some more?"

"Damn right. I'll get you some."

Still laying on his side, Wade felt around beneath the hair on his head and came away with a little blood. He'd cut himself and hadn't even noticed.

"Yeah, you're a mess, that's for sure," Wiley said. He fetched a pan and placed it down at Wade's feet. It had a big spoon stuck in a lump of rice and beans. Wade sat cross-legged and had at the food ravenously, like a prisoner just liberated from isolation. He listened to Wiley. Strangely, the man appeared to be in a better mood than he was farther upstream, when he seemed to be sulking over the loss of his truck, and their risky, near aimless journey.

"The others are down the river apiece, where there's good people, and even better food. I'll take you there later. I just came back to check on the raft."

"What river is this?"

"The Escalante. Ain't what it used to be. But nothing is now a' days..."

"You said you found some people?"

"Yeah, holed up in a slot canyon off the river. Damned if they haven't found a way to survive and thrive in this wasteland. They've got fish, and snake and lizard, and a cache of flour and eggs. They know how to scavenge and live off the land about as well as any..."

"Eggs..." Wade said dreamily, chewing and swallowing vigorously. "I could go for some of those..." He'd already wolfed down most of his food.

"And cheese!" Wiley exclaimed.

"How many of them?"

"I'd say about half a dozen families...about two dozen..."

"And you say they're friendly? They didn't mind seeing you?"

"Can't say they weren't hiding. We were lucky to find 'em. Jonesy pulled the raft over, because we were going to navigate the river and look for you guys. We never did give up hope. We thought we might find some food too, then that storm came. Javi and Carmen went up the river apiece, looking for a way to get to the top of the canyon with the dog, to look for Pepe. I have to say...Carmen was stricken with grief...thought she was going to do herself in..."

"I can imagine that..."

"You done a really good thing, you know, saving that child."

Wade only nodded. He thought of Kara, and the complex journey that lay ahead, the uncountable miles of desolate land, and his own needle-in-a-haystack chances of rescuing *her*. It made him feel less of a hero.

"Good Karma, you know," Wiley added.

"How do you mean?" Wade was now scraping the bottom of the pan and sucking on the spoon.

"You earned positive points for the Great Hereafter..."

"What I need is better luck here on solid ground, the rest of the way."

"That too..."

Wade stood up. "My backpack here? Oh Jesus, great!" He saw it leaning on a box and strode quickly to it. He felt renewed and pulled back together, if still mangy and famished. He began to search through it for the essentials: his pistol and ammo; maps, head lamp and flashlight; extra clothes, boots, medical supplies, the Bible, and its contents. It was all there; he picked the pack up and put it on, just to feel it there again. Along with his boony hat.

"Going somewhere already?" Wiley said.

"No. Are the others coming back soon?"

Wiley scratched the prickly beard on his chin. "Not sure. I believe the plan was to stay with those folks; they have food and shelter. And use the slot canyon as a launching pad to search for you guys, but now that we've found yah..."

"We should go and tell Javi and Carmen...hey Pepe!" The kid wandered out from behind the enclosure that encompassed the cockpit. "Had enough to eat?" The boy quietly nodded, and Wade noted that Pepe's stomach was slightly distended.

Wade wasn't looking forward to another hike, after what they'd been through, but he felt obligated to finally return the child to his parents. He'd had a short but deep sleep, as in total unconsciousness.

"No use doddling," he said. "Let's go."

The drought had reduced the Escalante to a meandering brown stream. It left them plenty of riverbank to hike on. Out of pure paranoia–he didn't want to lose his possessions as quickly as he'd found them–Wade wore the backpack. He felt relieved and back on track; on a path, if a skewed one, that might take him to Kara.

They wandered over the dried wafers and smooth stones of the parched riverbank. You could see the white sulfate stains of the prior river height on the canyon walls. The desert sun seemed to have burned out any shreds of clouds. Wade quickly became intensely thirsty, even though he had come away from ladling the stored water out of the raft's container and guzzling it down, so that it dribbled down his cheeks.

In his haste to fetch the others, he hadn't brought much more than a small water bottle, which he'd stuffed into the pack's side pocket.

The canyon rims around them were just as bleak and dizzying as they were upstream. The walls were bleached nearly white, like the color of desert bones.

They let Pepe straggle a bit behind, as there seemed to be no danger of flash floods or vile strangers, at least not yet. He padded amongst the rocks, picking some of them up and throwing them into the river. Wade thought it would be good for Pepe to experience a little mindless play.

Wiley took them into a narrow passage where the rocks had been smoothed into sculptural shapes and the water took on an emerald color, reflecting slants of piercing light from above. The walls formed natural coves and sitting areas, the smoothed geological shapes seeming impossibly natural and artful.

"These are the famous slot canyons of Glen Canyon," Wiley murmured. Wade had heard of them; they used to be flooded by Lake Powell, which now was drying up at a record pace. The drought had revealed the side canyons once more; now people were rediscovering and living amongst them, apparently, like the ancients once had.

The canyon was more like a small, spotless chamber now; a holy place.

"How far are they?"

"Not far," Wiley spoke back, his voice echoing.

Wade reached out and touched the rock, which was a pink color and shiny with tiny particles embedded in it. Any piece of it could be made into jewelry, and that made him think of Phoebe. He'd been really close to her, for a short period of time.

"How's Phoebe?"

"Surviving, like the rest of us," Wiley called back. "She really likes this place," he added, looking around.

"How do you mean?"

"I mean this little tribe we've found. I think she could join them."

Wade didn't say anything. He suddenly realized he didn't want to lose her, too. It made him feel more lost; emptied out. He promised himself to convince her to stay with them. They'd miss her spry pluckiness; her pure spirit.

They walked quietly, then let Pepe catch up. Wade allowed himself moments of fascination in that amazing place. Then a spicy admixture met his nose, like heavily marinated meat on a grill.

"That smells good," he said. "We must be close...they're cooking."

"And something else too," Wiley said. He'd stopped walking and was looking up the stream; it seemed to open up into another amphitheater, blasted by sunlight. "They're smoking the silly stuff."

"You mean weed?"

"Yeah. Just about everyone I've talked to is high as a kite, and with gentle spirits too. I think they're eating the desert mushrooms, and smoking great stuff from south of this border. In fact I might indulge myself if offered. I could use a break."

"You mean they're surviving here stoned?" Wade was convinced, by experience, that one needed to have razor-sharp wits to escape calamity and death in these regions, formerly known as the American West.

"Yeah, as far as I've seen. I'll take that over the crazies, and their rotgut, meth amphetamines, and whatever else they're sticking into their veins, any day. I think the mellow hallucinogenics are part of their religion, their cult, whatever they have going here."

Then through the piercing sunshine, Wade could see a man; a slim form, shirtless, long dark hair and beard, waving at them. He stood along the shoreline of the meagre Escalante.

"That's Rick," Wiley said. "Kind of the leader...sweet on Phoebe by the way..."

Oh no, Wade thought. Prying her away was going to be difficult. Against his will, being older and married, he felt this Rick guy's presence as almost hostile competition for Phoebe. He felt it as jealousy.

When they reached him, Rick came forward. He had a big smile and a welcome vibe. He looked like some depictions of Jesus.

"I'm Wade..." He stuck out his hand.

"Rick!" Rick gave Wade the Brah handshake and half hug that all the athletes were doing before the United States fell apart.

"So great..." Wade said. "To run into a friendly crowd. Strangers who don't pose a threat, if you know what I mean..."

"No worries," Rick said softly. "Everything's cool." He had a kind of hazy detachment, a lazy confidence. *Stoned*, Wade thought. He also reeked, the odor being sweet and not unpleasant. Rick was skinny, with knotted muscles and long lithe limbs. He was built and tanned like an agricultural worker.

"We've seen you guys coming for a long time," he said, nodding his head upwards. Wade looked up, and along the ridge line he could see the forms of maybe half a dozen men and women with what seemed bows and arrows. Wade was pleased himself to be back with his own crossbow.

"We're not *that* loosey-goosey," Rick said, suddenly revealing his higher place on the pecking order. "But I want to tell you now, upfront, that this place is about love and community and family...rebuilding, and that you're *welcome* here. You can stay here as long as you want. We've heard all about you already...you're good people we hear..."

From who? Wade thought, until he heard Pepe erupt, "Mommy! Daddy!" Both Rick and Wade turned their heads. Javi and Carmen, with Phoebe not far behind, were running up the shoreline towards them. Then the Santiago's were three people in a bustling huddle, with hugs and tears of joy. For Wade, it was a rare moment of timeless humanity, all so rare those days. They were a family reunited. His chin quivered with emotion.

Phoebe leapt up and down and was all over them with more eager joy. She hugged Wade; he stayed in that position for a moment, because it felt good. Then he realized how dirty and unkempt he was, a river rat, and he stood back, almost embarrassed.

"I thought you might be drowned, you crazy beautiful idiot," she said, smiling exuberantly. *I guess I know what you've been smoking,* Wade thought. The aroma was in her hair, along with the wonderful scent of wild flowers she seemed to always carry.

"Well, we were a little lucky. I guess it was just meant to be, all us getting together again…" The emotional outpouring taking place had exhausted his spent reserves, all over again. He stepped back to the river's edge to give Phoebe the space to greet and hug Pepe.

"Pepe, you little devil," she said gleefully. "Pint-sized muffin, come here to Aunt Phoebe! Where did you go? We looked all over for you!"

"In the river…at night…" he said, with a hint of mystery.

"Is that so? Well!" Phoebe stood with her arms crossed, miming a schoolmarm. Carmen was still crying and wiping her cheeks with her hands and showering an embarrassed Pepe with kisses.

"Is everybody hungry?" Phoebe said.

"You bet."

"We have food on the fire," she crowed, with what Wade thought was a holiday spirit. She sure was happy here, and sleeping and eating well, he thought. "Vittles!" she added, and they all started walking deeper into the amphitheater where Wade saw flames leaping against a pink wall, and a small crowd of people hanging around.

The atmosphere was one of atavism and wonder; someone played one of those Peruvian piped flutes, and another gently and steadily beat a drum. A wine pouch, he thought, was being passed around. A big pot of food, some kind of porridge or stew, brewed. He wanted to fill his stomach again, be part of all this, and sleep.

Amazement flowed through him; the people seemed like prehistoric humans, too content to realize how decayed and perilous the world had become. He was struck by the beauty of the place itself, bathed in the preternatural light that filtered through the narrow canyons. The smooth rock funneled a nice breeze over the shallow pools that branched off in another direction.

At some point, and soon, he would have to leave all this. He found himself standing next to Jonesy. They shook hands, and they sat down to listen to the music and eat.

"What's next?" Wade asked. He shifted in his seat. "We keep going down the Colorado? Glen Canyon Dam is coming up."

"Or what's left of it."

"What do you mean by that?"

"The Glen Canyon Dam is breached, they tell me. It's no more. It wasn't producing power, because Lake Powell dropped too low. The lake's almost dried up. The Dam isn't manned anymore and some gang blew a hole in it. From what I've heard, it's a giant white elephant."

"Wow, so what's the river like beyond it? That's the Grand Canyon. The breach must have still released a lot of water into it. The river must be moving faster through there." Wade bent over into his backpack and pulled out his southwestern map. He felt his spirit move faster, going south, toward his goal.

"Not sure me, you, or anyone else wants to keep going past Glen Canyon."

"Why? What do you hear?"

"You think *this* is a no man's land? It's all shot to hell down in Arizona."

"What about Lake Mead, the Hoover Dam, Vegas..." Lake Mead had been formed by the Hoover Dam, and Vegas "drank" from the lake. Someone passed them both wooden bowls of the stew, and they began wolfing it down greedily. With their beards, and the recently acquired, starving, uncouth natures, they looked like a couple of farmers in the Dark Ages, Wade thought. The men were all bearded and scrawny.

"Lake Mead is dried up more than Powell–that straw from Vegas has gone bone dry. That's what the folks here tell me. Seems more than one of them came north from there. They say that Vegas, what's left of it, has become a miserable chaos, a burning, decadent wasteland."

*Sounds like a more violent version of what Vegas used to be...*Wade thought.

"Not even the regime will go in there," Jonesy continued. "Crazy Land...maybe the regime is contemplating nuking it from orbit..."

"Oh..." The hollow drum beat more ominously in the background. Wade was disappointed; he thought at least he'd have a water route. He thought he could keep going down the Colorado.

He stopped chewing. "So you're saying you're probably not going to keep going."

"I promised you folks I'd go as far as the Glen Canyon Dam. I'll hold to that promise; I gave you my word. But then I'll probably scuttle her...or sell her if I can...and make my way back here. Ain't nothin' for me down there in that desert hell-hole. Can't say what the Santiago's plan to do. If I was them, I'd stay here...maybe there's a future..."

Where are they getting their food? Wade thought, then Jonesy read his mind.

"Can't see how they can continue cultivation here though– no soil to speak of, water's drying up...oh well beggar's can't be choosers..." He resumed shoveling the bowl's contents into his mouth.

Wade looked down at his map. He followed the squiggly line of the Colorado River past Glen Canyon, and he could see that it actually went due West of southern Arizona, where Sierra Vista and Kara were. The pitiable Colorado ended up reduced to a littered trickle, or simply mud-flats, once it reached the California coast.

A land-locked route into Arizona was a far more direct route to Sierra Vista. He looked up at the calm, convivial group, and they seemed to exist on another planet; not the increasingly uninhabitable one he'd gotten to know. He wouldn't begrudge them their contentment. But his mind raced ahead with the necessities of his own plans.

CHAPTER 27

All the things he didn't want to happen came to pass. Jonesy began to even reconsider going as far as the defunct Glen Canyon Dam. Phoebe loitered around Rick longingly, expressing too much unqualified fondness than Wade could stand. It was puppy-dog love, yet the times were too unsafe to let her emotions run wild, he thought.

The Santiagos were uncommitted about going as far as Nicaragua, as their transportation literally began to dry up.

Wade sat off to the side on a small rock, petting Pequeño by the river. He thought the dog was getting too scrawny, like the rest of them. The fish had been good but they hadn't gotten any in 24 hours; the dog was forced by hunger to lick the rice-dominated gruel they all were eating. Tough bits of lizard meat would show up in the stew, like chewy, hidden prizes.

It was morning in the canyon. They'd made coffee, but no one had awoken with the sun like he had. He was barefoot and he let his feet lay in the cool river, truly a stream now, on top of some smooth rocks. The water had been cooled by a brief evening shower out on the desert. Pequeño lapped at it, then wandered over to sit closer to him. He pet its scruffy head and felt sorry for the pooch, who was trapped in the same world they were. The dog's eyes were plaintive, and carried the same uncertainty he did in his heart.

"You're right Pequeño. We don't know where we're going, or what we're doing."

He gazed over his own legs, which were bony and covered in undifferentiated bruises and scratches. He'd used the propylene glycol in his kit to disinfect one of the nastier ones, then bandage it up. At least infections didn't thrive in this sun-blasted habitat, he pondered, but the dangers of the desert lurked ahead.

A noise behind startled him, and he quickly grabbed his nearby crossbow and stood up, nearly upending the cherished coffee cup, and spooking Pequeño. But it was only a young woman with long brown hair leading two wide-eyed infants to behind a rock. She was probably going to clean them up.

She smiled at him beneficently; her graceful, prepossessed manner and the silence of the morning had almost convinced Wade to stay with this group.

He thought of his own wife and children. It made him sad and wistful; the ordinary things they used to do together. A glass of wine with Lee on two chairs he placed outside with a sunset view of meadows and mountains. Drawing down a shade and sleeping heedlessly late in the cool darkness of a Sunday morning. Going to Little League games with his son Shane. Making love to Lee after they'd both gotten tipsy. He regretted the losses, but he admired these slot-canyon people, mingled with an acute sense of their naivete, for trying to recapture the old ways.

#

Jonesy and Wade got ready to leave. The early morning had passed. People had begun to stir, including Carmen and Javi. Wade saw them across the tiny river, with Pequeño trotting along the shoreline. It was just a question of who was coming with them, going south following the remainder of the river upstream of the dam. Wade thanked Rick, who'd walked over to the riverside where Wade packed his things.

"You sure you don't want to stay?" Rick asked. His tone suggested that Wade was insane for leaving. "Plenty of room..."

"Yeah. You see I'm looking for someone...my daughter. I'm needed elsewhere."

"I understand."

Phoebe wandered up and took Rick's hand. This was a definite development, Wade thought. She was introspective; far less bubbly, as if just realizing that part of her gang were leaving for good.

"Are you going now?" she said softly.

This was a turning point; her voice reflected that she understood. In this frayed world, people weren't very mobile anymore; goodbye usually meant goodbye for good.

"I decided to stay," she added.

Rick turned and smiled at her. They had a newlywed couples' sappiness, Wade thought. He looked away, not conferring his approval. Obviously, he wanted Phoebe to come. In a way, they needed her energy and presence for the rest of the voyage. He was beyond disappointed.

"I figured you did..."

She came forward and draped her arms around him. She rested her head on his shoulder, then pulled away. She leaned against Rick. Oddly, Wade thought right then, *are they going to have babies? In this isolated, desolate place?*

"Come back here after you find Kara. Come back through here on your way home," Phoebe said.

"I will."

"Thank you for picking me up way back there on the highway."

"It was all of us. We made it this far together." He picked up his backpack, shook Rick's hand, and started walking up the riverside towards the raft. Off to the side, he noticed the Santiagos pulling their things together, the duffel and backpacks. It had all happened too fast; finding Phoebe again and then having to split up.

He hadn't brought the subject up with anyone but Jonesy; he'd figured most of the people would join them. But it was only him, Carmen, Pepe, Javi, and Jonesy. The dog too. Wiley was staying.

"Hey Wiley! Aren't you coming?" Wade called out. He could see him over where they'd eaten the night before. Wiley was standing next to a younger man, drinking from a plastic mug and chatting amiably. He seemed right at home. He looked over, then he put the cup down and trotted over to join Wade by the riverbank.

"The food's better here!" he yelled back jauntily. "I don't know why you want to leave so soon...yeah yeah I know, your daughter."

"You gonna brave it out here in the desert, huh?"

"What else do I have?" Wiley shrugged. "Look what they've done here. From what I've seen, it's a miracle. There ain't nothin' for me down there in Medeeco, anywhere south of here's a pit of vipers..." Then he seemed to instantly regret what he said.

"Listen, I'd like to help you find your daughter. I really would. I just don't think I'd be much use to you, a raggedy old coot like me."

Wade raised his hand. "No worries. Good luck to you here. Maybe I'll see you again."

"We will meet again, I'm sure of that."

Wade thought about when Wiley picked him up in the truck–the blackness of the blotted out Denver sky, the empty, sinister highway; the deep loneliness he'd felt. They'd made some tracks together.

Wiley dug his hands into his pockets. He got serious, almost grim. "Listen, do you know which way your goin'?'

"We might not take the river the whole way. But I'm going to Sierra Vista...by hook or by crook, unless I hear otherwise about Kara's location."

Wiley looked down, scuffed the dry ground, and seemed to be at a loss for words.

"You took all that extra food, right?"

"Yeah."

"Okay, buddy." They gave each other a rough hug; Wiley smelled like a man who'd crawled out of the desert, mingled with pot, which was by comparison, perfume.

They all quietly marched back to the raft. Pequeño came along with them, following along behind Pepe. There wasn't any arguments about who would have the dog; as if they left the decision up to her.

When they got to the raft, it was still gently tugging on its line. It seemed to Wade that the river had evaporated another several inches. There seemed just enough depth to float without scraping bottom. He thought of all the water gushing past the breached dam, flowing in the direction of the Grand Canyon, then Lake Mead. Wade tugged his backpack, and an old canvas bag of rice, potatoes, and other provisions, onto the wooden deck. They got onboard silently, including Pequeño.

Wade undid the line, Jonesy took the tiller, and the raft slid into the gentle ripples. The sun blazed and he could feel the warmth from the deck's wooden boards on the bottom of his feet. He watched the little group of people waving at them from the shoreline, then they drifted around a bend and were alone again.

The river wound its way into solid rock canyon; not a strand of vegetation remained. The Colorado was still in shadow, and only a breath of wind whispered over the trickling waters. Ambivalence about leaving still gnawed at him; it was probably worse for the Santiagos, who could have made a go of it back at the slot canyon. Javi had still wanted to aim for the homeland, and Carmen was deferent.

They floated all day in the humid shadows. They encountered no rapids, or people.

CHAPTER 28

It didn't take long to reach the crumbling edifice of the Glen Canyon Dam. Wade had taken a turn at the tiller, when it loomed massively into sight around a bend. It was beige-colored and smooth and concave, like a giant shell excavated from the ocean. It blocked out the horizon, and the cliffs around it were red and arid. When they entered the dam's shadow, the water got rough and choppy. They were hit with a breeze that was relieving but chilly.

The shocking change in temperature seemed to involve more than just shade. The swirling waters breaching the dam had made agitated eddies and wakes at the foot of the structure, which lurched out of the desert like a monument to the recent collapse.

Wade handed the tiller to Jonesy, then he made sure that his backpack and the boxes of food and pans and other belongings were properly secured on the deck.

"Why do you think it's so cold?"

"Water's much colder down here," Jonesy yelled over the wind. "It comes from snowpack, or what's left of that. And it never gets full on sunlight."

Pequeño stood by on the deck, teetering on his skinny, short legs. He frantically had his nose in the air; everything had suddenly changed drastically, and the dog sensed it.

The frothy river slapped loudly on the sides of the raft, which drifted almost sideways in the quickened current. Wade couldn't take his eyes off the towering dam, more than seven hundred feet above. It had chunks of concrete gouged out of it in the way of the Greek ruins. Huge cracks that migrated down the concave surface. He could see tiny figures far above them, making their way across the rim of the dam.

Jonesy's scraggly gray hair and scowling beard gave him a wild look as he gripped the tiller.

"Maybe we should beach first," Wade yelled to him. There was far more wind in that part of the canyon; it carried away his voice. The boat seemed out of control.

"Where?" Jonesy grimaced, then stared at the swirling river just ahead. The current tugged hard at them. Off to the side were bleak rocky shorelines, where the greenish, riled-up waters broke up in a light spray against the canyon wall.

The river funneled the raft toward the main breach in the dam, which bubbled in the distance. Some people had simply blown a large hole in it, as far as Wade could tell. Although deeper and colder, the river sat far below its high mark on the dam. Wade wondered if the Colorado had equalized its depth on the other side of the dam, where the side canyons filled like suddenly engorged veins.

Javi stood beside Jonesy, his hands balled into fists. Wade thought he looked gaunt, with his wife and child huddled nearby. As men trying to bear the burdens of this voyage, this trial by fire, Wade related to him. They were all desert refugees trapped in survival mode.

"What are we going to do now Jonesy?" Javi asked, over the wind. Jonesy looked over his shoulder at the dam, getting closer. Wade thought, if they weren't careful, they would ram it, then capsize.

"We have to navigate to the side," Wade yelled. "There must be somewhere to moor–we're not the only ones coming down the river and aiming to pass through."

"Let me think, dammit!" Jonesy barked, then he yanked on the tiller at a sharp angle, aiming for a shoreline they were blind to. "Just let me think for two seconds, Jesus Christ you nervous Nellies…I've got you this far haven't I?"

Jonesy maneuvered the raft closer to the canyon walls, where the eddies calmed and the currents slowed. They began to drift beneath the ruins, which close-up showed blobs of black stains like oil, and concrete segments scrawled with spray-painted figures. They only could have been done by people rappelling from the top with spray cans. Wade had thought he'd seen most everything by then, but not this.

Like other places he'd been to–graffiti art he'd seen from the train–the images expressed both skill and anarchy. A wanton defacement, to make a point, about power. The loss of power, or a shift of power.

About half the graffiti spelled out RLA; one time it specified on the concrete in its entirety: Redboyz Liberation Army. It wasn't the regime calling the shots here anymore, he thought. A kind of blackness settled over him, one more profound than the shadows of the looming dam. He wondered what they'd find on the other side.

They saw the entrance to a tunnel in the distance. A man and a woman, with backpacks, stood at the entrance near their small boats. It seemed they'd kayaked up the canyon. More concrete had been gouged out and eroded at the water's edge, exposing nests of embedded rebar. As the raft drifted closer, Wade took the line and roped one of these steel rebars as they moved past it, then made the boat fast. The air down there was cool and strangely briny, like an ocean dock's.

He made the rope tight and they all stood silently on the deck. The raft could go no farther, at least at this juncture. They all seemed to realize this at once.

The two people looked normal; nonthreatening. Wade put his backpack on and stepped off the raft onto a traverse of broken-up concrete that led to the tunnel. He made his way over slowly, hoping his own mangy appearance wouldn't turn the people off.

He held out his hand, and the female shook it. They were going downstream, searching for a tributary that might bring them around the dam. They thought the passageway nearby was too risky. They were in a hurry.

"Have you gone through the tunnel?"

"No."

"Do you know how long it is?"

"About two miles," the man said. "It's too dangerous, I think." He had an accent, like a Canadian's in Montreal.

"You mean, to negotiate through the dark?"

"The people..."

"Up there? This RLA garbage?"

"Yeah. We have to go." The man walked over to where the kayaks rocked in the river's swell. Wade looked back to the raft, where all the people were on the deck, staring at him.

The woman spoke up, not wanting to maintain a silence. "We saw them throwing people off the dam. Yesterday."

"No kidding."

"Yes. There were a bunch of them, including one of their own, a guy in a red bandanna. They killed them. We're going to try to make our way around them. I think they own this territory. They're selling women…"

"What?"

"We heard rumors." She looked at her companion, who was sitting in his kayak staring at her.

"From who?"

"There was a group of guys in a boat; they had guns; some food. Came from Vegas. They'd survived. They were heading into the desert. They said this group is capturing women, from Vegas and elsewhere, and enslaving them…selling them…"

"Which way were these guys headed, the ones who told you this?"

"Are you coming?" the guy in the boat said impatiently.

"There," she said, pointing to the southeast, away from where the Colorado flowed toward Lake Mead and Las Vegas. Towards Mexico and southern Arizona.

"If you go into this tunnel, I think it's faster, but more dangerous."

"Where does it go?"

"Casey!" the man yelled out. He had one hand on her small boat to steady it. She shouldered her backpack and moved toward it over the chewed up concrete.

"It ends up at the top of the dam," she called back to him. "Only consider doing it at night–it's monitored in the daytime. They're not friendly…"

"Thanks for telling me this. And good luck."

"Good luck." The woman got back into her boat's cockpit, the man handed her a paddle, and they both pushed away into the river. They began to paddle furiously along the canyon edge.

The passageway was a black silent maw. He had the idea that they should go through that night; the dusk approached. No sense waiting; it was that or follow the kayakers, but he didn't think the raft could maneuver the same route they were taking.

They'd scan the top of the dam with Jonesy's telescope first. He didn't want to endanger the Santiagos, but they didn't have many options. Wade had to keep moving south.

Bruce W. Perry

PART III: THE DESERT

CHAPTER 29

Wade scanned the top of the dam as the sun went down. Through the telescope's lens, he swept it and he could see a railing and once, a line of men who seemed on patrol. Then when the sun dropped behind the canyon, it got pitch black. The dam was completely unlit; not even a torch flickered above. The giant concrete surface glowed in the starlight, like a Pyramid. It was time to move.

By flashlight, they all gathered their essentials into backpacks and duffels.

Jonesy had opted to stay with the raft. He couldn't let her go–just abandon the still seaworthy boat, which had carried them hundreds of miles down the Colorado. Wade saw the wisdom in his decision; keep someone with the craft, just in case they had to turn around in the tunnel. They'd also had to leave some provisions and tools on her, since not all of them could be carried.

Wade had a head lamp with two AAA batteries, the only working ones remaining. The plan was for him to go about 200-300 meters ahead, so that he could signal in the event of trouble.

It was 3 a.m. The tunnel was moist and cool inside.

"Wait for my signal," he said to the others. His headlamp stabbed the darkness and illuminated a ramp that proceeded gradually uphill. The floor had puddles and was littered with concrete debris and dust. He walked for a minute then removed his pistol, stopped, made sure it was loaded, then continued walking uphill.

It was silent, except for his foot crunches on the fragmented pebbles. He only had two shots left. He was tired, but alert. He kept stopping to listen; he heard nothing but water droplets and the wind that seemed to come down from above. Occasionally he'd come upon garbage like wadded up bags and empty aluminum cans; expired, rusted fire extinguishers. People-sized portals in the walls led to nowhere; they were meant for men on foot to step aside for vehicles, in the old days.

He wondered whether he'd run into any forks in his path–forcing him to decide which way to go–but the passage led to only one place, and that was daylight far above. One time, he sneezed loudly. The echo carried, and he swore softly to himself. He had two baseball sized chunks of concrete with him. When he thought he'd gone a long enough way, he stopped, pocketed the pistol, and tossed the chunks down the tunnel in the opposite direction. When he heard another knock against the wall, three times, he kept going.

The lady had said two miles, but she really didn't know. The total elevation gain was a bit more than 700 feet, the height of the Glen Canyon Dam, so the tunnel couldn't be much longer than two miles. That would be a six percent or so elevation grade, and the tunnel was traveling uphill.

He kept walking for 10 minutes, then 15, sweeping the small space ahead of him with the lamp. He saw a pin of light ahead of him. He began to think about their scant food and water, the mounting unknowns of his journey, and for that moment he had an overwhelming desire to turn back. Committing to the tunnel seemed doomed, because it wasn't a plan; it was the only card left to play. He felt hungry and fatigued; it was a moment of weakness rather than clarity, he told himself.

Then he heard a voice, not behind but in front of him. He reached up and shut off his head lamp. Two voices carried from afar, men talking, down at the end. He couldn't make out what they were saying. Then silence. He waited for a moment; he let the blackness and the quiet fill the tunnel. He couldn't hear the others coming, and he prayed that they could keep Pepe quiet. He forgot about the dog; *Christ, will they have enough sense to leave Pequeno behind?* He kept walking, with his headlamp turned off, feeling along the wall. It was like the inside of a subway tunnel. The pin of light grew larger.

CHAPTER 30

He put the pistol to the fat man's head and nudged his temple. The man woke up with a scowl, irritated, then looked at Wade wide-eyed. He sat in one of those fold-out armchairs with armrest pockets for drinks. One of them contained a tall can of something wrapped in a brown paper bag, as if he'd just bought it at 7 Eleven. The chair was located right at the tunnel exit, where it gave way to a walkway that overlooked the other side of the dam.

"Don't say anything," Wade said. "Until I tell you to." The bearded man wore a red bandanna, and had a cut-off sweatshirt with huge beefy, tattoo-covered upper arms.

"Where's your buddy?"

"He's gone." The guy, whose head was the size and shape of a ham hock, had a gravelly voice.

"What are you doing here?"

The man hesitated, then said "Watching out."

172

"For what?"

"...People like you...I guess. It's my shift." His red-rimmed eyes crept around the immediate area. When he shifted to look to the side, Wade said "Don't move your head, or anything." He heard foot crunches coming from the other side of the tunnel, whispering. It was the rest of the raft gang. Everything was dark, but a flight of stairs led away. It must have been approaching about 4 a.m.

"Where do those stairs go?"

"Down below."

"No shit. Then where?"

"There's a path, an old dam-operations road. It goes into the desert."

"I think you're going to have to come with us. If you make a peep, I'll blow your head off." Then he thought about how this whale was going to slow them down.

"Do you have a pair of cuffs on yah?"

"No." It was still dark and unlit.

"Get your fat ass out of that chair and keep your mouth shut." He still had the pistol to the guy's head.

"Drop your belt..."

"Why?"

"I'm securing your hands, genius."

Wade heard the others shuffle out of the tunnel. Javi looked surprised, eyes wide.

"Who's this?"

"Who knows," Wade said. "Is Jonesy coming?"

"He's a few minutes behind us, with Pequeno." *So Jonesy's coming after all,* he thought, and *Oh no. We'll never be able to keep the dog quiet, and they probably have dogs up here.*

"Hank..." the man muttered, unfastening his belt.

"Hank is our man of the hour. He's going to lead us out of

here."

When he'd taken his belt off, his pants slipped to halfway down his buttocks. Wade made him cross his wrists behind him. "Javi, I want you to do me a favor. Hold this gun to his head."

"Don't," Carmen said. She made Wade feel guilty for introducing this conflict and roughly taking a man captive, but Javi surprised him. Without saying anything, he took the gun and held it with two hands, aiming at the man's cheekbone.

"Don't move, clown," he said. Wade wore a half smile and bound the man's wrists with his leather belt. Maybe Javi understood better than his wife where they were; that they were amongst the animals.

"Are you packing, by the way?" Wade said. Hank grunted. Wade felt down his pants, reaching into his left pocket and removing a handgun. "I thought so. We can use this." He handed the weapon to Javi and took back his own pistol.

"Stuff that in your backpack for now," he told Javi. "Let's go. Walk ahead of me," he said, pushing the man forward. Hank shuffled along toward the stairs, just as Jonesy emerged from the tunnel, with a duffel strung over his back and Pequeno on a leash.

"Who the hell is this?" he whispered in a strained pitch.

"Just keep the dog quiet, if you can. In fact, you can go ahead first. Take the stairs. They lead to the desert, and Hank here is going to show us the way, aren't you pal?"

Hank looked back at Wade and scowled, which prompted Wade to poke the back of his head with the pistol barrel. The stairs led down, switch backing a few flights. The dog walked quickly ahead of Jonesy, sniffing. Then Hank, thumping over each step and holding onto a railing, with Wade and the others close behind. The sun still hadn't come up yet, but it would soon.

"You're not gonna get far you know," Hank mumbled gruffly. "They're gonna see I'm gone and they know I wouldn't go wandering off into the tunnel so they're going to look here..."

"Didn't I tell you to shut up, unless I tell you to talk?" Wade had no real patience left. They had a long way to go that day, even though he didn't exactly know the direction they'd be headed in.

"They ain't friendly either when someone messes with 'em and..." Wade clubbed him, gently he thought, on the back of his head, and Hank yelped in pain and leaned against the railing with Wade digging the metal handgrip into a soft spot on his lower back.

"*Dios mio!*" Carmen said. She hadn't seen this side of Wade. It had just come out, since Chicago.

Wade hissed into Hank's ear, "You're going to be the silent type and just show us where the road is, and we're going to take you and just let you go at a certain point. Got it?"

"Yeah!" The others went ahead until they got to the bottom of the stairs. Wade looked behind him; nothing. It was still quiet. Not yet five in the morning. He thought he saw a brightening on the edge of the dam and the canyon. They were lucky to get another hour on the road before Hank's absence would be discovered.

Soon they were on a dirt road that skirted the edge of the deep canyon. It proffered a long, dim view of the dark green river releasing from the bottom of the dam below. They shuffled along quietly, slowed by the things they carried, and Hank. Wade could hear Jonesy quietly cursing to himself. They would need water soon, especially Pepe. They'd only been able to carry so much, several liters worth, which wouldn't last long in the desert.

"What's the matter with you?" Wade asked. He already

knew; Jonesy regretted leaving the raft and the slot canyon tribe.

"As soon as I spot a road goin' the other way, back to the river and Arizona and the Escalante, I'm taking it. 'Specially if I can get a ride in a pickup. I didn't sign on for this friggin' death march."

"How much transportation they have on this road?" Wade asked Hank.

"Not much…a few ATVs."

"Any pickup trucks? Any horses?"

"A few come through. The Reds have Jeeps; a couple of technicals."

"The who?"

"The Redboyz; the group I'm employed with."

"Employed? Are you kidding me? They're a gang, and you're one of the peons."

"It's like a job, like any other." Now Hank actually sounded like Wade had hurt his feelings, his tender side.

"That's a stretch. Keep walking."

"It's hot–when are you gonna take this belt off my wrists? When are you giving me some water?"

"When you show me all the way out of here. And tell me where these Redboyz came from. How far do they stretch?"

"To Vegas. That's where we came from."

"What are they doing at the dam?"

"Less competition. Fewer turf wars…"

"Competition for what?"

"For what we sell–water, weed, food, mushrooms…"

"Anything you can steal, right?"

"Something like that."

"Are you selling women? Making slaves of them?"

"That's a lie. That's a crock. Where did you hear that? They have wives and girlfriends, like anyone else."

"They? Not you?"

"I don't have a girlfriend. You find that information shocking?"

"Not really. But don't let it get you down. There's someone for everyone out there."

"Listen, this road, it'll take you right to the main highway. Just stay on the dirt road. I won't say a fuckin' thing–you've already totally screwed me by doing this. Now I don't have any excuses–you're going to have to hit me over the head and make it bleed. Then I can tell them you knocked me out–so maybe they won't throw me off the dam, or crucify me." Hank was now shuffling along the path with his giant head lolling, like he'd pitch forward onto his face at any moment. He was slowing them down. The sun was coming up over the desert flats; the horizon smeared red and bringing out the sandstones own redness. No one noticed its beauty though.

"Where does the highway go?"

"South…"

"To Northern Arizona?"

"Yes."

They needed to go faster. The whole crew was strung out ahead of Wade and Hank. The time had come to part company.

"I'll catch up with you," Wade said to the others. Pequeno was now loose and running along the side of the path, frantically picking up smells.

Then Wade turned to Hank, whose slack posture expressed total exasperation. His mouth fell.

"Don't do it–I mean it! I didn't do anything to you. I showed you the way out of here. I did everything you wanted me to. Don't kill me!"

"Don't piss your pants. I'm going to do what you asked me to do–give you a little bruise to remember us by. Then you're going to cool your heels for a couple of hours while we catch a ride up there. This is going to hurt me more than it's going to hurt you."

"Alright alright, just don't cripple me okay?"

"Turn around and count to ten..." Wade was actually reluctant to do it. Hank was right; he hadn't done anything and seemed like a rather harmless dolt. But he'd probably lied about the women. Unfortunately, he turned his head just when Wade was bringing the butt of his pistol down, and the blow mostly glanced off his ear. Hank collapsed into the dust with a howl.

"What the fuck was that?!" He held onto the side of his head and his ear, sitting in the middle of the trail, a huge man that Wade thought was going to cry. For sure, it must have smarted like hell.

"Shshsh, quiet! I'd do it again, but you look bad enough." A wad of stuff had fallen out of his pockets, and he crawled around the trail collecting it. Wade looked back toward the dam and saw no one in pursuit, just a bone-dry sky and a blazing sun that seemed to have burnt away all the clouds. His own mouth was parched, but the others had the water.

A number of Polaroids were strewn around the ground. Wade picked a few of them up and looked at them. Hank looked at him sheepishly.

"What the hell are these?"

"They gave them to me to...," Hank struggled to his feet, out of breath. "Show people...because these are missing girls. Who other people like their relatives are trying to find."

The pictures showed a number of unsmiling women standing in front of a gray wall. Their expressions were impassive and forced, like those in a mug shot.

"You're lying! These are women you're trying to sell." Wade started to leaf through them, mostly young women with

178

long blond or brown hair, or Latino and African-American women. They were attractive but sullen, having been lined up and photographed at gunpoint.

He was appalled, as he looked from one to the other. Along the bottoms of each photo were four-digit numbers and names like ham radio handles or shoddy web usernames, like filly 0091. It was nauseating; it reminded him of the Holocaust. The people with numbers stenciled on their wrists.

"You have anymore of these?" He looked ahead where the others were waiting for him.

"I didn't have anything to do with this. I'd let 'em go if I could." Hank still sat on the ground with his hand on his wound; he pulled it away and looked at it.

"Just give me the rest of them." Wade took the whole pile of them, like a deck of cards, and shoved them in his pocket.

"Where are these women kept?" The open road pulled at him, but he just had to know.

"They're down by the river where they got a pier. Then they ship 'em to wherever…sometimes back to Vegas."

"Ship 'em," Wade whispered to himself. That sounded like bags of coffee, or UPS boxes full of imported junk from China.

"I'm going to leave you now," he said to Hank, righting the backpack on his shoulders. He still had the pistol displayed. "It's been special knowin' yah."

"Your gonna untie me, right?"

Wade had already started walking. "Nah. That wouldn't be a good idea."

"You're not gonna just leave me here like this? The coyotes will get me! The mountain lions!"

"Now that I think of it," Wade said. He walked over, snatched Hank's red kerchief from his head, pushed his head down onto the ground, and stuffed about two thirds of it into his mouth, around Hank's muffled protests. "I don't want you screaming like a banshee for the next half hour."

Then he turned and walked away quickly.

CHAPTER 31

They followed the dirt road until it reached a barren, beat-up highway. In the distance, they saw mountains and the glow from flames. The sun was like a giant spotlight trained on all of them. They had to stop, because Pepe had passed out on his feet; the others were close to curling up on the hard ground next to him.

They ate leftover rice and oatmeal and crackers by the side of the road, and drank lukewarm water from pouches and used plastic liter bottles. Wade craved an apple, an orange, a grapefruit; a fatty steak or a big stein of cold beer. Anything, from the old world of endless stuff. He wondered if they still grew fruit or tended cattle or fished in California. Or made wine.

Who was running that region now? From Phoebe's friends in the side canyon, he'd heard rumors of foreign invaders from Asia. At any rate, the West Coast was charred, and up for grabs; he knew that much.

There wasn't much of the water left; they needed new provisions. The Santiagos sat cross-legged on the ground beside Pepe. Pequeno was on his leash sitting in the dust by the side of the road. Wade stood in the road and looked what he figured was due south, toward Flagstaff, Arizona. The empty horizon was smudged by a brownish smog–they had mountains and forests there. It was probably the wildfires.

He could see utility wires leading down the road to signs of a town, the distance blurred at the edges by radiating heat.

Their options were limited; Jonesy wanted to return to the raft.

"No, that's out of the question. We'll run into that gang again."

"We could run into them anywhere! What do you think is down in that town? The church picnic? Main Street USA?" He lowered his voice. "Ain't no place safe in these parts, outside of the river. Even the Colorado has its hazards, as we found out. But I'd rather take my chances back at the raft."

"We need you to stay with us Jonesy. Just as far as the next town. Then you can catch a ride back to the river if you want. We'll get some provisions there, I promise. We've got gold coins left; a few things to trade. We'll be alright. We'll find a safe way south. Think of Pepe; he needs all of us firing on all cylinders. He needs you."

"Keep going, my friend," Jonesy quipped. "The rest of them will break out into applause soon."

"Seriously. I can't do it alone, me and Javi. You were our savior once–make it twice."

"Your optimism exceeds the probability of success, in my view. But now that you've laid the mother of all guilt trips on me…" Wade clapped him on the back and thanked him, before he could spit out the rest of his words.

The desert burned and glowed on all horizons. As if to emphasize its malignance, the breakdown lane they wandered along contained the buzzard-picked remains of dogs, coyotes, and a desert tortoise. The road sucked up the heat like a stovetop.

They stopped and they all took slugs of water from the diminished plastic bottles and pouches they'd filled from the raft's reservoir. They gave the desperately panting Pequeno a bowl by the roadside. Wade figured it was still about five miles to the town. It was difficult to get everyone moving again, which almost seemed futile. They hadn't even slept yet.

Only two vehicles passed them: a three-wheeled motorcycle that gunned it toward the town as if pursued, and a tiny electric car powered by a rooftop solar panel. It was vintage pre-2020, Wade thought, and a smart choice for the desert sun. As long as it could stay a safe distance from the crazies with their welded, armored Jeeps and weapon-equipped technicals.

Wade waved the car down; to his surprise, it stopped. A man in sunglasses, shirtless with a leather necklace on, rolled down the passenger window. He had shaggy hair and a friendly smile.

"Hi there. Need some water?"

Wade glanced back at the others.

"That, and a ride into town."

The man handed them a half-filled gallon plastic jug, which they accepted gratefully.

"You're very kind," Wade said.

"I heard things are tough around here...the dam. And you have a family."

"Yeah, we made it up the river. Say, do you know what the town over there is. Is it Page?"

"Used to be, but as you can imagine, it's nothing more than a desert outpost now, with a bunch of people squatting there. Trying to make do. People trade and sell; the gangs will raid it once in a while, but they're putting together their own defense force, I hear. I heard a rumor the regime will take it over, as a preliminary to seizing the dam. Rumors are everywhere. Gee, I wish I had more space in the vehicle."

"Maybe you can take me," Jonesy piped up.

"That's actually a good idea," Wade said after thinking about it for a moment. "You go into town and get us a bigger vehicle, then come pick us up."

"It's a deal," Jonesy said. "That alright?"

"Sure," said the driver.

Jonesy got his things together, opened the passenger door, shoved a duffel bag in, and got in beside it. "You can count on me. I won't be long–just hang in there."

"We will...we'll just be making our way towards town."

Wade took a slug of the gallon jug, then he handed it to Carmen, who drank and offered it to the others. Then he stuck his head into the passenger window and held out his hand. The driver shook it and they introduced each other. The driver's name was Sebastian and he'd been traveling alone from Phoenix, where he'd abandoned a ranch house and a small computer business. The city had mostly emptied out, he said, with the remainder of Phoenix going the way of Vegas–a lawless urban wasteland.

"What would I find south of here?" Wade said. This was the vast territory he still had to cover to reach Sierra Vista, past Flagstaff of the old Arizona, then Phoenix, east of Nevada and southern California.

"That's Navajo country–none but the most experienced

desert dwellers know how to survive it now. Long empty roads; desert and grasslands and buttes. There are some tall mountains down there; the San Francisco Peaks. Haven't lost all their snow but almost. Their flanks and forests are near burnt.

"The fires are bad, but in the desert they run out of fuel. I was lucky to make it; I just kept my foot on the pedal and only stopped to heed the call to Mother Nature. I can run the car on solar. Once I left Phoenix, it was eerie–I only saw a few people; lots of abandoned pickup trucks and rigs. I saw some human remains, sadly–people who died in the desert. It's all just a question of water. And sometimes, running into the wrong people. You gotta be prepared. I'm just going to keep heading north; hope to make Canada."

Then he regarded the whole crew standing by the side of the road, with a mixture of pity and disbelief.

"What are you going to use for transportation south? You can't hitchhike. You can't walk it. That's out of the question. Not too many cars or trucks around here for the having. Or fuel...as I said, I wish I had more room. But then again, you said you were going south."

"I have to–my daughter's down there."

Sebastian shook his head sympathetically. "There are alternatives–I'm going to write an address down for you." He had a notebook next to the front seat, and he ripped a page out of it then wrote something down and handed it back to Wade, who stepped back from the car.

"You guys better get going."

"Yeah, well, we'll try to send back a bigger vehicle," Jonesy said. Sebastian put his little car into gear, pulled back into the empty road, and left the Santiagos, Wade, and the dog standing by the side. Pequeno barked after the car, then went back to strenuous panting. Wade looked both ways and saw no refuges where they'd find shade, just spacious expanses of desert, abandoned barbed-wire fencing, sandy land mixed with yellowed grasses, and the ever-present cactus. Buttes appeared in the distance, like islands floating in the sky.

Above the land was a baking, seamless blue, with thin clouds like a white slash from a paint brush.

Wade was aware that their journey was ad hoc, badly thought out. Kara, he thought. Kara's the reason he's plowing forward and meeting each obstacle as it comes.

They walked for a little bit until they reached a rusted "Gas Food Lodging" sign. It smacked rhythmically off its metal sign post in the wind, like a bell tolling. Then they stopped and made a meagre encampment. Pepe had just reached a point where he had to be carried.

He wondered what kind of lodging they had in the town; probably nothing more than squatter's camps. He put his pack down and sat on it. He looked at the piece of paper Sebastian had given him. "Tucker's Desert Travel, Means & Supplies. Just off Main Street in the Page Historic Township." Historic, huh, he thought. The whole country was history. Its democratic and constitutional republic. Freedom, safety, and family were virtually consigned to history's dustbin. The only things you were free to do now were pillage, assault, and burn. Then he cut off the negative thought flow, for fear it would engulf him and his mission.

They'd try out this Desert Travel place. They had no choice or alternatives; this wasn't a country for walking. He had some gold coins left–nothing much else to barter.

Just when he was convinced that the weakest among them would expire under the sun, a large vehicle approached from a distance. Yellow, it grew larger through the filmy heat shimmer. It was was an old restored school bus, and it was slowing down for them.

CHAPTER 32

Wade could hear the engine knocking; it coughed black diesel dust into the air. The bus rolled slowly past them, then made a U-turn and pulled to their side of the road. Wade stood up. *Thank you Jonesy,* he thought. *...And Sebastian.* A woman was at the wheel, gray-haired, a wrinkled smile, and a sturdy arm leaning on the lowered driver's window.

"Whatcha doin' there by the side of the road, havin' a picnic? I'm just pulling your leg. Go on, hop in." She cranked open the levered door, just like a school bus driver.

"Next stop is town. You folks look like you could use a rest, and a meal."

"And showers..."

"That too. My name's Edna Grant. What's his name? The fella back in town? Jonesy? I swear I've seen him before. Never forget a face. Wonder if he did any roughnecking in North Dakota?"

"I don't know. Is that what you did? Roughnecking?"

"Are you crazy? I did bartending, and a little mistressing for an escort trade we had going, when times were good. Don't things change, eh? Jonesy…Maybe it was Oregon, fighting fires. I know I've seen him somewhere. I was part of the last stand out there in the northwest. We lost that one, but then again, you probably knew that. The fires are winning. Sometimes I think I've seen everything…Yeah, I'm old, but I'm wise. Faces just have a way of sticking in my mind. Don't think I've seen yours."

"I'm Michael Wade."

Javi stepped forward as Carmen climbed onto the bus with Pepe in her arms. "I'm Javi Santiago. We are grateful for this ride. We've come a long way. I don't know what we would have done. Bless you."

"Oh, no worries my friend."

Pequeno leapt up the steps behind them and then immediately into an empty seat, as though he'd been down this path before.

The exhaustion hit Wade hard when he slipped into a seat in the front of the bus. It's as if he'd been holding it off for a better time. Edna mentioned that there was an encampment, reasonably safe, outside of town near an old Red Cross tent. Javi and Wade said that they could stay there for now, then Wade tipped over on his seat and conked out on the window, using his hat crushed up as a pillow.

He woke up to squealing brakes. He had a stiff neck, and his knees and hip ached from the awkward position his legs were jammed into. He wondered how long his body was going to hold out, with endless miles still left. He ran his hand over the back of his neck, and he thought about how Lee would sense his tension in the old days. She'd offer a neck and back rub just at the time when he needed it most. Of course, *that* was minor-league tension, compared with what he'd gone through in the lawless lands west of the Mississippi.

He looked out the window. The scene resembled a daguerrotype from the early 1900s. The bus made its way through a busy intersection of horse- and oxen-drawn carts, walkers, and people riding rickety two-wheeled bikes.

Many of the homes, laid out in suburban tracks in the old cookie-cutter fashion, were burnt down. But efforts had cropped up to rebuild with wood and roofing scrap, even cardboard–new crude dwellings thrown together seemingly with hammer, nails, and duct tape. It was a shanty town.

The road was lined with objects for sale or barter; appliances, TVs, tires, ovens; sofas, bed frames and mattresses, stacks of books, magazines, vinyl records, computers; all the stuff you'd see from a home dredged of its belongings after a flood. It wasn't all useless in the fuel-deprived land: there were a few stands with what looked like bread and cloth bags of rice or flour. Native American pottery and tools, presumably from the local Navajo community.

He didn't see a single place that sold or distributed water; the most precious commodity in the region. Not a brook or a lake existed anymore, except beneath the San Francisco Peaks far to the south. Everything had evaporated, and it only rained hard once every month or so.

He watched the enervated people move slowly through the junk under a blazing sun. He got up and moved to the seat just behind Edna.

"How far are we to the camp?"

"Oh, just another 10 minutes."

"Where do you get fuel for this bus?" She glanced back at him for a moment as if deciding whether he could be trusted.

"Can you keep a secret?"

"Yes."

"There's leftover fuel tanks by the dam. We have jerry cans, and we sneak in there at night and replenish our stores. Not sure the Redboyz even know it's there; that's why it's so important not to say anything. Keep that under your hat–I'm serious. Those mongrels would be down on us in a jiffy, in numbers, if they knew we had a lot of gas."

"Mum's the word. Is it diesel you're getting?"

"Yeah. And propane."

"You have propane too?"

"Sure. We found a stack of still usable propane tanks. The hospital has an old Kohler generator. We've been able to run machines off it, like stoves, heaters, computers, and some medical equipment."

"You don't say…" He looked behind him and he saw Pepe collapsed in Carmen's lap, where she stroked his forehead. Javi was asleep beneath the brim of his hat. Good, they need the rest before we get going again. That is, if they *want* to go; these people here in the old Page seemed to have restarted something.

He rifled around in his backpack and found his old cellphone and adapter. Its battery had been dead for weeks– when he'd seen that last message from Kara. But now maybe he had a chance to charge it up. But there wouldn't be any cell phone service in this frontier settlement.

"You said you had computers running; do you have any Internet?"

"No," she scoffed.

"What about cell phone service?"

"People have been picking up G.P.S. signals lately. The little location thingies blinking on their phone screens. Some of the guys and gals with an engineering background think the regime is trying to put the system back together again. Or it's the invaders."

"Invaders?"

"News from the West Coast is that the Chinese, North Koreans, or both have landed. They've started taking over installations. Abandoned by the regime. They need the electronics running for their own armies."

Wade had heard the rumors before–but never from the regime's propaganda. They couldn't admit that they were losing the country, but power loves a vacuum, and it was just a matter of time for other countries to get involved. They wanted the USA's vast resources, the oil, minerals, and crop land. And the burgeoning American population for cheap, war-slave labor. They weren't going to find much but charcoal and roving bands of crazies and fleeing civilians, though.

He would try the cell phone anyways, just for the infinitesimal chance there was another message from Kara. The phone he held was a relic, given the new conditions in the stricken land. It reminded him of the pointless things that he used to do with it, like play with apps. It seemed pathetic now, an effete behavior trait from a brief, lost past.

Within minutes they pulled down a bumpy red-dirt road and ended up at a kind of baked plateau, covered with not only the white hospital tent, but hundreds, maybe greater than a thousand, other tents and encampments. It looked like an overflowing refugee camp from news footage of the Middle East and Africa; now the USA was undergoing the same kind of pain.

At least it was a place where they could sleep that night.

Carmen wanted a nurse inside the hospital tent to look at Pepe. He felt feverish, and was sluggish and reluctant to wake up. Once Edna parked the bus, they took him inside the Red Cross tent.

They piled their belongings outside the bus. Then Wade followed Carmen, Javi, Pepe, and Edna inside.

"Do you have any shelter, a tent?" Edna asked him.

"No. As far as I know, we're only going to stay the night." He wanted to contact that desert-provisions outfit asap, to stay on the move in a southern direction.

"You can stay in the bus tonight."

"Much obliged."

They found the Santiagos checking in with a woman at a fold-out desk. The hospital was packed, stifling, and busy with overworked staff. He could hear the generator motor running outside. Good thing, as it powered several electric fans whirring along the sides of the enclosure. Still, the humid, fetid air hardly moved. It seemed all the beds were taken, with many of the patients clinging to life. The space carried a stink of infection and death.

The shock must have manifested in his expression, because one of the ladies at the table looked up and said, "Yeah, this is quite the crazy busy place these days. Triage only. We can only take patients with serious conditions."

"What happened, here in town?" It looked like the front lines of a war.

"We've had a cholera outbreak lately, from drinking stagnant water; bad injuries from the last gang attack. Killer bee stings, snake bites, scorpion stings, Lyme disease; you name it. People come out of the desert in bad shape, if they come out at all, and they end up here."

"How's the medicine supply?" Then he thought of his own antibiotics bottle, from the Bible.

"Running out." She looked at Carmen and smiled wearily.

"My son, he has a fever and…"

"That's okay. A doctor will have a look at him—just have a seat over there and we'll find you."

Wade found himself standing uselessly in the middle of the hospital floor. He felt like a wreck with a bad neck and back ache.

"Is it possible to have a shower? We've come a long way," he said, running his hands over his heavy stubble, then greasy hair, which he felt had thinned in front.

"There's an outdoor shower behind a partition. Most of the time it has water."

"Thanks." He felt a little guilty for asking for a shower. He wrestled out of his backpack, then dipped into it for the Bible. He took the little antibiotics pill bottle, walked over, and handed it to Carmen, who was still waiting for a nurse. Then he came back to the table.

"Is there anything I can do? Need a hand with anything?"

She thought for a moment. More sickly, sweating people had wandered in and stood in line.

"Yes. Put some gloves on and take those trash bags outside and throw them in the dumpster. They're medical waste. Thank you." She handed him a pair of rubber gloves.

When he went outside it must have been 110 F. The sun lay in the empty sky like a molten pearl.

CHAPTER 33

He disrobed behind a wooden partition. The shower stall was open to the air on top. It felt good just to take the grimy, smelly clothes and shoes off, then pile them outside in the sun. He did have a change of clothes, one of a total of three in the backpack. If you could call another pair of grimy pants, "a change."

A small cracked mirror hung at head level, next to a rusty shower nozzle. He didn't recognize himself: the matted, reddish brown beard that crawled up to his cheekbones, the bloodshot eyes. Lee would have been aghast at his appearance, the bruised and withered aspect. He wondered how anyone could warm to him, as they otherwise had out on the road.

He pulled a cord to release the water. He had to hand it to this community, just to have the means to construct a shower at all. A cardboard sign said, "One minute max." Wonderfully, he found a bar of soap. He pulled the cord and splashed water on himself. He rubbed the wet bar over his torso and legs. He used it to lather up his beard, which he attacked in front of the mirror with an old disposable razor.

He wanted to feel civilized again; he watched some of the squalor and terror of the last several weeks flow into the drain with the filthy, soapy water. He chopped and scraped at the beard pitiably, but the soap and lukewarm water had the intended effect. The sun alone was all that was needed to make the water warm.

He let it run on the back of his sore neck for a minute. Then he toweled off, dressed, and walked back to the bus to secure their things onboard.

He ran into Jonesy out front.

"Well lookee here. I didn't recognize you. Is that really Wade? Don't you look smart."

"Not exactly ready for church or the office, but I feel better. Could use some more sleep." They shook hands. "Thanks for sending that bus after us. We were road kill without it. I think Pepe's sick now."

"Oh no, I hope he's okay. The poor lad has covered a lot of distance."

Javi had tied Pequeno to a stake in the ground at the hospital entrance. Wade knelt down and pet him. He did his best to bat away a swarm of pestering flies. The dog tugged on his leash and panted, then sat down, licked his chops, and looked up gratefully. Someone had even set down a plastic dish of the much coveted water. It was a place where they did their best to look after people, and animals.

Jonesy told him he had already bartered for a one-man tent; he was going to stay.

"I'm not making the same mistake twice," he said, referring to Phoebe's habitat. "This place ain't half bad. They're making a go of it. I've already got a spot over yonder, and they say the town itself will be rebuilt and they'll be looking for roomers. There's plenty to do around here."

Wade nodded. He figured he'd be going the rest of the way into the desert alone. He'd check in on Pepe and the Santiagos, eat as much food as he could, buy some provisions, then head out the next day. He had an Arizona map, and he figured he could get some advice from this local travel outfit. They must have horses and mules.

People of all stripes and ages were now lined up outside of the tent. Everyone was battling the appalling clouds of black flies that plagued the area. The bees are gone, except for the killers, and the flies thrive, he thought.

He went inside to the hospital and scanned the crowded beds for Pepe. On the table in front was a stack of Polaroids, similar to the one that the oaf he'd commandeered back at the dam was carrying. He picked them up and leafed through them while standing up, the grim female faces and the serial numbers along the bottom.

Then he stopped at one of them. He stared fixedly. The photo was of Kara Wade.

CHAPTER 34

His vision went gray and fuzzy, as though the swarm of desert flies had coated his mind. Then he felt weak on his feet, a dizziness that was quickly replaced by powerful, overwhelming rage. It was the face of his daughter, which he had never before seen unsmiling in a photograph. Serial number viola 9475.

She had a bruise on her left cheek, long hair in disarray, but the look of a fighter, staring at the camera. He sat down on a folded chair, put his elbows on his knees, and kept looking at it.

The woman at the desk had been watching him.

"That's my daughter," he told her. "Where did these pictures come from?"

"One of the people who came in sick had them. Oh my god."

"Which one?"

"They wouldn't be able to talk. They're bedridden. We

kept the pictures around, for the relatives. I'm so sorry this happened."

"Which one is them? I *have* to know."

"Edna might know. She brought in the guy who had the photos. Off the road."

He went outside and found Edna by the old yellow bus. He needed a direction to go toward, and fast. Sierra Vista might not be it.

"Edna, those photos, of women, in the tent. Who gave them to you?"

"Some rodent I pealed off the road about two weeks ago. His low-life friends shot him in the legs and left him, or so he claims. Why do you have to know? I probably should have left him for the buzzards. I think he was a Redboyz."

"My daughter's picture was in there."
Edna looked at him for about 20 seconds, a little stricken herself, but didn't say anything. Then she started walking toward the tent. "Let's find this vermin…"

It took them about half an hour of stepping from bed to bed in the packed ward, searching pained and weary faces, until finally they came to a black-haired and bearded man lying on his side. He was reading an old magazine. He put it down when they walked up. Edna said, "He's the one. Don't know his name. He's just road trash, but that's who had the pictures."

Wade held out the picture of his daughter, so the man could see it.

"Where is she?"

"Who are you?"

"None of your fucking business. I asked you a simple question. Where can I find her?"

He bent forward and looked at the picture brusquely. "I don't know this chick…"

Wade reached over and grabbed him by the throat, shoving his head farther into the pillow. Edna stood behind Wade and blocked the view.

"Where is she being kept? I won't ask you again."

The man gagged and coughed and tried to roll out of the grip, but Wade held him down by his throat, until the man weakly held up his hand. Wade released his grip.

"Fuckin' hell I told ya," he sputtered. "I don't recognize the face. They took about a hundred women. Maybe 500. I wasn't the guy; I was just an innocent bystander. I just happened to be there. It wasn't my doing."

"You mean guilty cockroach, not bystander. You're one of the Redboyz, right? They're the ones that have her?"

"I was with the Reds; livin' with 'em." He clung to his throat and massaged it. "They gave us all the pictures. We were supposed to help find buyers, go out into the desert and flash the pictures around. Girls for sale, you know. Some things haven't changed. It's still the desert, and it's still Vegas.

"Then I tried to run away, and they shot me. Swear to God, that's the truth! You can ask her!" He pointed to Edna. "She found me!"

"And a lucky one you were!" Edna said. "Maybe I shouldn't have wasted the fuel bringing you back here!" But if she didn't, I wouldn't know, the thought leapt to Wade's mind. This insect in front of them actually has a purpose; to help him find his daughter.

He took a bottle of water and handed it to the guy. "Here, maybe this'll clear your head." The man took a slug off it and handed it back.

"They've got to be keeping these women somewhere. Some central location. Down by the dam?"

"They're long gone by now. I mean, they get shipped around. Across the desert. They take 'em across old

Lake Mead; they sell 'em on the shore. I only seen it once–it's sad. Women held out like slaves, brought up to a kind of stage." Wade felt himself grimacing, as if he'd eaten something rotten against his will.

"Sorry, I figure you must know this lady," the man continued meekly. "They…she…might be in Vegas. That's where some of them end up. The others go south…west. Who knows?" He took another sip of the water and put it down.

"Where south?"

"Down where Phoenix and Tucson used to be. They get buyers comin' from down there; resellers you might call them. Buy the girls and sell 'em to someone else. That's sick isn't it? They're human beings." Then he'd realized he wasn't getting far with Wade, trying to appear thoughtful and humane.

"It could be anywhere, really. Sorry I can't give you more information. My leg's killing me…I think I'm getting gangrene…" He let his head drop back on the pillow and stared vacantly. Wade looked down towards the man's legs; he noticed the greenish, dark red stains on the bandages.

The man looked back at him, almost trying to seem innocent, but merely being stupid. "It's like you bought a car and took off, who could tell where you go…" he trailed off.

Wade wasn't going to get anything else from this guy, who didn't seem long for the world. He felt around for his cell phone and pulled it out of the backpack, with its white adaptor cord stuck into it. He looked for where the fans were plugged into the wall, with the coarse sound of the generator running outside.

Then he found one of those multi-outlet surge protectors that he thought didn't exist anymore. He plugged the adaptor into it. The phone beeped in recognition and displayed an "empty battery" symbol. This would take a minute. Wade curled up on the floor, put his head on his backpack, and fell asleep amidst the clamor.

CHAPTER 35

He went outside the tent and was met by a cloud of flies. He swatted at them angrily, then took in the burgeoning refugee camp. Almost as far as the eye could see, sluggish adults, oppressed by the sun, made camp and stood in glum lines in worn clothing. Nearby were their brave children. They kept on playing as if the world they'd been born into hadn't recently come to an end.

His phone was charged and he'd just switched it on. He had a hunch, or was it vain hopefulness? Maybe it would tell him something. He was headed for Tucker's Desert Travel; Edna would show him. Someone had made coffee in an ancient stainless steel dispenser and put it outside the tent on a table, mostly for the exhausted doctors and nurses. He took a Styrofoam cup, already with a coffee stain on it, filled it up, and drank the lukewarm liquid while he walked. The sleep, caffeine, and hope perked him up.

Amazingly, the phone came to life and instantly displayed new messages. How could that be? he wondered. Probably the regime; someone, somewhere, had kept the network's servers and cell towers (or one tower) up and running. He brought up the messaging app, feeling his heart soar. There were half a dozen messages from Kara; he read them from new to older, with the newest being 10 days old:

"Coordinates: 33.548983, -111.940426"

"Check the coordinates. lov u K"

"I'm in Phoenix I think. I'm OK dont reply"

"Please come get me oh please!!"

"dad just tell me where u r luv K"

"Im still in sierra vista maybe we can meet? luv K"

He slugged the rest of his coffee and washed down the lump in his throat. He felt his eyes burning, and he rubbed the grief and guilt out with his fist. Coordinates–he'd programmed a simple app and given it to his children for their phones. It allowed you to message your current location to certain recipients. She'd used it to send the coordinates–smart girl!

It followed that, if there was messaging then there might be a maps application available. Yet, when he opened up the ones he'd installed on his phone, none were functioning.

He followed Edna to Tucker's Desert Travel, which was outside an old wooden fence that surrounded what was probably a fairgrounds, now the giant squatter's camp. Then they walked about 300 meters down an isolated dirt road outside of town.

The Tucker's place was like a small ranch, single-level homes and corrals and barns. Thick brown dust hung in the air, like a stampede had just thundered through. It smelled gamey and ripe, like manure.

They walked up to one of the buildings and when they neared the entrance, the door opened and a man with a bush hat and long white beard came out. He had a quick and gap-toothed smile.

"Hey there Edna! What brings you out to the barrens?"

"I got an interested traveler here."

"Oh yeah? Where're ye headed?"

"Well, south, toward the old Phoenix, I think."

"You think?" Then he had a big belly laugh. "I'm sure you're well-intentioned young fella, but around these parts, you better know exactly where ya goin', or you won't likely get there alive."

"Knowing exactly where you're going seems to be a luxury these days," Wade muttered. "My daughter's been kidnapped."

He pulled the picture out of his pocket and showed it to the man.

"Good God Almighty those animals!" The man spat in disgust onto the parched ground. "If it isn't one thing it's another. Now they're trying to sell women. Well, it ain't going to work, they'll find that out fast enough. And I'll blow their faces off if they come near here, those red-headed devils. I got several loaded shotguns back there. Don't worry–you'll find your daughter. Sure enough."

"I have her coordinates–latitude and longitude. Do you have a map? A detailed one?"

"That I do."

"By the why, I'm going to hire your services. Do you have pack animals? I can pay you, well enough."

"I'll take what you have and leave you with enough," the man replied, somewhat vaguely.

"Mules?"

"Camels. The best in the region. As many as you need."

CHAPTER 36

"Camels?"

"You heard me right fella. It's the best way–I'd say the only way–to get across that desert. If you're fixin' to look for your daughter. I'll tell yah everything you need to know. You get used to riding them after day one. Believe me, it's like the Australian outback out there; there's no water. The towns are dryin' up as fast as the wells are. Only the Navajos and the Comanches know how to live in it. You'll be goin' through their country first. Why don't we look at the map."

"Yes, let's do that," Wade mumbled, still wondering whether this old coot was pulling his leg, or had simply lost his mind. Camels?

The man's name was Terry and ran the outfit with his brother Bud, who was out back with the animals. Wade walked into the cluttered office, which was buzzing with flies around the screened windows, one of which was broken.

Gratefully, he saw one wall covered with a map that had been pinned to it.

"Okay..." Terry said. "You said you had coordinates."

The map was annotated with latitude and longitude, not quite to the scale that Wade had from his message, but precise enough to pinpoint Kara in the area of old Scottsdale, Arizona. Terry pulled on his beard thoughtfully. "So you're going at least 350 miles into the desert, and that's if you don't get turned around, navigation-wise."

"I have a compass," Wade said. "I know how to use it."

"Right," Terry said, with a skeptical air. "I've heard that one before." Then he looked at Wade and sat down. "You look like the competent type, like you can handle yourself. And you're going to find your daughter...I know it."

He propped his legs and cowboy boots up on the table and picked up a pad of paper, a pen. "So I have to make some calculations here."

"All I have is gold."

Terry arched his eyebrows. "That'll do," he said, then clicked his tongue. "How many people are going?"

"So far, only me."

"So far...well if you find some partners, we can always make some adjustments later. You're going to need one animal to transport yourself; one to pack your belongings and water and food, and another for companionship and backup."

"Companionship? I think I can get away with one."

"You definitely won't make it with one, without a lot of luck. You're going to have to carry a lot of water, at least two and a half weeks worth, maybe three. Also, if a camel dies on you or wanders off..."

"Wanders off?"

"It's been known to happen. You don't tie them down at night, like horses. It's an animal that prefers freedom but sticks with its fellow beasts, and its owners. They're a pack animal, and a feisty lot. Best to keep three together and keep them happy; because if you lose one, it could get bit by a snake or shot, you're guaranteed to have two, to handle your water and yourself. All the way to the Land of the Desert Sun."

"By the way, are these the kind with two humps or one?" He laughed at himself inside. He could hear, and smell them, through the open window–stamping, snorting, and grunting. They made phlegmy, unpleasant noises deep in their throats. He walked over to the window and looked out.

"These are Arabian camels, one hump," Terry said. "Best in the business."

"How fast can they go?"

"About three miles an hour. You'll be able to go up to 25 miles a day, but don't try to push it beyond that. That makes…14 days, if you don't get sidetracked."

"Where did you get camels around here? A zoo?"

"Roped 'em wild, like you would a mustang pony."

"Wild, are you kidding me?"

"Desert's full of 'em, runnin' wild as I said. In fact, that's the other thing I…"

"The Arizona desert is full of Arabian camels?"

"One of the few things that can survive and thrive out there, with the fires, drought and all. And the fact that millions of humans have pulled out of the region, migrated, or got sick and died. You'd be surprised at the kinds of animals that have thrived over the centuries in the North American West, dromedaries and wooly mammoths…"

"In fact, the dromedary started in North America then crossed the Alaskan straits, and made their way into the Middle East. Then they divided up into the two-humped Bactrian camel and…"

"Thanks for the history. But how did they get down in these parts recently?"

"Rumor has it they came from multiple sources, one being a Texas rancher who had a herd, and some Saudi sheik who lost his herd in the fires in Tucson. At any rate, you're going to have female camels; less volatile. If you run into a wild male camel, in rut, just shoot it. No questions asked. They can get downright ornery and will attack the females."

"I'll remember that. By the way, do you have any handgun ammo?"

"No, only shotgun shells for my own use. Ammo's hard to come by around here."

"OK." He saw one of the camels looking at him. They were tall, with brown and even white-and-black spotted, mangy coats. They had big, innocent, bulbous eyes, with two layers of eyelashes, giving them almost a doe-like look. A man forked a pile of grass and weeds for them to feed upon. There had to be at least three dozen milling around the high, well-fortified paddocks.

"That's Bud out there. So we have three pack animals for you. This is essentially a purchase, you must understand."

"How's that?"

"If you come back this way, I'll buy 'em back from you. That's a promise; it's a good deal. Otherwise, it's a one-way deal. I've got no one here who can march down 350 miles and fetch 'em back. See, it wouldn't be worth it, by a long shot. This isn't like dropping off a used car."

"Got it. I'll need provisions; do you have canned food? For me? What do the camel's eat?"

"They graze…they'll eat the scrub, weeds, even bones that they find. They can go a week without water. That doesn't mean if you encounter an oasis, you shouldn't water them."

"And the hump stores the water right?" Wade mumbled,

staring out into the dried up ranch, blazing in the intense heat. Terry chuckled, taking delight in his own specific knowledge.

"No, the hump stores fat. They can live off that fat for days on end if they're not getting any food. If the body draws off it too much, then the hump actually flops over. I've seen it, a comical sight…eating restores the hump's former firm position…you'll be riding on that, you know."

"I gathered that. I hope the saddle's comfortable."

"I'll put all this together for you—camels, saddle, reins, other gear…food, water for one person for two weeks plus—in an invoice. It's pretty scientific, actually. You'll need to drink at least three liters per day. We'll train you for a day with the camels, tomorrow. It's free…"

Wade went back outside into the concentrated heat. He vaguely remembered old trips to the southwest, being in A/C-equipped hotels that were actually cold, then going outside to Arizona suburbs and meeting air that felt like a blast furnace. Now no one had A/C.

He wandered back down the road alone. At least the sun was going down soon. His stomach growled. Edna had said they were cooking pots of cheap food outside the hospital tent for dinner, and there might be some meat. He needed some; he wanted to build up his strength for the long haul. He noticed in the shower that he was getting awful scrawny, losing not only fat but muscle. Eat fat, he told himself, and protein, as much as he could. He squinted into the desert horizon, glowing with the fires that had consumed a nation, then he wandered into the bus and fell fast asleep.

CHAPTER 37

He started out at dawn. The Tucker's had packed two camels and saddled up another. The animals sat with their legs curled up under them and waited for him in the grainy light. He hadn't been able to sleep that much, and was grateful he'd passed out in the bus the few afternoons before.

This was the only moment he'd seen the sprawling settlement almost peaceful. A cool wind gathered strength over the flat pan of sand and stone; the horizon to the east burned magenta. That was New Mexico, the old territory, he thought distantly. He only heard tent flaps and clothes hung out to dry, whipped around by the breeze.

He swung his legs across the saddle and the beast grunted and stood up on its hind legs first, almost pitching Wade forward off the saddle. He leaned back, hanging onto the saddle horn, and the camel stood up straight on its forelegs, until he was seven feet off the ground, perched on the hump.

It smelled like a moldy, wet blanket and its five-foot tail lazily swatted at flies. The camel put its nose to the wind and began to walk, Wade's hand insecurely tight on the reins, his boony hat strapped on the chin. He swayed back and forth; another tether dangled behind and connected to the two other camels. They followed along passively.

He gave it a whack on its flanks with the stick Tucker had given him, and the beast bellowed and bawled. "You have to show 'em who's boss..." Terry had said the day before.

He'd taken some bearings; they were headed due south toward Flagstaff. It was a dirt road at first, with sand and gravel blown over it. "Never seen Flagstaff, not for myself..." he said out loud, aware of his loneliness. They were headed in the right direction now, the camels made steady progress, and it gave a boost to his spirits.

The sun cleared the mountains on the horizon; soon, it would seem like there were three suns. The southern horizon was smudged by smog, as though they were headed to Basra or Jeddah. "The fires," he mumbled to himself. "It's the fires that does that..." Flagstaff and its suburbs must be ashen.

He had an image, as they loped along, of the complexed wildfire like a tsunami, rolling with a terrifying fury across the west, to the midwest. He wondered if the winter would stop them. He wondered if North America would have a winter.

At one point, he swiveled around on the saddle and looked back north. The low rooftops and defunct power lines of what used to be Page, Arizona had disappeared. He listened to the crunch of the camels' two-toed feet on the gravel. It made a pet-pet-pet sound. The beast picked up its pace if he gave it a nudge with the inside of his boots. "It's better to be alone..." he declared, because he'd been thinking it. He felt the loneliness in his gut as they moved farther into the empty desert; but he'd go faster this way.

He'd bid farewell the night before to the Santiagos, who had to stay with Pepe. The meds Wade had offered had helped beat the fever, but the child was still weak.

Terry was right; the saddle was hard on his ass. But the swaying movement and southerly direction had a calming effect; he knew the tortured flow of his journey still pointed toward Kara. Who was now for sale by human traffickers.

He'd be there in as soon as 12 days. Then someone would pay.

The Santiagos clung to their dreams of returning to Nicaragua. He thought of floating down the Colorado, on essentially a wedge of sticks, with Pepe. He hoped the young boy would eventually find harmony, a safe calm rhythm, like the flow of a river in the wilderness. Javi insisted Wade would meet them again on the road south.

When Carmen hugged him and kissed him on both cheeks, his eyes had moistened. Riding along and watching the desert scenery, he vaguely thought of Phoebe. He had 340...perhaps 335...miles to go.

He reached into a pocket, took out a lozenge, and chewed it. Terry had sold him some caffeine pills, which came in handy. He'd be traveling by night as well. The pills made him feel a little jacked up. He had his crossbow strapped to the back of his saddle, and a handgun in the side pocket of his pants.

Halfway through the morning he stopped to drink and take another bearing with his compass. His legs were cramped and back stiff; he stretched, drank from a gallon bottle of water that was strapped to one of the other camels. The sun was punishing. The camel he'd dismounted rested on its knees; the two others towered over him. He was still a little wary of the beasts. As he watched, they lowered their heads and nosed around the scrub, then began to chew at it and graze.

He was impressed at the ease with which they took to such harshness. They ignored him; it seemed they mostly looked straight ahead, or up into the sky.

They were making good mileage, but Terry had warned him about pushing the camels too hard each day.

The trail they followed petered out into plain desert landscape, strewn with coarse sand and red boulders and clusters of cactus, some with yellow blooms. No crumbled communities were visible, or vehicles. In the near distance, he saw swathes of yellowed, dry grasses. The map had indicated that he was generally following a highway south; he couldn't make it out, but it was about two miles to the east of them.

He thought they'd stop beside some boulders, for the early evening. He didn't want to go too far off-trail, but he took the beasts through some of the grasses. They lowered their heads, and quietly fed, looking up once in a while and chewing. He thought he was getting the hang of this ride, by shifting his position to aid his sore hips, about as much as he ever would.

Everything had changed. In travel mode not too long ago, he'd be driving a rental down that highway, with a gallon of Poland Spring in the backseat, maybe a Subway sandwich of cold-cuts on the seat beside him. He'd make the drive to Phoenix in one day, stopping over at something like a Holiday Inn Suites. A Super 8. He shook his head and laughed, watching the ground amble by, hearing the steady, crunchy footfalls. Things change in an instance; you never see it coming.

He reached a point where he saw a falling-down billboard, hulks of cars, some of them blackened and stripped. The flat landscape had a sameness in all four directions, like the bottom of a coral sea, but without the varicolored nature. The few clouds were motionless, frayed, and white.

"I'm going to call you Moe, Curly, and Larry," he called out, as the camels meandered along. He began to think of what he'd do when he got to the Scottsdale region. Would he know he was there in the first place? He kept the most minimal juice in the cell phone–maybe an hour of activity left. He'd answered Kara's texts; told her to "sit tight" and that "Daddy's coming."

Just when he'd almost fallen asleep in the saddle, his camel raised its head and bawled, a detestable sound. Instinctively, he reached for and displayed his handgun. The camels stopped. He trained his eyes on the ground, and there was a large, thick-bodied, coiled snake in front of them. It was hard to distinguish–yellow and black scales that blended into the surroundings. It was stock still; until, without thinking, he shot at it two, three times, killing it. He saw a second snake, which had been sunning nearby, slither away speedily.

He dismounted; the camel crouched down and settled on its stomach. He got out his Swiss Army knife, carefully approached the body, put his boot on it, and sawed the snake's head off. He took down his backpack from "Curly" behind the first camel, removed a plastic bag that contained some food, and stored the limp snake body in the bag, skin and everything. He took the opportunity to snack on some crackers and old government-issued cheese. He'd cook the snake-meat that night; he'd have to make a fire anyways. At least he hadn't encountered any rain or cold yet. He wondered how the camels took to bad weather.

This wasn't a good place to stop yet, he thought; too snake-ridden. He scanned the horizons. On one side, to the northeast, were beautiful red spires, maybe 25 miles away. That was the edge of Monument Valley, he thought. He'd always wanted to see that place, during peaceable times.

He liked not having to look after the camels much. The

Tuckers were correct about them being a better mode of desert travel–despite their terrible dispositions. They had the ability to convert the fat in their humps to water, Terry had told him, not just calories. Their bodies recycled water, rather than flushing it through the kidneys and pissing it out. Wade couldn't imagine finding any standing water until maybe outside of Flagstaff, which actually had a snowy mountain range.

He awkwardly mounted Moe again, giving the flank a whack with the stick. It hissed and bellowed; he feared the teeth if Moe turned around to take a bite at him. Abruptly the camel stood up, hind-legs to fore. Wade leaned back and gripped the saddle horn for dear life, with one hand holding his hat on. He aimed for what looked like low mountains, with the late afternoon sun dipping toward the Grand Canyon and the Colorado River.

CHAPTER 38

The nights were surprisingly cold. They approached the mountains of northern Arizona over ground that was hummocky with thorny vegetation, a surface of coarse sand. He slept maybe three hours at most in a row. He had no problem traveling by night; the pristine clarity of the webs of stars were like companions to him.

The camels rested huddled together at night; a strategy they used in the sun as well.

He avoided lying on bare ground, due to the scorpions and especially the fire ants. Tucker told him a gruesome story about a man who'd fallen off a camel and broken his leg; what the desert fire ants did to him afterward, when he couldn't get up. So he put his bed roll down on flat slabs of rock when he found them, and did the best he could.

The first night he made a fire and placed the whole snake in it, skin and all. He ate the roasted meat with his hands, and crunched the small bones ravenously, grateful for both the fire and the food. He couldn't get over the fact that the temperature typically dropped about 80 degrees F. at night, from almost 120 F. or 49 C., to as low as 40 F. or 4 C.

The snake meat was a nice break from beans, crackers, cheese; there wasn't much processed food left in the river or desert communities, due to most of the factories being closed and regional food transport having ground to a halt.

He heard a chorus of coyotes the second night. After they cried and bayed through his sector, inspiring loud grunts from the camels, he didn't sleep a wink.

He was traveling fewer and fewer hours during the day; it was a cauldron. He couldn't stay on Moe for very long at a time either, perhaps two hours at most, before he urged and cajoled Moe to let him down, usually precipitated by a solid whack on the hindquarters and a spitting response from the camel.

Once, he saw a small group of horsemen in the distance. You could see clear 50 miles across the baking flats. Then they disappeared into the shimmer. He figured they were Navajos.

By the fourth day he was within 50 miles of old Flagstaff. The southern horizon darkened during the day into a chocolate brown, interspersed with flashes of yellow, as if a bombardment took place. The ponderosa forests, the lower flanks of the San Francisco Peaks, must be aflame, he thought. He wasn't surprised; it must have been 115 degrees F., at least 46 C., during that day. Wherever the wildfires found fuel; it was like one insatiable beast coursing across the countryside.

He had to water the camels soon. They were remarkable–complaining bitterly whenever he made them get up or down, but seemingly impervious to thirst or brutal heat. His days and hours were marked by the "pet pet pet" of their feet on the sand.

sand.

He guzzled water during the day, huddled under his tarp or whatever shade they could find, and shivered at night. He felt his strength being sapped. If he was 100 percent in Vermont, he was down to about 90 percent in Chicago, 80 in Denver, and 60 now.

Please God, he mumbled to himself, head bowed, in the boony hat, under a blazing sun. *Keep me strong. Alive. At least for her sake.*

Early on the fifth day, they ran into an armadillo, waddling through the dry underbrush. He briefly thought of putting a bullet into it for food, until he felt sympathy for it. It was only doing what he was doing, trying to survive. It didn't even lift its head as man and three camels lumbered by.

Just before sundown, as he was making camp, he saw a helicopter, metering across the sky from east to west, near the mountains. He felt afraid to make a fire then. He figured it had to be the regime. He thought he recognized the black tone and the logo. It was the only night he didn't make a fire. He ate two cold cans of beans and lay under double blankets and tried to sleep. He could smell the distant desert fires. He finally got up, shivering, and roused the camels, just as a fiery orange sunrise appeared. For once, he wanted the sun.

He took a piss and it was dark yellow, almost brownish, like some of the ash was mixed in. Some misery had set in; he had a little diarrhea. He squatted in the rocks a long time, and when he came out, buckling his pants, the camels were gone.

CHAPTER 39

He frantically looked everywhere, all around him, and saw nothing. All of his stuff was still there. So he didn't think the camels were stolen.

"Mo Larry Curly!" he yelled out, expecting them to at least grunt. The desert was silent.

He grabbed half a liter of water and his pistol and he ran at a slow trot, which he couldn't keep up beyond a fast hike. He thought he would cover 360 degrees about 50 meters from his camp, which he didn't keep out of his sight. Everything looked the same in the desert; he'd be a pile of bones soon if he got lost.

Thoughts galloped through his mind about the camels walking back north, like a loose dog might return homeward, when he came over a small rise and saw them, not far, dragging their tethers and grazing on tufts of sparse heather. "Moe!" he screamed, grateful for the mangy beast. He caught up with them and took Moe's reins, making sure the lines to the other two camels were connected, and led them back to the campsite.

Part of the way there, he saw two other camels in the distance. They held their heads high in the air and were trotting in his direction. Moe suddenly got agitated, pulled on her reins, bawling and growling. The camels were bigger and shaggier, had no saddles or restraints on them.

They got closer; the one in front didn't seem at all afraid of him. Then he thought about what Terry told him about the male camels. When it got within about 25 meters he noticed that gobs of frothy white saliva dripped from its swollen lips. It was huge; he figured 800 to 1,000 pounds. He pulled out the handgun he'd taken off the guy at the Glen Canyon dam; he figured it had six to nine rounds. His old pistol only had about two.

He couldn't lose the camels. Distressed grunting and whinnying came from all three of his animals, which he let go. The big, crazed one stopped about 20 meters away, growled and bellowed terrifically, then began to trot toward Moe. Wade aimed for the shaggy neck and shot once, twice, four times; the sounds crackled across the hard desert floor. He saw the brown coat leap where the bullets hit. The beast's knees buckled and it collapsed. The other one had run away.

"Damn," he said out loud. That was close, and now he probably only had abut four to six rounds of ammo left. His own camels, carrying his essentials for the next week, stood still as if in shock. He gathered them, led them back to the campsite, and loaded the rest of his stuff onto Curly.

It occurred to him that the dead male camel was a useful store of meat now. He could make some use of that; if he didn't, the coyotes, the fire ants, perhaps a lion, and the other surrounding desert species would. But he didn't want to spend the day butchering this corpse and trying to figure out how to store the meat.

He pondered this for a moment; that was a lot of calories there, meat and fat. He was feeling weak lately. Survival was about recognizing opportunities when they arose; taking advantage of them. Then he thought of Larry, his third camel, which was so far expendable. He hadn't strapped much to carry on it; Curly had most of the water and food, and he was drinking up almost all the water that had been loaded onto Larry. He thought he ought to keep free a round for Larry, in case he started to starve.

It was a relief to get moving again. He'd taken a few minutes to get another bearing with his compass and look over his highway map. They'd been making more than 20 miles per day/night, and today's march would take him damn close to due east of Flagstaff.

He swayed atop Moe; listening to the "pet pet" of her feet. He thought of his wife Lee and his son. Hopefully, they were comfortable and safe in Ottawa. He'd dreamt the night before that he was waking up in his bedroom, next to Lee in Vermont. Like all of this had been a nightmare, a twisted vision concocted in his subconscious, and that's all it was. He had this awful deflated feeling, sitting up in the desert, that this was reality, and he couldn't put it behind him like you can a bad dream.

Maybe when he found Kara and got back to Canada, things would settle down a bit and he could put the pieces of their life back together again. He'd sent Lee a message back in Page, mentioning nothing of what had happened to Kara.

The smoke rose from the San Francisco Peaks to the west, like a volcano.

He saw a man trotting along the desert, about a quarter mile away. It was the first person he'd seen since the horsemen a few days ago. The guy looked like a long-distance runner. The man stopped; Wade waved at him. It was a gut feeling; he doubted this was a predator. Maybe he was out of his mind running through this desert. But Wade needed information.

The man didn't wave back but he walked toward Wade, slowly.

Wade got his crossbow out. The man had his hands behind his back. "Hey," he called out. "Can you help me, man?"

"Maybe." He had long black hair, ruddy skin, and wore shorts and sneakers without socks. He turned around and showed Wade his hands, which were bound together with a zip tie.

CHAPTER 40

"Who did that to yah?"

"Weren't family or friends. Regime people did."

"Then you escaped?"

"You might say that."

"How long you been runnin'?"

"Don't know. Twenty miles?"

"Wow, then you probably need some water."

Wade still sat on the camel, then he slapped its flank and Moe grunted and squatted down. He swung his leg over the hump and dismounted. He took a gallon of water off Larry, opened it, and held it over the man's open mouth and cracked lips. The water poured in and the man gulped greedily, desperately, and some of it poured down his cheeks.

"Thanks," he said, breathlessly. "Can you take this off me?"

"Why'd they put it on you?"

"Because I didn't want to be their slave. I come from the Navajo territory up north–they came in with helicopters and trucks at night...took a bunch of us. They're using the Navajos, Apache, and Comanche as fire troops on the front lines. It's suicide duty. The fires have to do their thing, burn out, then maybe people can live by the mountains again. I hear they're working 16 hour days; the regime will kill you, shoot you on the line, if you don't work all day or night. They might kill you anyways when they're done with you. Saves on food."

While he was talking, Wade got out his knife, unsheathed it. "Turn around."

The man turned around and held up his wrists to expose them. Wade sawed away at it with the knife, until it finally snapped loose. He gave him some more water.

"My name's Michael Wade."

"Johnny Ironcloud." They shook hands. Ironcloud gripped and ungripped his hand, as if to make sure it was still working.

"What are you doing way out here? With them camels?"

"Trying to get to Phoenix."

"Ah."

"Hey, do you know where I can find water around here?"

"There's a river, about 10 miles, that way..." he pointed south.

"Do you think you can show me?"

"Yes."

"You probably want some food, right?"

"I'm starving. I haven't eaten since yesterday, and I've been running for miles."

"I've got crackers, a little jerky, beans..." Wade went over to Larry and unpacked some of the food and brought it over. They unwrapped the crackers and jerky, started eating. Wade gazed around the empty desert.

"You know there's a camel carcass back there. Fresh one."

"Really?"

"You could help me butcher it. Real meat."

"How far is it?"

"Not two miles, that way."

"How long has it been dead?"

"About 40 minutes."

"We don't have long."

Wade paused before his resting camel. "Ever ridden one?"

"I'll walk."

Ironcloud did seem indefatigable. When they backtracked and reached the carcass, it was covered in flies. When the two got close they all buzzed away. Wade took out his knife and unsheathed it.

"Let me try," Ironcloud said. He handed it to him. Ironcloud knelt beside the huge carcass in the sand. He got in close to the underbelly, with the beast lying on its side, then he turned to Wade. "Knife needs to be sharper and longer. But I'll do what I can." He began working furiously on a section where the hide and the coat wasn't as thick. A black bloody stain grew in the dirt around the camel. Its tongue lolled out of its mouth. The other three camels, fidgeting at a short distance, ignored it.

Ironcloud eventually reached into the camel's insides with both hands, as though it was giving birth. Wade laid out on the ground a cloth bag he'd been using to store rice, which had all been eaten.

Ironcloud emerged with a large dripping liver, which he severed away from the entrails. He smiled and lifted it up, as if to say, "You first?" Then he took a big bite right off, and tore away a piece of raw liver, chewing vigorously. He did it as naturally as Wade would take a bite of a large watermelon. With his mouth full Ironcloud said, "Good. Have some. It'll keep you strong."

Wade knew Ironcloud wasn't barbaric; he was knowledgable, about how to survive out here. If you're fortunate enough to have a fresh animal carcass you should eat the mineral and vitamin-loaded organs.

"What's it taste like?"

Ironcloud shrugged. "Not as good as Buffalo liver, but pretty good."

Wade was still desperate for food and he was lucky to find Ironcloud, who was also fortunate to come across Wade. The typical U.S. suburbanite, who'd recently had their comfort zone detonated, wouldn't have the least idea how to live in the desert.

"Give it to me." He took a tentative bite, holding the wet liver in two hands. It was still quite warm, and that bothered him. Ironcloud laughed.

"Arizona delicacy, huh?"

"The camel special," Wade said, around the chewing. He took a sidelong glance at the other three camels. He handed it back and his companion took another big bite, then Wade said,

"Tastes like uncooked meat marinated in piss..." Then he couldn't help but laugh with the Indian. He had to admit to himself, it was filling. He was getting iron, protein, minerals...it felt good to laugh. He went to get some water.

"It would have been rancid in 30 minutes," Ironcloud called out after him. "We were lucky." He was up to his elbow in the camel again, with the knife, trying to extract the heart.

"You sure that 30 minutes hadn't already expired?" Wade said. Ironcloud had one knee on the carcass and hacked away inside it, bloody now to his tricep. Then he emerged with the heart, handling it again with both hands. It was sheathed in veiny fat and dripping dark red. The heart was the size of a heavyweight fighter's clenched boxing glove.

Ironcloud ate the liver a little bit more, then he went into the nearby shrubs and came back with some leaves. He wrapped the heart and liver with the leaves, then placed them into the cloth bag. He tossed the bag over his shoulder.

"We'll cook more over the fire tonight. I'm finished with this camel. It's too hard work to butcher it with this knife. Let's leave it to the jackals and the vultures."

They spent the rest of the day crossing the desert to nearby what used to be Winslow, Arizona. Ironcloud knew where to find the river. The waterway still ran well with fast-flowing, clean water. The camels stood on the banks and drank copiously, absorbing dozens of gallons at once. They hadn't drunk water in six days. There were tire tracks all over the place, but so far, no people.

Wade swam in the cool water, and refilled his own water bottles. They made camp for the night.

CHAPTER 41

He still had about 180 miles or 300 kilometers to go, which he thought he could make in nine days or less. They cooked the camel heart over another fire. They skewered it with some sharpened sticks and roasted it good and well-done. Wade ate several large pieces until his belly was full and it made him tired, so he'd sleep deeply. It tasted infinitely better than the liver, somewhat like beef. They saved the uneaten roasted chambers and returned them to the bag.

Ironcloud cooked the liver too, so they had meat for several days. They just had to keep it away from the flies.

Wade fell over onto his back, on top of his camping pad, and stared at the stars…as long as he didn't lose the camels or something happened to them…he didn't think he had too many bullets for more rutting male camels or worse, a marauding gang. Ironcloud was, understandably, worried about being recaptured by the regime forces. He was going to join Wade and planned to aim for a reservation close to the Mexico border.

When they awoke the next morning they saw a mule-driven wagon parked across the river. The river must draw many people who are trying to cross this desert, Wade thought. They waved at some people, which from a short distance looked like two families. They waved back. Then he and Ironcloud gathered their bedding and food, loaded up the camels, and headed southwest.

Ironcloud's initial walking pace slowed them down, so Wade finally cajoled him into riding atop Larry's hump. Larry carried hardly any provisions, but still bawled and complained bitterly when Ironcloud threw a blanket over the hump. Then gripping the reins, he awkwardly climbed aboard.

"I need a horse!" he yelled out. He was red-faced and angry; Wade laughed when he fell off once, but they were able to cover almost 14 miles when they finally stopped in the middle of the day.

They followed old Arizona highway 87, which headed into a recently burned forest of the high plateau. Columns of grey smoke rose on the horizon. They steered away from the highway, and its cracked and uneven surface, since they figured the regime would be using it. The camels' feet worked better on desert soil than deteriorating concrete, but they could still follow the southwesterly direction of the highway, while staying hidden at a short distance.

Outside of Winslow and well off the highway, they crossed some train tracks. The tracks led east-west. It was getting tough going, as the desert was pockmarked with ditches and arroyos; the land was hilly and cloaked with rocks and cactus. In places, it was thickly forested with saguaro cactus. Wade liked the saguaro standing against the red sandstone cliffs and monuments, when the sun went down.

One time they saw two wild camels ambling off in the distance, but the animals never came closer.

They emerged into the fringes of a large, mostly burnt pine forest. The route was beginning to climb; he worried about their slowing pace. They stopped and began to unpack. They were going to eat, rest, then get going in a few hours. They'd travel as far as they could at night. They decided to stick to the road, because the topography was becoming too difficult, and it led to where Wade wanted to go.

About a half mile away they saw a train coming. A single engine trailed by wooden railcars. Wade walked to the top of a nearby hill to get a better look. Some of the cars said Southern Pacific along the side in faded, flaking paint. But others flew a small version of the flag the regime used at the moment, a rather trite and uninspiring black-and-red design. The trains had small windows, and he saw people's faces crowded around. He couldn't believe how many wood railcars trundled past; it reminded him of when he was little and the freight trains took forever to go by.

He thought he saw grim, distressed faces from a distance; once in a while an arm dangled out, as though to touch the fresh air. Halfway through, an open-air car went by containing troops in black uniforms. Wade ducked behind a rock. There must have been a hundred, two hundred cars in the train, and it just continued on past. He looked at Ironcloud and said, "They contain people. They're transporting people in boxcars."

"I know. It's a forced migration. A forced deportation. They round up the Latinos, the Apaches, Navajos, and Comanche people. Other 'undesirables,' they call 'em. They ship them to the fire. They clear out the old peoples."

"What do you mean 'clear out'?"

"Southern Arizona was full of old folks; millions. There was no room for them anymore; no food, water. They're expendable; they're old, taking up space and resources. So they get rid of them."

"Where did you hear this?"

"Friend of mine had been down to Phoenix–said all the old retirement towns in southern Arizona were ghost towns. All the old people were gone. They either got out on their own, or they got rounded up and put on these trains. Which is what happened to most of them, because they were too old to move long distances. They put 'em in camps in the desert. He said that he saw about a thousand old people behind the wire, but I didn't believe him. That seemed too far-fetched for me, and I've seen a lot."

The last train finally rolled past. Wade had a vision he tried to dispel from his mind, of Kara packed in one of these cattle-cars. That's all they were, cattle-cars, containing besieged human cargo. It was an obscenity. The regime had finally gone mad, panicked–they couldn't manage the millions of people driven out of their homes by the fires, so they resorted to vile, brute-force methods. But the regime didn't have Kara, as far as he knew. It was the Redboyz he was looking for. Maybe that made it easier; that the regime didn't have her.

The sun was going down when they went back to their camp and the camels. They made a fire, cooked and ate some leftover organ meat. He saw curtains of rain in the distance, flashes of lightening. They'd have to find cover by some cliffs, or make a roof out of their tarps.

Except for the train, they didn't see anybody go by on the highway as the darkness enveloped everything.

CHAPTER 42

They traveled by night through the forest, with its bed of ash and charred tree trunks. It wasn't camel country anymore, and this concerned him. He was barely halfway through the trip now. They traversed a high plateau more than a mile above sea level. The landscape was composed of mountains, canyons, and burned wooded hollows; the aftermath of a very recent fire.

The air was permeated with a pine-scented fog. The vapor would rise into the air when they stepped on the ash, like some mushrooms do. He and Ironcloud walked with buffs pulled over their faces. At least the camels had eyes and nostrils that could withstand sand storms.

It was difficult to navigate, if not impossible, so they veered over to and stuck to the road–Arizona highway 87. There were ruins about; roadside franchises and small towns reduced to piles of black rubble. They still had plenty of food and water so they didn't try to scavenge.

The only birds were ravens. He heard their squawks and saw their black forms against a purple sky. It was morning again. At some point they'd sleep. They wandered through the ruins and the blackened landscape silently. He heard a dog barking, but couldn't see it back in the flattened rubble of the neighborhoods. Then they found themselves in quiet tumbled-down woodland. The road ahead sunk down into a gray wasteland. They had no choice but to follow it.

The heat mingled with the dust by mid-morning. They were forced to stop. It was almost like nuclear winter, with a grey mist blocking the sun, which, seemingly out of spite, doubled up on its pouring down of heat upon them. There were mountains around that topped out at seven thousand feet or higher.

Ironcloud had a head band on and he'd taken his shirt off. Wade thought, with his long black hair tied back and wiry, taut muscles that looked sun-burned, he looked more Indian, like from old photos in libraries. Or paintings. Ironcloud swung off Larry's hump and declared, disagreeably, "If I had a rope, I'd get a horse. Even a wild mustang. Anything but this…camel," he said with disdain. "This is horse country. Or used to be."

"You come from the Navajo territory, up north?"

"Originally, Fort Apache rez, just west of here. They still have wild horses; tall mountains with snow. I'm Comanche, not Navajo," he talked, while he fetched something from the bags. "I had a single mom. My real dad killed someone in a fight—he claimed it was self defense. They put him in prison. My mom met a Navajo boyfriend and we moved to a rez up north when I was a teenager. I was in the Army—ended up in Kuwait, Iraq, and Syria. I was code talkin'!" Then he burst forth with a paragraph of native language that Wade didn't understand.

"Really?"

"No, I'm just kidding man. They wanted me to be a rifleman. That's what they needed."

So he can handle a rifle, Wade thought. That might come in handy.

"This place, it reminds me of there. Syria. Bombed out cities, streets full of refugees. Gray, everything gray, caked with dust, depressing, baking under the sun. It would get into your nose, eyes, under your fingernails. You couldn't see." He looked around. "Yeah, it was like this. The Middle East. Polluted, by hate. I was glad when I got out. Came back to Arizona and worked in the almond orchards and on a farm breaking horses. The places closed down due to the fires, then the regime took over."

Wade chewed slowly, then drank some water. It just felt good to talk, to hear voices other than the noise of ravens and buzzards; the wind blowing through brittle trees and ruins.

"Got a girl?"

"You bet; her name is Marina." He took a photo out of his pants pocket. It was bent on all the corners and somewhat stained. He handed it to Wade. "She's third from the left."

The photo showed a group of young, fashionable Native American women standing in front of what looked like a Tex-Mex style nightclub. Halters and tight jeans and makeup; long combed out black hair.

"She's beautiful. Think you'll marry?"

"Oh yeah, I want to. Soon as I get a chance. She's waiting for me. I'll get her and bring her back to the good country, down by the river and the mountains–grass and horse country, untouched, as far as the eye can see. We'll plant an orchard, keep some horses. I'll bring her there."

"That's precious." Wade kept the image in his mind; it was

restful.

"You married?" Ironcloud asked.

"Yeah, her name's Lee. I've got a son Shane. They're waiting for me in Canada. You know about Kara." Thinking of her brought him back from the lofty perch of his imagination, to the scoured gray earth they tread upon. The violent and uncertain legacy of the future prospects. The camels raised their heads and looked around at the sky and ground. They'll need water again, he thought.

"It's good to have someone waiting for you," Ironcloud said, looking down and fooling with a stick.

"Aren't women great?" Wade said. "I didn't know how to relate to girls when I was younger, high school or college. One would come on to me, I wouldn't know how to act. I'd fumble around, then I'd think later, 'You idiot. Just talk to her.' I still don't know how to relate to women. I'm emotionally distant. That's why I'm so lucky with Lee. She seems to understand everything; I don't really have to try with her. It's just dumb luck, that I found her and she stayed with me."

"Do you like marriage?"

"Yeah, with her. If you want kids, you have to work out a marriage."

"I want kids," Ironcloud said. "But I want them to have a good home; not stuck in a slum on the rez. Maybe Flagstaff or Tucson will come back. Maybe I can get a farm by the river…"

"Yeah, I can picture that. I think you're going to do that. You'll do well, when this is all over."

They finished eating, put some more scrap wood on the fire, and tried to sleep some. They lay down off to the side of the empty road, with their buffs pulled over their faces.

At night, they heard in the far distance a train going west. Wade imagined it was the same one they saw, but this time emptied out.

CHAPTER 43

It had been nearly two weeks since he'd left the dam. It seemed like two months. The water had lasted and he had plenty of food, so he considered himself lucky. They were on the outskirts of the ruins of a town called Payson. The three camels had been able to graze, and they were approaching a river. He was glad to be out of the wasteland of the toppled forest and scorched canyons.

They were at most four days out of the Scottsdale area.

When they reached the river, they found the wagons they'd seen before, overturned in the sand. The mules and people were gone. He took two of the camels to the shoreline to drink. The water ran clear and shallow over rocks; long yellowed grasses grew on its banks. He brought a couple of empty gallon jugs down and dipped their open tops into the running water.

Ironcloud had lingered behind; at that point, he was

disgusted with riding the hump. He'd dismounted finally and led Larry along by the reins. They were a few hundred feet upstream of Wade.

When Wade came up the hill from the river, carrying the two jugs, a man with a rifle stepped from behind the wagons. He pointed the gun at Wade.

"Stop right there, pard. Put the bottles down and empty your pockets. I want to see the weapons." Wade put the bottles down, then reached into his pocket and carefully put his handgun on the ground, never taking his eyes off the man. The camels wandered up the hill and passively meandered among the grasses grazing. The only sounds were the water, wind, and the two men talking.

"Where's the rest of your crew?"

"I'm alone."

"Shit you are." The man looked around him. He was bulky and bearded with long, unkempt hair under a kind of bowler hat. He had a buttoned up shirt, a string tie, jeans, and muddy cowboy boots.

"Anybody else out there, come on out, or I'll shoot your man." He looked at the camels.

"Money bag over there?"

"I don't have any money." That was true; he'd spent all his gold on provisions. "I'm just like you; all I'm doing is migrating west."

"Shut up and get on your stomach." Wade did, then the man approached cautiously, bent down, patted down his clothes, took Wade's gun off the ground, and backed off. Wade was just glad the guy hadn't bushwhacked him from behind the wagon. This one seemed a little smarter; he had reasons for keeping Wade alive.

"How much food and water you have on those camels?"

"Some. Maybe a couple days worth."

"You're lyin' to me about the money." He walked over to Moe the camel and took a closer look. He hadn't seen Wade's crossbow yet; it was strapped to Curly, who'd wandered off a short distance.

"I could use one of these animals for food," the man muttered, mostly to himself.

"I'm all out," Wade reiterated, buying some time. "That's the truth. Spent it all on camels and food back in Page. I'm just looking for my daughter." It felt strange telling the truth and appealing to this highway thief's sensibilities, but he sensed that concocting a lie wouldn't be any more effective. Besides, the truth was easier to tell.

"Well, I'm going to take the camels. I might have to kill you. I'm sorry about that. You see, that guarantees that you don't shadow me and kill me back. It's a simple equation; one minus one equals zero."

"Where's the rest of your gang?" Wade said.

"I'm asking the questions here. But since you asked, I'm on my own. Things got a little rough down by Phoenix–that's putting it mildly. It's the badlands down there. They're all dead. Or most of them. It's rob or be robbed; a sad state of affairs. When I get to a place where it's not, I'll stop doin' it.

"I'll feel better about your future prospects, however, if you just show me where the gold is."

Just then, a voice came from behind the man. "Drop the rifle, on the dirt. Now!" Surprised, the man swiveled, with a pissed-off look, as at himself. "God dammit!" he exclaimed. He dropped the rifle.

Wade quickly got back on his feet and went and fetched the rifle. "Now *you* can get down on your stomach."

"I've got a few gold coin, and some ammo," the man said, pleading somewhat, as he got down on his knees. The wind blew off his bowler hat, exposing a scraggly, sun-burnt bald spot. "You can have it all, and the rifle. I'm used to this; I won't tell anyone about you, I promise. No one knows about you; I just came back here to check the wagon. Just don't shoot me."

"Shut up asshole!" Ironcloud said. "How many innocent people have *you* killed lately?"

"None, I tell you. If you shoot me, the others will hear the shot." He looked back at Wade, sheepish as he was exposing a lie. "They're a couple miles out in the desert with those mules and people. But you can take my gold pieces. I wish I had more, but I blew it all down at the fairgrounds they have in Pleasant Valley."

"Fairgrounds?" Wade said. "You just told me it was a killing fields down from here. What fairgrounds can there possibly be?"

"It's bad between here and old Phoenix. For sure. But if you take the Highway 188 south instead, they have the remnants of a town. I just call it a fairgrounds; that came out of my own memories. It's not too bad; the regime runs it. They want to keep the dam running on Lake Theodore Roosevelt; use the energy and the water. They have a kind of tent city built up there, for services and entertainment. They accept real money–it's all food, drink, music, circuses, strippers, and tents full of women they're selling."

"Selling? Did you say selling women?"

"I did, unfortunately. Poor souls. I'm not into that, believe me on that one. Find it kind of disgusting. They offer them by the hour, and longterm. Hundreds of 'em. It's just not right…"

Acid rose up to Wade's throat. "You bowl me over with your empathy. Where exactly is this? You said south? 188?"

"Keep going on 87. Then south on old 188. Less than a two-day ride on your camels, I reckon. Why, are you going there?"

"Maybe. But you just managed to delay us."

"Just don't get caught by the regime. They'll make you fight the fires in Phoenix, and that's like slavery itself. If you stay close to 188, you can't miss this tent city."

"The regime runs it, you say?"

"The regime, but they tolerate what the entrepreneurial gangs and syndicates do."

"Entrepreneurial…that's a fancy word for a highway man. Is it the Redboyz down there? Those low-lifes with scarves?"

"Yeah."

Ironcloud had come over to the man and was looking over his rifle, which Wade handed to him. "Give me the rest of your ammo," he said. He'd put a shirt on, but the oddly formal man eyed him like he was some kind of a savage. Wade got the impression that he was petrified of Ironcloud, what he might do to him. As in, hammer him into the ground and let the fire ants start in on his face; an old Apache special.

The man emptied his pockets and handed over some shells. It wasn't a great rifle, just a bolt action, but it was something, other than a handgun.

"What exactly is going on down on 87 that's got your panties in a tangle?" Ironcloud asked him.

"Nothin' good. I'd turn around; I could show you a better way out of here, through the mountain passes…"

"We don't need you," Ironcloud said, evenly.

The man looked at him with more suspicion and fear. "Don't kill me, ok? I've got a son, two daughters. Over in Texas. I'm tryin' to make it back to 'em. You seem like a family man," he lied. "We're all in the same boat, trying to escape back to our families. There's been enough killin'."

"There's been enough talking," Ironcloud said, strapping the rifle onto his back.

"We're not going to kill you," Wade declared. The man

exhaled an audible sigh of relief. His eyes calmed.

"You should take a wide arc around the highway. Then connect up with 188, if you're headed down that way."

It was rough, hilly, and mountainous country around the highway.

"We need to go the fastest route. Who's controlling the highway toward Phoenix?" Wade asked. "The regime?"

"No. Crazy people, that's all. The regime haven't taken them down yet. Maybe they want people to think they're responsible for it, to keep everyone in line."

"Responsible for what?"

"You'll see," he said ambiguously.

"Take your clothes off," Wade said.

"What?"

"Down to your skivvies. Now…you can keep your money pieces. We're not criminals and robbers like you. But we're going to tie you up a bit so you can't alert your friends."

"Don't leave me here like that."

"You were going to kill me, pal."

"No I wasn't. I don't have it in me, if you want to know the truth. That was just tough talk. They've got coyotes and wart hogs and everything else here! It gets cold!"

"Yeah, only at night. You'll get loose by then. Clothes, off!"

Wade looked over his shoulder and saw the three camels calmly grazing in the grasses. They'd been down to the river to drink. Ironcloud was standing on a rock, scanning the horizon.

CHAPTER 44

They side-tracked about a quarter mile south of the highway and headed down, first west toward Phoenix. They would intersect with Highway 188, or what was left of it, eventually. Wade had gone through the wagons; he wanted to leave anything useful for the owners, in case they got away. But he tucked into his backpack an old bottle of liquor he found there.

Ironcloud walked behind the camels with the new rifle on his back. They figured they'd walk west-southwest, and thus avoid any trouble on Highway 87. Wade had a hunch about the tent city, the so-called "fairgrounds."

Dark curtains of rain drifted over the rolling, uncluttered landscape of painted desert. You could see the weather patterns approaching from 50 miles away. They took shawls and threw them over their shoulders. The rain swept over them, like someone spraying a hose into the air. The water dripped off the top of Wade's hat. A hush came over the desert as pattering rain flowed in graceful rivulets over the gravel and the rocks. A rainbow arched over a portion of the mountains in the distance, then the rain parted to a spectacular range of clouds on the horizon, like a foamy wave breaking. Everything had cooled off and been cleansed. They took a moment to stop at a rise.

Wade wanted to try and see if he could see the intersection of the two highways. They both dismounted from the camels, and stood looking out on the edge of a butte. The barren, vast country they'd wandered through looked huge and unwelcome; he couldn't believe they'd crossed it. Then he saw Highway 87; a long row of what looked like small telephone poles went down one of the road's sides. He could see shadowy forms fastened to the poles, of men.

"Holy shit!" Ironcloud said. "This is what the idiot back there was talking about."

At least two dozen people were crucified along the road. From a distance, Wade could just make out the heads hanging down. Birds of prey had settled on some of them. He wanted to get back on the camels and turn away from that benighted landscape, as if he'd dreamt the hideous images, and he could dismiss them as a figment of a stressed mind.

Ironcloud brushed the flies away from his face. "Damn insanity," he said. "These lands have gone over to the devil."

"What do you think we should do?" Wade said. He was completely at a loss; he wished he hadn't seen it, could turn the clock back and never stop and dismount on the butte. All of the frames of images over the intervening minutes could have stopped at the rainbow.

"I don't know," Ironcloud said. "What if there are women, or children? It's torture. We can't let 'em die like that, with the vultures. Dammit, I need a horse!"

Ironcloud seemed braver, less demoralized, and Wade wondered if it was because he'd been in desert wars across the world. He'd seen this kind of horror before.

"How much ammo do you have in the rifle?"

"About six shots."

Wade looked up at the vista; he saw that a short-cut could bring them close to the intersection of 87 and 188.

"Okay, let's go."

# # #

They made their way down to a flat dry plain below the butte, keeping their eye on Highway 87 for intruders. Wade's stomach growled; he reached into a bag hanging off the saddle, where he kept some of the cooked, leftover camel meat. He handed some to Ironcloud, then placed another piece into his mouth, chewing it to take his mind off everything else, and stop the growling.

"Are you coming?" Ironcloud said, nodding his head to 87, in the distance.

"No, I'm staying with the camels."

Ironcloud, the rifle slung over his shoulder, began at a fast hike towards the road. On his belt, he had a small canvas bag of intricate animal bones he'd found in the desert. Wade hadn't asked about them. He figured they'd go onto a necklace, or were simply good-luck talismans.

In the distance, he saw five people on horses. They halted about a mile from the first crucified victim, and formed a huddle. They shimmered in the heat off the desert floor. Wade watched as his partner raised his hand in a friendly signal. One of the horsemen waved back. Wade thought he saw two women and three men. Three of the people, including one of the women, drew pistols when Ironcloud approached them on foot. He pointed up to Wade, and they talked for a few minutes. Then he pointed to the people hung up above the road ahead. One of the women dismounted and gestured toward Highway 87. Ironcloud handed her his rifle. Then she handed him the reins to her horse.

Wade watched this standing next to the camels, with Moe by the reins.

Ironcloud mounted the horse, then quickly attained a speedy gallop down the highway. The posts, and the people nailed to them, were as still on the landscape as trees or cactus. The heat was unbearable; Wade's body was bathed in sweat. Ironcloud made his way slowly along the ghoulish scene until he'd reached the end. Only one or two of the birds flew off as he rode by. Then he rode at a gallop back to the woman, and he took the rifle back, having apparently won back her trust. He went back up the road.

He raised his rifle three times–Wade heard the reports crackle and echo across the desert. All the birds flew away except for one, which Ironcloud shot off of a man. Then he shot a fourth man from his horse; Wade wondered whether the gunshots would bring the crazies or the regime's foot-soldiers down on top of them.

The desert was silent; not even a bird cried, only the wind blowing through cracks in the rocks that lay like giant red tortoises on the desert floor. The camels shifted their feet on the ground; their ears twitched at the gunshots. Ironcloud returned to the horsemen at a full gallop. He got down off the horse, handed over the reins, shook the lady's hand and one of the man's, and began walking again.

CHAPTER 45

The bright moon that night cast long shadows amongst the rocks. They stopped and made a fire. They had continued south with the camels towards Theodore Roosevelt Lake and the makeshift, honky-tonk fairgrounds he was looking for. Wade didn't ask Ironcloud much about the prisoners, except that the young man had said that some of them had begged to be killed. It would have taken tools to actually bring the live ones down, or bury the bodies, and Ironcloud had wanted to burn the whole thing down anyways. Neither of them wanted to talk about it, especially him. One of the dying men had told Ironcloud that the Redboyz had done it.

Ironcloud took his sack of bones and made a circle around the fire with them, while humming a song softly to himself. Then he stood up straight and raised his hands to the moon, and spoke in the language Wade didn't understand. When he sat back down, he rocked back and forth and continued the song. The flames cast their elongated, distorted shadows into the night.

Wade heard howling that night; he slept restlessly on the ground, turning over and over again on his hard bedroll. Partly what they burned was mesquite bush, the tart smell of which permeated his few dreams, which lay close to the surface of his mind. They both got up at roughly the same time, when the sun cracked brilliant orange on the horizon.

They were less than a day's ride to the current, ad hoc settlement in Tonto Basin. They were almost out of water and the camels needed to drink again. They'd reach Tonto Creek by early afternoon, then they could stop. They drank some of the remaining water, including some he made tea from by heating it over the fire, then they mounted the camels again and kept going.

Mountains rose on either side of them, the Mazatzals to the west, and the edge of the Mogollon Rim to the east. They looked like mountains on the moon, grayish brown and denuded of everything. You could see no snow on the peaks anymore. Wade heard thunder in the distance; black clouds careened across the southern horizon, below which he could see the large lake.

It was dark blue against the dun brown of the desert. The lake itself was the result of an old dam built years ago on the Salt River. The large river had hosted human settlements that included the Salado, farmers and hunters who made beautiful pottery, more than 700 years ago.

From higher up, they could look down on a ramshackle shanty town scattered along the parched lake's shoreline. Then the piecemeal town spread to the surrounding desert, the collapsed society's version of sprawl. He saw a few tiny vehicles, trucks and Jeeps, bumping slowly along 188. They raised small plumes of dust. The drying lake was pale blue and brown around the edges. That was their target, the tent city somewhere down there. Wade mused that the ancient Salado people were infinitely more civilized than what had only recently sprouted up in "Pleasant Valley."

The asphalt on Highway 188 was in an advanced state of disrepair; tough to traverse for the camels. Once off the higher plateau, they were also wide open and too visible to whatever noxious groups, including the Redboyz, that occupied Tonto Basin. They moved off the road and diverted into the desert again.

This part of the desert had been junked, left to decay. What used to be quaint and kitschy was now like a rotting museum. They passed falling over Burma Shave signs, and at one point, a torched, blackened junkyard containing acres of discarded bikes and motorcycles. They passed behind a falling-down roadside diner that had a toppled neon sign that reminded him of Denver and Union Station. They saw nothing useful in the rubble, and moved on. The priority was water now.

At one point in mid-morning, they were forced to hide in a hollow about a half mile from the road, as a group of motorcycles and a single car–an old Buick or Oldsmobile missing three of its fenders, rumbled past. Finally, they saw Tonto Creek, barely flowing through rocks and bone-dry desert. They led the camels to it. Ironcloud stood by the road with the rifle and kept watch.

They'd eaten all of the camel meat, and now they were down to nothing but a few crackers and cans of beans. It had been all about calories and calculations, Wade thought, remembering Tucker and his camel ranch. They each needed more than 2,000 calories per day, at a minimum, and much more than that to deal with the intermittent violence and stress of the voyage, all the days that raised a question about whether they would survive them. Ironcloud wanted to go hunting with the rifle, but Wade preferred saving the ammo for self defense. He'd hunt later that day with his crossbow.

His mind was suffused with worry and dark images of his daughter's plight, which he tried to banish from his head. He swore he could sense her presence, smell her from a far distance, like a horse or a wolf. It was all intuition, which at this point, along with hearsay evidence of the wanton selling of women, was most of what he could go by.

He remembered the other thing that Ironcloud told him about the dying, crucified men. One was a Redboyz member, barely alive; he'd been caught in an affair with a gang leader's woman. They'd made him pay the price. He'd told Ironcloud that women were being sold from a building next to a circus, then the Indian had taken pity on him and shot him.

With the camels watered and several of their own gallon containers filled from Tonto Creek, they headed back up into the hills for the afternoon.

It was slow-going, with a steep, gravelly minefield of chollo, prickly pear, and saguaro they had to steer the camels around. The animals issued bitter complaints that were harsh on the ear, and Wade couldn't do anything to quiet them. Maybe they'd let the camels go and walk from there, he thought; perhaps shoot one for food.

Farther up they found a cliff dwelling in a hollowed out part of a hill. It had two stories, dated from centuries ago, and seemingly was not occupied full-time. Wade thought it was possibly from the lack of nearby water, but still they considered it a windfall for the night. Wade fetched his crossbow from where he'd stored it on Moe; he slung the quiver of arrows over his shoulder. Ironcloud stood nearby, unloading a bedroll onto a red sandstone floor.

"I appreciate you staying with me all these days, you know," Wade said. "I'm going into the town tomorrow. You don't have to come, because you know it's going to be rough."

Ironcloud held up his hand. "I will help you find your daughter, then we'll steal horses or a car," he said. "You saved my ass in the desert."

"You don't owe me…" Still, Wade depended, to no small extent, on having Ironcloud at his side. For this final push.

"I want you to get your daughter back. I do. Then I have to go back north to Marina. I want to make sure she's safe. I want to start up our life again."

"You don't owe me a thing. And I hope you reunite with your lady."

Ironcloud looked down at the ground, where he tossed mesquite sticks and other scrub into the fire. "Maybe I have no luck anymore, because of what happened back on the highway. Maybe Marina is with someone else now."

He was still vexed by the mercy killings, which weighed on his soul.

"That had nothing to do with you, back on 87. You did a good thing, the humane thing. It was the Redboyz–it was all their doing. You ended those mens' suffering. It was the saintly thing to do." Wade wouldn't have had the guts to do it, he thought to himself. "And we wouldn't have gotten as far as we did, without you. I'll never forget it, Johnny."

Wade hiked into the nearby hills. He made sure to fix various landmarks in his memory, because it was easy to walk endlessly and lose your bearings; the desert landscape had a sameness to it. But he got lucky, and within an hour he had shot a jacaranda with an arrow. They skinned it and cooked it over the fire, then they put the fire out when they'd finished eating, and went to sleep.

CHAPTER 46

They left the camels at the cliff dwelling in the morning.

Wade disguised himself as a beggar, which wasn't difficult to do. He had scraggly hair, an unkempt beard, and already looked the part of a haggard drifter. He draped the shawl over his shoulders, pulled the wet hat down over his eyes, and when he walked down into the town or settlement, he assumed a bent-over posture. He'd rubbed more dust into his face; he didn't make any eye contact with people on the street. Around his belt, beneath the shawl, he carried a Swiss army knife stored in its sheath, the almost empty pistol, and the crossbow and quiver.

Ironcloud followed closely behind him. He planned to steal two horses. He carried the rifle with him.

Wade walked down the barren, empty road. He thought he must appear like death warmed over, possessing nothing worth stealing. He entered the shanty town, which was crowded with bereft-looking families, men of all ages carrying tools, and groups of loitering, predatory young men. The buildings were all patchwork structures made from plundered metal or plywood, and even scrappy pine logs, or tents. The "town" was not put together nearly to the level of old Page, Arizona, or especially Grand Junction, he thought. It looked like a monsoon or a habib, the giant sandstorms that now plagued the southwest, would come through and sweep it away, and that the occurrence might be a blessing.

He heard loud voices and music coming from some of these shanty bungalows, and occasionally a man, drunk or zonked out of his mind on some cheap controlled substance, would stagger out the front door to fall face down, as one did in front of him, in the dusty, pot-holed street.

At times, on a street corner, stood a man in a dark uniform, looking bored and uninvolved, one hand resting on a holstered sidearm. He figured they were part of a regime cadre, but they didn't seem to be enforcing anything. If the settlement was governed at all, it was by malign neglect. At any rate, he was glad they weren't randomly checking his papers, so he never was forced to lift his shawl. His outfit otherwise made him stifling hot under the cloudless sky, which felt like an oven on high.

He kept shuffling along, paying nobody any mind. He read every poster he saw, as many things were posted for sale: dogs, horse and camel meat and desert game, shabby rooms for rent, and many kinds of useless detritus. The settlement apparently had no running water or electricity, except for the occasional generator. He remembered the circus; there was no mention of one on the posters.

He found what seemed the central strip, the "Main Street," and he walked to the side of that. He could see the lake, pale blue and like a mirage, so out of place, through the ramshackle buildings. One time, three beefy louts with Mohawk haircuts sauntered up to him; one gave him a shove, and he fell back onto the ground pathetically.

"This one's a true weakling," one of them said, with a malicious gleam in his eye, like he wanted to deliver another pleasurable blow; a swift kick. Wade was aware that a confrontation now could blow everything. Luckily, a regime person stood kitty-corner from him on the street.

Another of the toughs gave him a nudge with his boot. "He's half-dead drunk–let's move on." Wade didn't get up until they were gone around the corner.

Finally, he ventured to speak with someone. He chose an innocent person, a woman who was selling potatoes on the corner.

"Where's the circus?" he said.

"The circus?" she ran a hand through her graying, but long-flowing hair. She seemed nice, dressed in jeans and a buttoned-up shirt. "You might mean the boarding house, down two blocks and around the corner. To the right. They have an old circus sign, but it's not a real one. I don't know of any other circus."

"Thank you." He kept going, following her directions. Once in a while a man would come swaggering down the road with a woman on his arm, who looked anything but compatible and happy. He was drunk; her mouth was a straight line, and her overall countenance suggested she was counting off the minutes, until she could go on her own way.

Before he turned the corner, he looked around for Ironcloud. He didn't expect to see him, because his companion had to keep the lowest profile and not draw any attention. He figured Ironcloud would keep him in sight; at least, he hoped so, as he turned the corner off the main street.

An intact wooden building stood on the side, and sure

enough, someone had placed an old pealing circus sign near what looked like the front door. For decoration or to appeal to a passerby's fondness for antiquity, he didn't know. Wade looked around for a tent or "tent city," but he didn't see one. A man who might have been forty, but looked as grizzled and used up as someone twice his age, loitered near the circus sign. Wade shuffled over to him.

"Say friend, where might one find a woman, for rent?"

"For you?" the man scoffed in a gravelly way with his throat. "That'd be a laugh."

"No, it's for another fella. You see, he pays me to find a woman for him, once in a while. When I'm lucky."

"Got any of that money now?"

"Nah. He doesn't pay until the goods are delivered. Money, me? I couldn't pay for a pot to piss in, sorry to say."

"And sorry you do look," the man laughed. Then he looked around, with a pitiable attempt to seem in charge and authoritative. "What kind of woman is your man boss looking for? White lady, black, Latino, Indian? A younger one; an older one with experience..." The word "older" rolled off his tongue, as if he was just getting started with a sales pitch.

"A child?" That one made Wade want to wring his wrinkled chicken neck right then and there, but he had to keep his cool.

"Young one, I'd guess. About twenty. Pretty..."

"Of course! They have to be pretty! They only have pretty ones! Now, I'll point you in the right direction, and once you get your payment, you be sure to give me my cut for doing the favor, say fifty percent? I'll be holding you to that one." And he put his finger on his right cheek and pulled down the lower lid of his bloodshot eye, as if to suggest he was the all-seeing one.

Crouched in his hunchback, Wade answered, "I'll be sure

to drop by…"

"Come along," the man said.

He brought Wade about three-quarters of a block to the only brick building he'd seen on this whole journey; it looked like a former bank branch.

"They say this place," the grizzled guy said, "has a woman you can buy, and if the price is right, she's yours' for the taking, forever, in a manner of speaking…for the correct price."

Wade's heart was beating faster; his blood was rising. "Thank you," he said, and he shuffled up to the front door. He went up the stairs, opened the door, and walked into the darkness.

CHAPTER 47

"Now, who do we have here?" a man said. He got up from a rocking chair; he wore one of those strange, out-of-place bowler hats, with a dusty black coat and skinny tie of the same color.

"We don't take beggars here, old feller. Now why not move along...before I throw you out."

"I'm inquiring about a lady..."

"I'll bet you are," the man laughed. He came forward gruffly. "Don't waste my time–I told you to leave."

"...For another man...he has money. He's interested in her." Wade handed him the picture of Kara, the one he had with the serial number along the bottom.

"Ah *yes*," the man said, looking at it. "We do have this one." *This one,* Wade thought, with menace in his mind.

"Where is your good man?" the man crowed, with a fake, proprietary flourish. "Maybe he'd like to come in and meet her?"

"He's just outside, with his horse. I'll go get him."

"And I'll fetch the girl," the man said. "Any message I can give her?"

"Yes. *Daddy's* home…" Wade said, and out from beneath his cloak came the army knife, which he jammed up to its hilt into the man's thorax, which instantly spouted black blood onto Wade's shawl. The man let out a sigh like it was coming from a bag, Wade withdrew the knife, and the body crumpled to the floor in a heap, the bowler hat coming loose and rolling part-way across the wood. Wade dragged the body into the shadows on the side of the room, sheathed the knife, and readied his crossbow with an arrow.

The first man he met, emerging from the hallway nearby the staircase, wearing a Redboyz headband, got an arrow point-blank in the forehead. It gave him a sudden shocked look, the feathers protruding just above the wide eyes, before he fell heavily backwards, dead. Wade left him there; he had a whole quiver left.

He went up the dark stairs with its stale odor and pealing wallpaper, calling out, "Kara! Are you there? Kara! It's Dad!"

Instantly a man turned the corner on the second floor and came down the stairs at him, and he received one of the steel projectiles center chest, which knocked him more than half dead onto his back. Since it was easy, from this angle, Wade put a foot on him and yanked the bright red arrow out, rearming his bow with it. The recipient gurgled and died at his feet.

Another man appeared at the landing on the top of the stairs, this time with a pistol drawn. He fired twice; the bullets went astray, one grazing Wade's shoulder, and seconds after an arrow pierced the shooter's neck, appearing out the other side with a small portion of bloody flesh dangling from the tip.

The shooter pitched violently sideways over the railing and landed dead on the first floor.

"Kara!" Wade cried out. "Where are you! It's me!" he added, somehow knowing she'd recognize his voice.

Then he heard, it was unmistakable from the other side of a door, at the end of a hallway. "Dad! Dad! It's me, Kara!"

The building had a third floor, and a staircase. An armed, bulky man came down the stairs, with a red, sweaty, angry face and wearing the Redboyz headband, all the buttons of his coat unbuttoned and his belt loosened and hanging free, and he leveled both barrels of a shotgun at Wade. Before he could squeeze the trigger though, an arrow struck with an audible thud just below his ribcage and all but disappeared into the ample, torn-up abdomen. He smashed down onto the stairs issuing his final guttural cry, just as Wade, mechanically and with a steady hand, loaded another arrow into the crossbow.

He turned toward the front of the building beneath, as three more armed men came through the front door. There was a shot from outside; the third one fell onto the floor of the front hallway, as the other two turned and returned fire.

Ironcloud, Wade thought. As he was looking down there, a door, near where he had heard his daughter's voice, burst open, followed by a man in suspenders who fired a pistol, at will. Bullets flew all about the hallway; Wade ducked completely to the floor, but one of them passed thoroughly through his left shoulder, partially shattering the shoulder blade. It felt like someone had whacked the arm half off with a sword, but with a primal force of blind vengeance, he stood up out of a crouch and fired at close range; the projectile passed into the man's mouth and took part of the back of his head off. He slumped into the door jamb with eyes still wide, expressing nothing, for his efforts, than vacuity and emptiness.

Wade ran over the man's body, and found his daughter

cringing and crying by an open window. She put her arms out for him.

CHAPTER 48

He hugged her with one arm; her tears felt wet on his neck, mingled with his own.

"We're getting out of here!" he yelled. He wasn't able to rearm the crossbow, but right outside the open window, he noticed the shingled roof of the lower floor. He still had the pistol with one or two bullets left, the crossbow slung over the shoulder. Both of them climbed outside the window and dropped about five feet onto the roof. Wade could hear commotion in the room they'd just left.

Beneath him was an empty street with trash, dust, and disheveled shanty structures along it. He wondered whether he and Kara would have to drop all the way to the road, when around the corner came Ironcloud on a horse. He led another horse by the reins, looked up, and caught their eye. Although ten feet separated them from the ground, Ironcloud rode to just beneath where Wade held Kara. She lowered herself limberly onto the bare back of the horse behind Ironcloud. "Come on!" he yelled to Wade, steadying the other bareback horse in the air clouded with dust.

Wade lay on the roof bloody and wounded. "Go!" he yelled; "Take Kara and the horse!" A man pushed the muzzle of a rifle through the window, and Wade turned and emptied the last of his pistol ammo into it. A shower of broken glass spilled onto the roof, amidst the smoke of burnt cordite.

A small crowd had gathered, not far away on the dirt road; women in jeans and country skirts, groups of grimy kids, and dust-covered men holding their hats, watching.

"We have time!" Ironcloud yelled. "Take the other horse!"

"Dad!" Kara cried, muddy tears streaking down her face as she held onto Ironcloud from behind.

"Go! I'll be right behind you!" Wade said, unsteadily using one arm to get to his feet.

Men approached from about 100 meters down the dirt road; a shot was fired in the air. Many in the crowd turned to look at them, but only a few in the gathering parted to open the view for them. The dust was almost blinding, as the horses galloped in place and whinnied, Ironcloud turning the reins on them. He and Kara galloped in the opposite direction, as Wade dropped perfunctorily, rolled, and lay in a blood-stained heap on the ground. He looked up and he could see the two people and the horses disappearing around a bend.

CHAPTER 49

The once quiet roadside was chaos. Dry yellow dust filled the air, permeated with the odor of spent gunpowder. People milled around yelling and pulling curious children away; armed men approached on the road, and clamored onto the rooftop. As the road had no sidewalk, he scuttled in a half run alongside the buildings, holding onto his arm, until he ducked into an open door. The first room had blinding, mite-filled sunlight that streamed through a glassless window. It seemed unfurnished; he stumbled about. In the confusion, none of the armed men had seen him slip through the door.

The inside of his mouth was bone-dry and pain radiated through his left side. It was wet with his blood, some of which had already trickled and dried, staining his shirt down by the rib-cage. He staggered through the room, dizzy, and found a door, which he went through. A woman stood leaning against a counter in semi-darkness. Cracks in the wall emitted weak strips of sunlight. She was vaguely familiar, startled. She reached for a kitchen knife.

"I'm hurt bad..." Wade said. "Can you help?"

She stared at him for a moment. "Aren't you the one who came to get his girl?"

"My daughter, yeah..."

"Come with me." She was the lady who was selling potatoes outside. He was getting more dizzy; she led him by the arm out into the sun again.

"Help me," she said to someone. It seemed like a teenaged boy grabbed him by the good side. The air got furry and dark, then he blacked out.

# # #

He was being trundled along. He was on his back, covered by a sheet. Two people pushed him along a bumpy route. He heard whispering about "Get him to a doctor."

Then he was lifted upon a table inside a room. They tore the rest of his shirt off. The light was weak, as if powered by lantern, but the hands on his body assured. They mopped up the encrusted blood, then began to sew him up. Someone had him bite down on a stick, before the needle went in.

He murmured, "Put this on my wounds," and with his good hand, dug out the plastic bag of white powder from the Bible. He blacked out.

He found himself in a bigger wagon, laying beneath a canvas. He heard the clipped footfalls of the horses; voices. It was intensely hot. Thirst had robbed him of both voice and strength. He pushed the canvas partly off and whispered, "water." Someone put a canteen down and up to his mouth, and he gulped at it desperately until the trickle stopped and he ran out of breath. He saw the desert all around.

Then he was on a train; the sounds were familiar. The wheels scraping along the track and the shift and bump of the wooden flooring. It was hot and dusty inside, with a few open windows at eye level. He looked around; about a dozen silent people, all sitting down. Next to him, a canvas bag, his crossbow, and a quiver, containing a few arrows. He recalled what he had done with the rest of them.

He reached down into the bag and found a liter bottle of water. He drank it down and set it aside. A dust-covered, raggedly dressed teenage boy sat across from him.

"Where is the train going?" he asked him.

"West."

"Where west?"

"I don't know." The boy looked away; reluctant to converse with the man who looked like he'd been dragged behind a horse.

"Where did it leave from?"

"A town."

"What town."

"Phoenix. It used to be called."

Wade looked around, confused.

"How did I get here?"

"You was lyin' over there, when I got on."

Wade took another guzzle of the water. Rooting around, amazed, he found his army knife, wiped off and stored in its leather sleeve. He'd been looked after, meticulously, given the circumstances. He idly chewed a small package of crackers, savoring the salt.

"Want some?"

"Okay." He gave the open package to the boy.

"Where are you going?" he asked the kid.

"California," the boy said. "The ocean. My uncle lives there."

Wade got up, unsteadily with one arm. He wore a sling; the bandages were secure, in a tight wrap.

He ambled over and looked out the window. A baking brown desert, with sand dunes and greenish-brown mountains in the distance. The horizon glowed ruby red. He looked around at the others.

"Did anyone see an Indian, with a bone necklace, and a teenaged girl?"

They all shook their heads silently.

"Where's the end of the line on this train?"

An old man sat in the shadows, with a woman rocking an infant.

"South of L.A., where the Colorado flows into the sea. Follows old Highway 10 west."

"How long does it take?"

"We'll be there in a few hours." The train rumbled along its route with purpose, he was glad, and never made another stop in the desert.

PART IV: THE SEA

CHAPTER 50

He sat back against the wall of the railcar, before the wheels screeched and the train slowed. He stood up, went over to the open window. He thought he smelled the sea. There were more trees than sand, including a few palms leaning into a breeze off the water. The air was cool, briny. Squinting into the sunshine, Wade could see nothing threatening, like camps or barbed wire, yet.

He picked up his things; he heard the heavy wooden doors of the freight cars slide open. People had begun to disembark with meagre belongings, and walk in groups alongside the tracks. Finally, the door of his own freight car slid open; he joined the line at the exit, then he hopped gingerly down onto the black railroad bed. They were in California.

Down a hill and through a woods, he could see the pale blue, sunlit ocean. The hills were crowded, thousands of people moved about either toward the beaches, or inland. He saw troops, directing traffic, and organizing groups of people. They had brown uniforms trimmed in red. Some of the people were leaving on buses; others got back on the train, but far fewer than had gotten off.

A long line of people, hundreds, awaited a docked freighter. The Pacific, eggshell blue and with a perfect swell breaking meters offshore, lay beneath the rail yard. He scoured the crowd for Kara and Ironcloud. Nothing but preoccupied, unfamiliar faces. People who were looking for other people, like him. He joined the line for the freighter; it made more sense for them to have gone to the sea, for a passage north. They came west, and they wouldn't have turned back. Or they're waiting for him here, he thought.

He asked the person in front of him, "Where is this ship going?"

"North. Towards the Bay area. They want people up there— the rumor is that they need laborers for the city and farms. The cleanups; the firefighting. They're trying to grow vegetables again."

"Who does? Who's in charge?"

"The Chinese. They've taken over these parts."

"Is it violent? Are they rounding people up?" He looked back around at the troops, nudging people towards lines, watching over the crowds. They had a calmness bordering on arrogance. A quiet, iron authority. "Do people have freedom of movement?"

The man lit a cigarette and blew the smoke the other way, as if to dismiss the confusion and chaos.

"See for yourself—you can go where you want, within limits, I suppose. They're not charging for the ship. It's better than under the regime, that's for sure. I haven't seen any forced labor or prison camps...so far. No rough stuff."

"Is this the only ship?"

"No. One leaves about once a week. I've heard."

So Kara and Ironcloud could have been on an earlier freighter, he thought. He continued to scour the crowds for them; the sunny hillsides.

"What's going on in L.A.?"

"There is no L.A. It burned, then it flooded in a cyclone. It was a giant squatter's camp, then these troops cleared it out."

"Cleared it out…"

"A lot of them died, the residents…" the man said, looking away. Wade was sick of smelling his cigarette smoke. He was going to go search the crowds further.

He kept his eyes trained on the people gathered at the shoreline. "You haven't seen an Indian and a young girl, have you?" he asked, uselessly, in his mind.

"No," the man said. "But I hope you find them."

She's safe, Wade said to himself. He trusted Ironcloud. They'd freed her from bondage, he knew that much. She was alive, and now she was on the move, in a general direction homeward. He reasoned, they would make an effort to find a central location and wait for Wade.

He left and walked the dirt pathways, the crowded hills with grass whitened by the sun. He thought of the bullet that smashed his shoulder; he'd be with Kara if it wasn't for that. Then again, she could have caught a bullet, or he could have gotten one in the head, so he supposed things had worked out, better than they might have.

He couldn't find them so he returned to the line. After several minutes, he shuffled up the metal gangway and onto the freighter.

The boat seemed a bit of a tinpot, he thought, with a rusted hull and pealing paint. Everything on it was iron-hard, and showed the beating the ocean had given it. He wondered where they scored the diesel for it, or maybe the antiquated vessel ran on coal. He could feel the thrumming engines in the metal deck; the hydrocarbon exhaust was thick in the air. It was every man for himself to find comfort inside; he chose outdoors, on the deck.

All this was avoidable, he thought. Everything that's transpired, for the masses of suffering people in this region. They knew global warming was happening; it was as plain as the nose on someone's face. Every year was hotter than the last. They knew exactly what were the levels of CO_2 and methane that spelled catastrophe, as well as how to cut the emissions. Inertia and status quo ruled the world, however. Now chaos did.

He found a place where he could sit down, in a sea breeze. He still wore the boony hat, which had somehow survived all the miles he covered. He looked around once more for a familiar face, then still drowsy from blood-loss and travel, put his head back and closed his eyes.

Phoebe Tate came onboard, with Wiley in tow. Wade struggled to his feet. He waved with his good arm. She looked fresh, vibrant, despite everything. She rushed forward toward him across the deck, all smiles, bright eyes, and hair flopping around.

"Where's your daughter?" she said, eyes wide. "I heard!"

"You heard what?"

"That you got your daughter back! I want to meet her!"

"She escaped, yeah, we got separated…"

"But you'll find her again!"

"I will. What about you? How come you're not in Glen Canyon?"

"Oh, I got sick of it. Needed a change."

"They broke up," Wiley said, ruefully. Wade shook Wiley's hand. "Looks like you broke a wing," Wiley quipped to him.

"It's healing. Where're you going? Got a specific destination?"

"Same place you are," Wiley said. "Same place..."

Phoebe looked at him thoughtfully, in a way he found penetrating.

"I'm *so* glad you're alive," she said. "I prayed for you when you left the river. I remembered the dark road in Colorado, when you pulled over for me. It was a moment in time. The moments that make all the difference in the world. We went through a *lot* together, and we became close.

"I saw you kill, and I said to myself, that's not the Michael Wade I know. Not the true one. He's not a killer by nature; he's a kind man, at the core. The world changed, not him; he had to change with it, to find his daughter. The men who held Kara, did you kill them?"

"You bet I did."

"You had to."

"I need to find my daughter for good."

"You will," she said. "She wears the Saint Michael medal. Remember that, from the old days?"

"I do. Years ago, I came back from a fishing trip once, down in Florida, with a bad case of Staph, on my back. An infection, came home with it. Kara was only a baby, an infant. Right after that, she had her first epileptic seizure. She kept having them, dozens per day–we felt helpless. Lee and I. I blamed myself. I thought she got sick from me. The doctors told me the epilepsy wasn't related, but I was sure it was my fault, with the timing of it. She was so helpless, lying in bed with the fits. That's why I had to get her back. It's why I had to do everything I could to save her."

A loud clanging on deck startled him. He opened his eyes. They were serving watery potato chowder to the crowd on deck out of a big heated steel container. He stood up to eat.

CHAPTER 51

The freighter pitched in the open seas. People were getting sick on deck, over the sides. Wade clung to the rail with one hand. It felt different, to be cold. He watched the hull rise up in a swell, then strike back into the sea, lifting a spray of froth that felt like mist. A bulbous, angry cloud drifted over them, then there was rain. He joined a group of people pushed against some steel bulwark, but the rain was brief. It subsided, then he returned to his place in the sun.

He could still see the coastline, appearing in and out of a shroud of fog. He didn't have a map of California. But he knew that even going only 20 knots, they'd be within range of Monterey Peninsula by evening. The sea voyage had already gone about eight hours.

Phoebe's and Wiley's presences were still palpable for him. Somehow he thought he'd see them again.

That chowder they'd served had been like prison gruel. He

thought of Ironcloud, and the heart and liver that had been a banquet by comparison.

Then came a loud, vibratory shudder from the stern. There was a crack, like lightening had struck, or a big transformer had blown out and sizzled. Black smoke poured from the stern behind them. People screamed.

Barely a minute passed. He pushed against the crowd that fled to the bow of the boat; he wanted to see what had happened. The ship seemed to be drifting. He reached the stern and craned over the railing. He saw crewmen lowering wooden lifeboats with thick ropes and pulleys into the swollen seas. Soldiers in the brown uniforms pushed back the crowd; then panic. The boat listed. Clouds of the black oily smoke clouded the deck. She was going down.

He took his canvas bag and his bow and joined a crowd that choked the stairs leading below-deck. When he reached the bottom deck, he continued to press along the railing until he reached another flight of stairs. The ship listed hard starboard. He ran into the man he stood behind in the ship line, who recognized him. The man leaned dissolutely against the rail; he made eye contact with Wade.

"They're scuttling the boat," he said, bitterly. "They set charges back there. They're letting her go to the bottom, to thin out the refugees. I could have taken the bus–I knew it!" Then he and Wade were swallowed in the crowd that surged toward the next flight of stairs. Wade had the bow and bag slung over his good shoulder, and he fought not to be trampled. He found himself on the lower deck.

He looked over the side at the overcrowded lifeboats, already pulling away heartlessly. Mostly full of soldiers and crewmen. The boat then listed acutely to starboard. People fell from the upper decks, somersaulting into the choppy waters. Making sure everything was secure on his body, everything precious, including the crossbow, Wade draped his leg over the railing, and jumped overboard.

CHAPTER 52

Kara and Ironcloud had finally reached the California coast. It was a place they could stop, eat, and rest. Kara Wade was quiet, and since they'd barely escaped on horses, she was agreeable about the route Ironcloud took: first to the west on the horses, then he sold them for a pocket full of dollars, and they boarded the train. The freight cars took them past the desolation of Yuma, Arizona, and they'd ended up in Tijuana, which was a massive refugee camp of escapees from all points of the compass.

Ironcloud thought Michael Wade was dead. In fact, he was sure of it. He sensed a special responsibility for the daughter, and he thought he could get her over the Canadian border up north and eventually onto another train. Wade had mentioned Ottawa, Canada.

People were resourceful. A wagon train had formed. In actuality, it was a motley collection of mountainbikes, single horses, and horse-drawn wagons. There was even a rickety old school bus that had some diesel. All these people who'd wanted to go north had banded together. Some people simply walked next to the wagons. Ironcloud got a place in a wagon with Kara. They had food, water, and they were going in the right direction. Ironcloud told her that Wade would head west, and they'd keep an eye peeled for him the whole time.

There was a chance, if small, that they would run into each other. If he was alive. Civilization was in such bad shape that there were only a few places that people congregated regionally; the open-air train depots, the ports, and the makeshift refugee camps. They all had roughly hewn resources for looking for someone, like public wall boards where you could pin a picture and a note.

Ironcloud kept dreaming of returning to Arizona and his girl Marina. He kept his spirits up by imagining her beautiful face. Once they'd made love on a leather skin laid on the ground in the hills, and she'd said she felt his heart beating through his chest, and that told her he was a good man. He didn't forget that Wade pulled him out of the desert. He saw that Kara cried to herself sometimes in the wagon.

But Kara was also talking to and making friends with other young girls. He saw her picking flowers in the fields with them next to the wagons.

It took them two weeks. They followed the Pacific Coast north. The soldiers watched them passively. The crazies seemed to have gone somewhere else; they weren't attacked or harassed. If a wagon broke down, they all stopped and fixed it. There were occasional disagreements, but no one went on and left an individual, or a broken wagon. No one was abandoned. People were remarkably stoic and relentless, he thought, like Comanches. The view of the ocean was beautiful from the hills. They'd finally made a beach; it wasn't ruined, or massed with people. It was called San Luis Obispo, someone said.

CHAPTER 53

They were fortunate the sun shined. Everyone on the boat was soaked from sea spray, or from having been in the ocean, like Wade.

He'd hit the water hard, then awkwardly side-stroked to the nearest boat. There wasn't any alternative; the ship was going down. He had to make some space between himself and the listing vessel, which leaked burning oil. People were screaming, drowning, and he heard creaking, groaning, hard metal joints breaking apart, from the ship. He couldn't be swamped by the suction of the sinking vessel. That would drown him, guaranteed, especially since he was trying to swim with one arm. He kicked his legs furiously, and his face, with the hat still hanging off below his chin, gasped at the ocean's choppy surface.

He made one of the rubber rafts and threw his one arm over the side. Two crewmen, an Asian man and a woman, pulled him the rest of the way on. He fell onto the floor of the raft, grateful once more to be alive.

He was cold and wet, but the sun warmed him, and the floor of the raft kept him out of the sea breeze. He felt that he would have gotten hypothermia otherwise. They passed around a kind of hard tack, and emergency water. His shoulder killed him. The people on the raft chatted in Mandarin. After things had settled down a bit, he said, "What happened to the ship?"

The men ignored him. The woman gazed at him, as if forming the correct answer. Then she said, "The ship was sabotaged." She had carefully pronounced English, conscious of it.

"By whom?"

"We don't know."

"What about all those innocent people?"

"This is a very dangerous place," she said. "We're doing the best we can."

After a moment, she looked at him again and asked, "What were you doing on the boat?"

"Trying to find my daughter."

"Oh," she seemed to reply in a whisper, and turned away.

He looked around. The storm had passed. The horizon was empty again. It was the perfect placid blue he'd first seen.

They floated on the empty sea, and the men were paddling. You could see the coastline, about four miles off. He judged that it was 5 p.m., given the location of the sun towards the Pacific horizon. The men chattered amongst themselves endlessly, discussing survival, he figured. There wasn't a whole lot of potable water. At one point, one of the crewmen gestured toward him, with spite in his tone. He figured they might try to throw him overboard. That would be his last stand, he thought. He still had his knife, and the bow. He'd signal to them that he would knife holes in the raft, if they tried to kill him.

It might be a good idea to show them he had a knife, he thought. At least the woman. She seemed more humane; she also seemed to have a higher rank than the others. She spoke to them in remonstrative tones. He might have thought her pretty, in another context, with her long dark hair and pale, calm face. He took out his knife and said, "Maybe we should fish…"

"Yes, maybe," she said. One of the men looked at his knife with hostility, then he spat, "No fish! No knife!" Then the woman said something to the man in Mandarin, something like "Calm down." Wade pulled himself into the corner of the raft and kept the knife out. The sun felt good, like salvation.

# # #

A fishing boat found them and attached a tow line to the raft. They were brought to shore just when the dark settled in. Sullenly, a couple of the sailors had given him a pad to sleep on in a kind of barracks one block off the docks. He saw the lady walk away and he smiled at her; she nodded, then turned around. Maybe she noticed something in my eyes, he thought, because he otherwise looked terrible. Or was it that comment about looking for Kara. He got depressed thinking about Kara, wherever she was, and tried to get some rest.

He went to sleep, exhausted, but he woke up in the dark. Soon, the sun came up over some hills. The light filled the window in the barracks. He'd heard snoring during the night, morning. He got up before the others and went outside. He stood on a bluff above the water; the coastline was pretty and silent. People began to gather outside the barracks, then he smelled cooking. He spoke to another ragged man–they were like two homeless bums. The man said that the beach was part of Carpinteria, and that he'd heard the ship had gone down near the Catalina Islands.

"You were on it? No kidding?" he said incredulously.

"Yes."

Bodies had washed up on the beach. Thank God Kara hadn't been on the ship, he thought.

He walked back toward the barracks, and he saw the Chinese woman from the raft the day before. She seemed to give an order to a man, then she caught his eye and gestured him over.

"This man will show you where you can wash up, clean up, you know, have a shave," she said in a clipped tone. "Then you can have some food. Do you need a doctor?"

"No," he said.

"Come!" the man said, in a too loud voice. Wade began to follow him, then turned back and said, "Wait. What's your name?"

The woman laughed, in a sophisticated way as if it was funny to introduce such informality. "Biyu," she said, and walked away.

At first he thought she said, "Bye you." He followed the man to an outdoor shower, and using one hand, rubbed soap all over his body and hair. He hacked away at his beard with a much-used metal razor that lay in a soap dish. Then another soldier with a towel wrapped around his waist screamed at him in Mandarin, and he left the shower. He toweled off, and put his grungy clothes back on. He caught a look at his face in the mirror and ran his good hand over the remaining stubble. "Isn't half bad," he murmured to himself.

Then he went to breakfast, where he was able to eat a lot of boney fish, rice, bread. He drank several mugs of tea, and that with the shower and food, greatly revived him.

CHAPTER 54

He went down to the beach at Carpinteria afterward and scanned the area for refugee settlements. He didn't see any, nor did he see any sign of Ironcloud and Kara, although the chances of that seemed slim. There were only fishermen in small boats just offshore, and two trucks with crews collecting bodies that had washed up on the beach. He didn't see any groups of people gathered to stay there on a permanent or semi-permanent basis.

Feeling better, he walked up the road north. Everything was burned on the collapsed hillsides to the east, off his right shoulder. Then, strangely, at least in his regard, he reached a point where the giant burn and ash mark on the hills stopped. The bare hills gave way to beautiful slopes of greenery, even a copse of woods, sunny and untouched by the fires. They must have leapt them, like wildfires will.

To the west, the ocean was still and sunlit, a desert plain of rippled blue that hid the previous day's tragic outcome. Sand and ash had blown over parts of the road, which was otherwise busy, including with troop trucks and the occasional wagon. He studied the wagons and people that went by, hopefully.

He came upon a bus idling by the side of the road. He'd only walked about two miles and a half. He asked the driver where he was going. The man had enough fuel to make the coast near Monterey, but he didn't have any empty seats. He was leaving in an hour–Chinese soldiers took up at least two-thirds of the seats, and that's the only way he was able to negotiate for gas. Wade told him his story–how he'd journeyed at least a thousand miles through desolate, perilous lands. The man said he could sit in the aisle, if there was room and no one objected.

Wade was grateful; he thought of Ironcloud, the people who'd patched him up back at Tonto Basin; Wiley and the Santiagos, all the people who'd helped him along the way. They'd given up something of themselves, sometimes in return for nothing. Basic humanity survives amongst the squalor, he mumbled to himself.

# # #

Kara could see Ironcloud sitting in the sun on a grassy bluff, watching the ocean. He was one of those men who didn't ask for help, but she was helping with whatever she could; setting up camp on the beach, washing clothes, cooking food. They had some rice, Ironcloud had caught a fish, and Kara collected crabs amongst the rocks. She'd got a couple of new outfits from people she met in their caravan, including an old jacket that Ironcloud could wear at night. She asked nicely, and people would share things and not make demands in return. She'd slept well on the beach. She hadn't had any seizures the whole time out of the desert, to the coast. They'd stay awhile, Ironcloud said, on San Luis Obispo, where an ad hoc community was cropping up. But she knew he wanted to get going; he wanted to get back to his own girlfriend in Arizona. Sometimes she wondered where his loyalty sprung from, as in the beginning they were perfect strangers. At times of stillness by a fire or the ocean, she thought of her father. She felt sadness, remorse, mixed with hope.

Then she saw Ironcloud stand up on the bluff in the sunshine. A smile broke across a face that she thought of as serious, handsome. He waved. She looked down the beach and she could see a man striding quickly along the water, where the sea slid back into the waves. She got up and ran, bare feet on muddy sand, the Saint Michael medal around her neck glinting in the sunshine.

THE END

Made in the USA
Middletown, DE
24 September 2019